YEAR OF

THE

ROOSTER

Also by Tim Mahoney

Reverse Lightning
The Resurrection of John Dillinger
Dead Messenger
Dead Like Lazarus
Dead a Long Time
If the Dead Could Speak
Secret Partners
We're Not Here
Hollaran's World War

Year
of the
Rooster

Second edition

ISBN: 978-0-9908974-7-7

To the memory
of Mary Matsumoto,
and a kind deed, long remembered.

Aloha

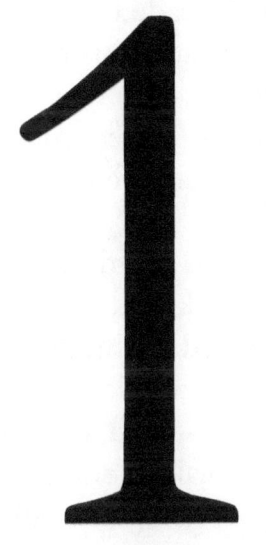

When the Estonophie brothers boarded the jetliner in Newark, they pretended they didn't know each other. Terry, the bruiser, flew first class. Larry, the pipsqueak, sat in coach, back near the restrooms. You could take a magnifying glass to the flight manifest, but you'd find no one named Estonophie listed.

Ah-Ston-Ah-Fee. It was pronounced like the *aston* in *astonishing,* but with a *fee* at the end. How often they'd had to instruct nuns, police officers and probation agents in the proper pronunciation of their name. They had often pestered Mom: All our friends are Irish, Polish, or Italian, so what kind of people are we?

You're Proud Americans, Mom replied.

At Honolulu International, Terry, first off the plane, marched through the tunnel, a death grip on his suitcase. Heading for the cab stand, he glanced neither left, at the lei stands, nor right, at the hula girl greeters, nor back, at his brother.

Larry was the last to debark. In the flash of a camera's strobe light, he allowed a hula girl to kiss him. Then he lounged at the airport's Flying Aloha bar, sipping Primo beer and watching TV. During commercials, he gawked at gorgeous wahines as they walked by.

After a restless hour of watching *Danger, Hawaii* on the bar's TV, Larry, carrying no baggage, headed for the bus stop. Buses were for losers, so Larry hated this part of the plan. But Terry had insisted, and this was Terry's show. Larry hadn't taken a bus since he'd dropped out of school at age fourteen, two years sooner than New Jersey law allows.

At an outdoor lei stand he bought $2 worth of sun-wilted flowers, strung them around his neck, and studied a bus schedule. A perfumed breeze signaled his brain that he was a long way from Jersey. As he turned to look for the bus, Larry gazed upon Honolulu's blue-green, cloudy hills, and was overcome by the first mystical experience of his life. This flood of emotion convinced him he had visited these islands in some other lifetime.

It was such a strong feeling that he was breathing hard when he boarded the crowded bus. He sat sweaty next to a fat lady who wore a bright flowing muu-muu and a straw hat. His legs kept jimmy-jumping. The fat lady gave him the Evil Eye.

He tried to calm himself. Perhaps Oahu's green hills seemed familiar because he had watched so many reruns of *Danger, Hawaii*. He snapped his fingers. That was it. But a moment later, he already wasn't sure. This deja-vu was a scary feeling, so Larry avoided looking at the mountains.

He plucked a newspaper off the floor. The big headline read:

Governor Resigns!

Well, that might have been news to the mopes who lived here, but Terry and Larry knew that a week ago. It was, like, knowing the future before it happened. It was like, pre-déjà vu.

Deja-vu of the future, that's what it was.

He flipped to the comics and horoscopes. What kind of weird place had they come to? Where was Gemini? All these horoscopes were named for animals!

The fat lady, reading over his shoulder, rasped: "I'm a Rat."

Larry gave her the Evil Eye.

"What's your birth year?" she asked.

"Nineteen fifty seven," said Larry.

"You're a Rooster," said the fat lady. "This is your special year, 1981, your third Rooster cycle."

"Is that so?" Larry asked.

"Oh." She nodded. "You're in a very fortunate year."

Larry was spooked because the woman had white hairs sticking out of her chin. That could only mean she was a Hawaiian witch.

Normally he wasn't much of a reader but he decided to dope out his Chinese horoscope. Maybe it would predict a change in the lousy luck he'd been having.

> "It is difficult for Roosters to accept advice because of their independent spirits. Today: The crowing Rooster awakens to new possibilities. Direction of your wind: Mauka."

The meaning of that last word escaped Larry. But wind, yes. The bus windows were open, like they'd never heard of air conditioning here. In blew a breeze that smelled of auto exhaust, sea rot, tropical flowers. Larry sucked in a deep breath.

So, my lucky year, he said to himself. The Year of the Rooster.

The Big Call

As they awaited the Big Call, the Estonophie brothers wasted the sunny days as prisoners of luxury at the Royal Hawaiian Hotel. They smoked Big Tent Filter cigarettes, their favorite brand, and one of the few tastes they had in common. They drank $12 room-service cocktails that arrived topped with floating flowers. Terry worked crossword puzzles. Larry watched TV.

After five or six cocktails, being trapped in that fancy room didn't seem so bad. Second floor, with a lanai overlooking Waikiki Beach. Terry kept the drapes closed, but when Larry peeked he saw Diamond Head and the shimmering turquoise ocean. Half-naked wahines buttered with suntan oil lay on the beach below their salt-stained window.

The room furniture was like, European. The bed was fancy, like in a high-class porn movie, and big

enough for sumo wrestlers. But no way would Terry
allow Larry to sleep there. Fortunately for Larry, the sofa
pulled out. Although Larry had registered under an alias
at the $40-a-night Tiki Torch Hotel, he couldn't sleep in
its cockroach-infested rooms.

"This is like being a king," Larry said. He peeked
out the window at the buttery bathing beauties. "Cooped
up in your castle. What do they call that, a coupe, right?
When the king..." Larry ran his finger past his throat...
"off with his head."

"Stunod, don't worry about the king's head."

Terry pronounced it stoo-nod, accent on the nod.
He wondered if he'd ever see the word in a crossword
puzzle. *Italian moron. Six letters.*

"You know why it's called the Royal Hawaiian?"
Terry asked, looking up from his crossword puzzle. "The
king needed some place to stash, what do you call them,
dignitaries. Back in the olden days, they had a crowned
king on this island. Read the brochure."

Larry waved his brother off.

"The nuns wasted their time," Terry said, "when
they taught you to read."

Terry was built like a football lineman. Larry was
shorter, skinny, with dark short hair that stood up like a
shoe brush. Terry's hair was the same utilitarian cut. Mom
had given them haircuts in the kitchen, saving money,
and they honored her now, with the simple butch cut.
But Terry was the fussier brother when it came to
appearance. Terry owned suits in many fabrics, cuts and
colors. Larry went with jeans and t-shirts, except that
every few months, he donned a shirt and tie for an
associate's funeral.

The brothers had settled the who's-tougher question long ago, with a wrestling match on the threadbare carpet in Mom's living room. Larry, arm twisted behind him, had screamed in pain: Uncle! Uncle! Uncle, you sick bastard! Since then, his every victory over Terry had come by wits alone.

"You're not going beach-bumming," Terry said, "so forget about it."

Terry glared at Larry, then focused on the puzzle page of the *Honolulu Record*. He muttered: "No Jumble. What kind of newspaper is this? Pathetic crossword, could be solved by a numb-nuts in ten minutes. And anamalistic horoscopes. Ridiculous."

"They have the Phantom?" Larry asked.

"Of course they have the fucking Phantom," Terry said.

"Look at this chubby bunny," Larry said, staring out the window.

Terry turned the page. "I don't let babes lead me around by the dick. That's your game."

"They got gorgeous women here," Larry muttered. He snapped his fingers. "Wahines, that's what they call 'em."

Through a part in the drapes, Larry watched eight women playing volleyball in the sand. All but one wore a bikini. Some of the bikinis, thank God, had a tendency to slip. Some of the women were blonde and some were dark. Larry had known plenty of blondes, bleached and otherwise. He watched a plump dark girl, the only one wearing a modest one-piece bathing suit, her breasts jiggling.

Ah, the one-piece suit. Flashy babes, they hadn't worked out for Larry. Maybe it was time to go for a modest girl.

"I wish the fucking phone would ring," Terry said. "Is that too much to ask?" He stared at it. The phone was a white fancy thing, historical. It somehow made Terry think Beethoven could have talked into it. But he was pretty sure they didn't have phones in Beethoven's time.

Larry snatched up the phone.

"Put the phone down," Terry said.

"I want room service."

"We just ate two hours ago."

"I'm hungry."

"You got no interminal discipline. Put the phone down, stunod, we're waiting for a call."

Larry dropped it. He sulked in the stuffed chair. Then he threw open cabinet doors to reveal a television. He flipped through the channels. This, he knew, would piss Terry off.

TV, Terry said, was for stunods.

A commercial for cockroach killer faded out, and there it was: *Danger, Hawaii,* a show that would be rerun in Eternity.

Big guys paddled a canoe. Hula dancers swayed. A steel guitar hit a long sweet note just as a plainclothes cop in a Panama hat appeared. A handsome rogue, he tipped his hat and grinned.

The camera pulled back to reveal a flower lei draped around the cop's suit jacket. TV viewers knew this rogue as Mick Danger, the most famous imaginary Hawaiian cop since Charley Chan. He was played by Hollywood legend Bix Sanders.

"Look at that, our guy's on the TV."

"Could you turn it down?" Terry said.

"We're going to meet him?"

Terry just glared.

"Bix Sanders. He's our guy, right?" asked Larry.

"Yeah, he's our guy because, intentionally speaking, it's the other guy who's really our guy."

"That's what I said, he's our guy, so it's the other guy."

"That's the guy, stunod."

Terry sniffed at his underarms. This was a tropical heat city and he might smell bad, even with the Old Spice.

"You smell okay," Larry said. "Don't worry."

"Who asked you?" Terry said. He picked up the Sunday New York Times crossword puzzle, four days old, which he'd started on the plane. A few times, just one blank corner had stood between Terry and a Sunday Times winner. He had mastered a few weekday ones, without cheating, and he'd clipped those, keeping a scrapbook of his winning puzzles. It was a marbled composition book, like the ones he'd used at Holy Infant to keep track of football bets. He brought a scrapbook, and a coffee-stained Webster's dictionary, along on every job. He consulted Webster's exclusively. He despised crossword dictionaries. They were crutches, and people who used them were weak.

Larry had already seen this episode of *Danger, Hawaii*. A hillbilly family came to the islands, trying to pull a scam on Mick Danger. But you can't scam The Mick, so the hillbillies were bound to fail. But it didn't seem fair. Larry was puzzled by the popularity of a show where the criminals lost every single time.

He flipped channels.

A good honest criminal, like for example Larry Estonophie, didn't hurt people, but just snatched whatever was lying around their houses when they weren't home. Everybody had homeowner's insurance, right? So really he was robbing from the rich, the insurance companies, and giving to the poor, Larry Estonophie.

He flicked the TV off and walked to the tall window. The air conditioner underneath it blew a cool breeze up to his sweating face. The volleyball girls were brushing sand off their suntanned bodies. One of the blondes was unpinning her hair, another waded in the ocean. The thick-set dark girl was bending over, giving Larry an enticing view of her ass.

"I'm going out for a burger," Larry said.

"Sit tight." Terry frowned at his crossword. "They deliver cheeseburgers. Deluxe. What you call, custom upholstered room service."

"You said don't use the phone."

"Make it quick."

"But I want a Big Mac."

"Have some class, order a room service cheeseburger."

"A Big Mac's got that special sauce."

Terry grunted.

"I'll be careful," Larry said.

Larry was like a restless mutt, you had to let him out or he'd piss on the rug.

"I shouldn't do it," Terry said, "you do nothing but prevaricate. Be back here in ten minutes." He held up his index finger. "No babes, Larry, this is serious business, okay?"

"You want me to fetch a couple of burgers for you?" Larry asked. "No onions?" Terry despised onions, they made his breath stink offensive.

Larry made that honest, lost-little-boy look come over his face. When people saw those wet innocent eyes, they gave in. Even Terry, who knew better.

"No. Get out of here." Terry waved him off.

Larry, biting back a victory grin, walked out into the hall. All up and down the hallway, room service trays lay with their disgusting remains. Were the waiters on strike or was the help lazy here?

Larry had been a room service waiter once, in the olden days of A.C. Then one day, what do you know, the Service Manager accused him of a dishonest act, and they argued in the kitchen, and Larry accidentally spilled hot coffee, and, okay, the guy somehow ended up with burns on his face. Unfair as it may seem, after that one mistake, Larry had found it difficult to obtain employment in the hospitality industry.

Larry padded along the thick posh carpet and into the sunlit lobby. But the volleyball girls were walking away. They funneled down a concrete pathway into a shady palm grove. The big dark girl had the volleyball trapped between her waist and arm. He watched in sorrow as this fine wahine, and her girlfriends, disappeared into the shadows.

Not even his wettest puppy-dog eyes would work on a woman surrounded by other women. You had to get a woman alone, bring tears to the rims of your eyes, tilt your head and say: Could you help me?

Damn, his heart was crying as he watched that big girl get away.

Back in the Prince Kuhio suite, Terry was thumbing through the dictionary pursuing a clue about flower gardens when the phone rang. Perennial, that was the answer.

"Yeah?"

"That you, Stone?"

"Depends who's calling."

"You ready?"

"We been waiting impatience here."

"Plan A. Get off your ass."

Terry didn't say anything.

"Go, you hear me?"

"I heard you," Terry said. "Plan A. No problem."

He hung up the Beethoven phone. Beethoven was deaf, wasn't he? Or was that the other guy, Mozart? Either way, it was good to know your song writers, they came up in puzzles all the time.

He peeked through the purple drapes at Waikiki Beach. He always felt some mysterious darkness whenever he stared at the sea. He wasn't no swimmer, and being on boats made him nervous. His first memory of water, his old man nearly drowned him in the cold waves off the Boardwalk. Sink or swim! Terry had swallowed a lungful of seawater before the old man dragged him out of the surf.

On the flight here, he'd fought off dread panics that the plane would go down and he would sink into the ocean, still strapped into his seat. Somehow the thought of salt water, miles deep and full of sea snakes, sharks, killer whales and other vicious creatures, terrified him.

He turned his back on the ocean, opened the closet and there hanging in a shoulder holster was his Army Buddy, a 1911 Mil-Spec model. It wasn't the crude weapon like they issued to grunts, but a gorgeous stainless gun with walnut grips. He dropped the clip, slid each of the seven rounds out, sat on the bed and polished their brassy jackets with spit and a white handkerchief. Then he clicked the rounds back into the clip, counting, even though there was no question there were seven. He was a counter. Was this discipline, Terry wondered, or habit? He'd look those words up. You'd be surprised what you could learn from the dictionary.

He took another peek out the windows and son of a bitch, there was Larry. Big Mac my ass, he was walking along the beach, flirting with bathing beauties.

Terry shook his head. It would only be worse if he burst out there and started screaming. It would call more attention, when what they needed was less attention. But no problem. He'd learned a lesson in Vietnam. He'd been a convoy guy, scout jeep, facing all the dangers. Somewhere on every road was a landmine, trip wire or ambush, you could depend on it.

He could handle Larry. Some men were just suckers for women. Why else would a guy, only twenty-four, have been married three times? Okay, he'd cut Larry slack on the divorce from Karen. She took off while Larry was doing time in Rahway. The Karen problem, that was not the kid's fault.

Fickle, that was the word for Karen.

Terry pictured all three of Larry's wives, babes every one. Terry would have been happy with any of them. But he was cursed with women. He'd get near a beautiful babe and all of a sudden he couldn't think of the right words. Maybe he smelled bad, maybe he came across crude, maybe he scared them, hard to tell. Half the time, the women would go off with Larry. And the minute the women walked away, wouldn't you know, the words Terry wanted would come to him, a regular brainstorm.

Terry found himself staring at the phone, like he was giving a dirty look to his most recent caller.

What, we're a couple of skids, they talk to us like that?

This Vegas guy, Terry said to himself, could learn phone manners. You could call him crude, you could call him ... he snapped his fingers. He couldn't think of a better word right then.

This was the big move of Terry's career, in which there had been some embarrassing failures. None had been Terry's fault. A couple you could blame on Larry. And a couple more, things just went wrong. The brothers had sunk to the bottom, in the estimation of impressive people in Jersey. So Terry had relocated to the Western desert, to get some new action. Now Terry had to deal with this Vegas hot shot, code name: Management.

It came to Terry then. The word he'd been looking for to describe his new employer. Not crude, Management dressed too nicely for that. You could call him ill-mannered.

Homey

The more Larry thought about it, the more he figured the Year of the Rooster would bring the luck he deserved. For one thing, his brother had got them this Honolulu job, which paid like they were movie stars. If they got it done in 50 hours, that would work out to $500 an hour. Each!

For another thing, as luck would have it, they knew somebody useful who lived on this island. The guy's name was Lazarus Patrick McCabe, or L.P. as everybody back in high school called him. He'd been editor of the school newspaper at Holy Infant. He was one of the smartest guys in Terry's class, although it was only Atlantic City, so he was a pinhead compared to, for example, Einstein.

Instead of going to Rutgers like a normal pinhead, McCabe had enrolled in a California hippie college. Somehow he got drafted into the Army, was discharged in Honolulu and had gone to work for a newspaper.

They were parked outside McCabe's apartment now.

Apparently the newspaper racket didn't pay. McCabe lived in a drab neighborhood of condos and apartment buildings, and rickety wood houses that belonged in a jungle. Opposite his building stood a dusty cinderblock building with a sign:

KAZA SCHOOL

Terry shut down the rental car and its engine ticked in the heat. Sunlight glared off the windshield. Larry adjusted his dark glasses, cleared his throat and said: "I'll bet McCabe's fat now."

"I do the talking," muttered Terry.

"You got your Army Buddy with you?"

"Now why would I bring it here?"

"Intimidate," said Larry.

"This ain't Nevada. They got gun laws in this city, strictly reinforced. I been what you call debriefed on the subject. Besides, you didn't know McCabe too good, Larry. I did. He's got no stones."

The school doors burst open and out ran a stream of children, shouting with joy at their release into a shady playground.

Larry watched them through the tinted window. "What's a Kaza school?"

"Don't bother me," grumped Terry.

"You're the word man," said Larry.

"I'm thinking of subsequent words. Words to say to McCabe."

"Why do we need McCabe anyway?"

"You didn't get it the last time I verified it to you?"

"I forget what you called him."

"The Missing Link. Things go wrong, he goes missing, there's no link, nobody can pin nothing on us. It's smarter ..." he tapped his head "than what you call the direct business model."

"I don't know," Larry said. "McCabe never did nothing to us."

"Don't worry," Terry said. "It's gonna work smooth. McCabe keeps his mouth shut, like we all should, and he could live a hundred happy years."

McCabe lived on the ground floor of a two-story cinderblock apartment with eight green doors. His was #7, and so it said in a brass number nailed to the door. As Terry was assembling his verbal troops for combat, door #7 opened and out slipped a female.

"Oh ho," said Larry.

She was a short Asian gal in dark t-shirt and jeans that were spattered in white paint. She opened, without using a key, door #8 and shut it behind her.

"Hanky panky with the neighbor lady," Larry said.

"Good to know," said Terry.

"Do we want her home or not?" Larry asked.

"Nope," said Terry. "We wait."

"Well, start the fackin car and run the air, or we'll bake in here."

Terry was good at waiting, Larry was not. Larry's legs danced the jimmy-jumps whenever he tried to sit still. He couldn't help it really. But the nuns at Holy Infant, did they understand? Oh no. A guy needs action, the nuns label him a troublemaker, and then it's a week's detention and Mom sobbing in Sister Matilda's office.

"Easy does it," said Terry. "We could be here a long time."

Larry, from the pocket of his green aloha shirt, whipped out a pack of Big Tents.

"Not in here," Terry said. "Enclosed space. You know how I am."

"Fack," said Larry.

But they weren't watching more than ten minutes when door #8 opened and the woman appeared, dressed in nurse's pale green uniform. Flowery purse flung over her shoulder, she hustled toward the main drag and planted herself at a bus stop.

"Not much longer," Terry said, watching the nurse in the rearview mirror.

Larry looked over his shoulder. "McCabe's got taste in ladies."

"You ever met a girl you didn't like?"

"Yeah, I met an old witch on the bus coming in."

"I mean girl. Of eligible age. Nubile is the word."

The bus came along and took the nurse with it.

The brothers eased out of the car and crossed a hot asphalt parking lot that was lined with dying papaya trees. Papaya fruits, buzzing with flies, were lying tire-smashed on the sun-melted asphalt.

Larry knocked on #7. Terry stood back.

A stunned-looking McCabe opened the door, dressed in shorts and
t-shirt, hair wild like he'd just rolled out of bed.

"Surprise!" yelled Larry.

McCabe stood in the doorway like a statue.

"You guys!" McCabe said.

"It's us," said Larry, "do you believe it?"

Terry shook McCabe's hand. "Lotta years," Terry said.

"Who's the neighbor babe?" Larry asked.

Terry glared at him.

"Reiko?" McCabe said. "She's helping me paint."

McCabe stepped out but left the door open. He was a guy of average height and heavy weight, platinum hair, pale face, shifty blue eyes.

A whiff of fresh paint wafted out behind him.

"Look at this guy," Larry said and elbowed his big brother, "he's got the babes doing the painting for him. Like Huckleberry Finn."

McCabe said: "You mean Tom Sawyer?"

"See?" Larry said to his brother. "That's why I shoulda gone to college."

"I'd invite you in," McCabe said, "but, as you can smell ... what are you guys doing in the islands?"

"We needed a vacation," Larry said.

"We're here on business," Terry said.

"You should have called ..." McCabe said.

Terry cut him off. "You never wrote."

That cracked Larry up. "Neither did we," he said.

"Stunod had plenty of time to write," Terry said. "In Rahway."

"Fack you, calling me stunod," Larry said and stepped back.

"He would have mailed a postcard," Terry said, "only the prison ran out of stamps."

The prison bit embarrassed Larry, but he understood the strategy: intimidate McCabe by making Larry seem prison-tough. Intimidate, that was the word of the day.

Larry said: "Mom died."

"Sorry to hear that," McCabe said.

"She wasn't feeling well," Terry said.

"Facking emphysema," Larry said.

"I hadn't heard," McCabe said.

"You left for California," Larry said, "and after that, ungotz."

"We see your sisters around," Terry said. "They're proud of you, college grad and all."

McCabe took a sharp breath, like maybe the mention of his sisters bothered him. Which was good.

"I'm really surprised to see you guys here."

"Yeah," Terry said. "We can show up anywheres."

Larry nodded. "It was a long facking flight. I got the phone numbers of two waitresses."

"Stewardesses," Terry corrected him. "My brother the stunod. Yet, he's the ladies man." He craned his neck to snoop into McCabe's apartment. "Nice place you got here," he said. "I mean the Hawaiian Islands. They're real nice."

"How long have you guys been in town?"

"Two fucking minutes," Terry said, "and stunod gets lost at the beach."

Larry turned sideways and posed like a muscle man. He made his bicep bulge by putting one fist behind it. He grinned. "Wahines," he said.

"Yeah," Terry said. "Hey, Lazz. I figured, guy like you, pretty good job. But you ain't spending on luxury accommodations."

"You've got to be rich to buy a house in this city," McCabe said.

"That's where we can help," Terry said.

"Absolutely," said Larry.

McCabe backed away. He put up both hands, like the brothers were trying to punch him.

"I'm real busy," he said.

"It looks like you're loafing right now."

"Well, I … come around the back, we can talk in the shade."

He led them around the building, where they squeezed past bushes. McCabe's concrete back porch faced an eight-foot chain link fence and the gray machinery of an electrical substation.

"Quite the view," said Terry. He was being sarcastic, Larry understood that. Terry was like, a put-down artist. He did that so's you knew he was in charge.

"It's private, though," McCabe said. "Can I get you guys a beer, an ice tea or…"

McCabe's porch was furnished with rusty cheap beach chairs. A giant spool that once held electrical cable had been turned into a table. He kept plants in pots, tiny trees, like they were meant to shade a dollhouse.

McCabe padded through the screen door and returned with two sweating bottles of Bass ale.

"Oh, fancy, thank you," said Larry.

Terry sipped beer, sat back in a lawn chair.

"Where's your beer?" Terry said.

McCabe patted his gut. "Had to give it up. The weight."

"So you're not married," Terry said.

"Nope," McCabe said, and sat on the spool table.

"Good," said Terry.

McCabe wore a sick grin. It was like the grin of a guy who knows, when you stop him on the street and ask for a light, that he's going to get robbed.

"We got an adventure for you," said Terry.

"Perfect fit for you," said Larry, "since you know all the…"

"Shut up," said Terry. "What my brother means is, we need a small favor, and we pay handsome. Maybe up to five thousand for an acceptable performance."

"I've already got a job," said McCabe.

"We know," said Terry. "That's why we picked you. How well do you know this guy Uncle Sam Wing?"

McCabe shrugged. "I've seen him here and there. It's a small island. He's just another politician."

"That's where you're wrong," said Terry.

Terry leveled a look that McCabe dared not challenge. "I don't like this British shit," Terry growled. "It's what you call…" he snapped his fingers. "Snob brewed."

He poured beer over one of McCabe's little trees.

"Hey!" McCabe said. "Beer could kill them."

"When are they going to grow up?" Larry asked. "Your trees."

"They're bonsai," McCabe said.

"What's wrong with them?" Larry asked.

"They're miniatures. They're not mine, they belong to my neighbor. There's better sunlight on my lanai." McCabe flooded the baby tree with water from a battered tin watering can.

"Uncle Sam Wing is running for mayor," Terry said.

McCabe stroked the baby tree like he was apologizing to it. "Sure, Sam's a candidate."

"What if he wanted to spend more time with his family?"

"I'm not sure what you mean," McCabe said.

"You may have went to college McCabe but I matriculated from another school," Terry said. "And here's what I learned from a very wise teacher. We call

him The Management. He related to me that no
Republican has a chance to be mayor of this city, which is
like eighty percent Democrat. The Republican candidate
is just a punching bag, right?"

McCabe nodded.

"So whoever gets the Democrat nomination is
guaranteed to be mayor."

"Essentially true," McCabe admitted.

"So there are two Democrat candidates. Bix
Sanders, former TV star gone native. And Uncle Sam
Wing, boss of the City Council."

"Chairman," McCabe said, "of the City Council."

"If Uncle Sam drops out," Terry said, "let's say a
few days before the vote, it's too late for another serious
candidate to come out of the closet."

"Probably."

"So, minus Uncle Sam Wing, TV hero Bix Sanders
wins. That is the pertinent result our Management seeks."

"Be right back," McCabe said. "Bathroom.

Terry, on the bright lanai, watched McCabe in the
dark apartment.

"He picks up the phone, I'm going to clock him,"
Terry told Larry.

"He's got no stones, like you said."

"You never know," said Terry.

"I kinda like this beer," said Larry.

"Me too," said Terry.

"I shoulda known," said Larry. He shook his head
in wonder. "My brother. You shoulda been an actor.
You'd a been a bigger star than Bix Sanders." He held his
bottle of Bass Ale out to toast his clever brother.

The toilet flushed and McCabe appeared in the
doorway.

Terry said: "McCabe, we're going to send Candidate Wing a message, but not of the verbal variety."

"Verbs," said Larry. "We're bad at verbs."

"You could make personal contact with Sam Wing and explain to him exactly, in no uncertain words, what the message means."

Terry looked around the fence at the other porches, and up at the porches above. No eavesdroppers in sight.

"The message means Uncle Sam has gotten over his head in an ocean of doubt. And in an ocean of doubt, you could fall in and drown. Am I mixing my metaphors? Plain speaking, Sam's gotta go. Don't worry McCabe, we got plan A, B and C. And there is no rough stuff in Plan A, is there, Larry?"

"Nope," said Larry.

"This could turn out lucrative for you and for Sam," said Terry. "But remember, you are impaled by secrecy."

"Okay," McCabe said, but Larry could tell he was just going along.

"So what role do you play, McCabe?" Terry said. "You are the peacemaker. Because of your verbal skill, you will deliver a message that's perfectly understood, and gets us the ultimate result, without so much as a black eye or a bloody nose. That is what our Management seeks."

"Management?"

"Oh, you'd know their names, well some of their names." Terry crossed his arms over his massive chest. "These guys are so wise, they stay one inch on the fortunate side of the law."

Larry tapped the side of his head.

"And the beauty part," said Terry, "is we keep the peace, and we all get a piece. How do you like that for, what are those words, harmonizers, right?"

"Give peace a chance," Larry said.

"Sam drops out," Terry said, "Bix Sanders, your next mayor."

Beautiful flower

Larry Estonophie walked barefoot over the sands of Waikiki. He was astonished to find that anybody could walk onto any beach, no charge. He kept thinking he'd see a booth, like in Jersey, where they sold beach badges. See, back in Jersey, they had a Beach Badge System. This kept the skids off the nicer beaches and funneled them into crap holes like Wildwood and Seaside. If he ever met the mayor of Waikiki, Larry might suggest the Jersey Beach Badge System.

He walked over the hot sands whistling. That Terry, staying in his room all day, what a jaberk-jaboff. That was their private word because Mom had forbidden them to say curses like *jerkoff* in the house. So they called each other jaberk-jaboff and made up words like fack.

What could Mom say? She was proud of her inventive boys.

On this next beach, volleyball. Larry sat on a stone wall and watched the games. No wonder volleyball was so popular here, the women played it almost naked. Back home, guys wasted their summers in taverns watching the Phillies. Over here, half-naked chicks gave a better show for free.

He'd been watching maybe five minutes when his chubby bunny walked out of the shadows of a coconut grove. She wore that same dark one-piece bathing suit. She seemed like a saint, in blinding light, doves cooing at her feet.

She talked to a blondie on a blanket, then walked back into the tree shadows.

Larry stretched real casual, jammed his hands into his cutoffs pockets, and ambled over to where blondie sat. He let that eager puppy dog look come over his face. He didn't have to try hard. This was him. He was a people kind of guy.

The blondie had a picnic basket on her blanket, but nobody to share her lunch with.

"Mind if I ask you something?"

In that space before she answered, Larry took her in. Her short bunched hair, sign of a college diploma. A shift mostly covered her bathing suit, which meant sex hang-up. The bathing suit was a cheap job, so this chick was broke. She had the pale white skin of a tourist. She was alone, so she was some kind of loser. She wore a tennis visor, so she was a snob. Even though she was long and lanky, she wasn't playing volleyball, which meant she was like, afraid to come out of her shell. Most noticeable of all was her bug-eyes, like the eyes of a frog.

He kneeled in the hot sand.

"You live here?"

She nodded.

"I need some advice," Larry said.

That line never failed.

"You know," Larry said, and clenched his fist, "If I could just get a job." He smacked his thigh to show his sincere determination.

The blondie turned her tennis visor so it no longer shaded her face. Her bug eyes fixed on Larry.

"What kind of work do you do?"

"Car mechanic," he said.

"I don't know any..." she glanced at the volleyball players... "anybody in that business who's here right now. But I can ask around. Have you tried looking in the newspapers?"

"Yeah," Larry sighed. "It's hopeless."

"Oh," she said, "I don't think anything's ever hopeless."

The chubby bunny emerged from the palm trees, carrying a cone of blue ice. She licked her ice, and stood watching a rally.

"I know that girl, don't you?" Larry asked.

"Pua?"

"Right, Pua," Larry said.

The blondie curled into herself, like a turtle pulling in.

"Where did you know Pualani from?" blondie asked. "I thought you were new to the islands?"

"Volleyball," Larry said. There was nothing to beat the one-word lie.

Blondie looked him over. Doubt crept into her eyes. So now Larry had to backtrack and build trust. A shy smile. A flash of the puppy dog eyes. A cocked head. Harmless, lovable Larry.

"See I'm from back East." He smiled. "What about you?"

"Born here," she exhaled. The way she said it was like, what a terrible tragic tale to be born in paradise.

From her picnic basket she brought out a can of pineapple juice, it was sweating so much its paper label slipped off. Larry looked at the label and freaked, the hair rising on the back of his neck. The label showed a young blonde with a ponytail drinking from a straw stuck into a pineapple. The label girl, maybe twelve years old, had blue bug-eyes. She could have been the little sister of the woman right across the blanket from him.

It was like one of those deja-vu feelings again.

A look at Pua's ass refocused Larry.

"So what teams are these?" he asked.

Blondie put her hand up to shade her eyes. "Team Kaza versus. ..." she hesitated "versus the Mormons."

Larry nodded. Kaza. He had seen that word somewhere.

"Team Kaza doesn't play to win," she said. "And nobody ever beats the Mormons."

"The Kaza team likes to lose?" Larry asked.

"Ideally," she said, "we seek a fifty-fifty record."

Larry nodded, but it was the stupidest thing he'd ever heard.

"So you're on the Kaza team?"

"It's my team."

"You own it?"

She curled up like she hated that question.

"I've seen Pua play," Larry said. "She's really good. What did you say her other name was?"

"Pualani. I guess you saw her play for our semi-pro team, the Fierce Loving Amazons."

"The who?"

"Kaza's all-women team."

"Right," Larry said.

"You play?" blondie asked.

"Too short for volleyball," Larry said. He'd found that when you acted inferior, people just naturally trusted you. Hell, if you did it long enough, they'd come to love you.

"Fierce Loving Amazons," he said. "I heard that name somewheres."

"Where are you from?"

"Originally? Pennsylvania," he lied. "Near Philly."

"I thought I recognized that accent. You were in the Navy?"

"How do you know that?"

"Your tattoo."

Larry closed two buttons on his shirt and said, "I don't like to talk about it. I lost a lot of close friends."

He looked out to sea as if mourning all the fine sailors consigned to Davey Jones Locker. But what he actually saw was Pua. He gawked at her breasts, they looked like pillows. Like Mom's breasts. Larry wanted to lay his head there and go to baby sleep.

"Kaza's the fastest growing religion in Hawaii," blondie said.

Oh it's a religion, Larry said to himself.

"You ought to come out. Everybody's welcome."

"Listen, my name's Larry, Larry Stone."

They shook hands. Her hand was light, it was like holding a bird.

"I'm Christina Grotton."

Now it was getting just too weird for Larry. Hawaii. Grotton. Pineapple. Those three things went together like ham and hash browns and eggs. Grotton Pineapple, that was like, world-famous, the rings in the little can. Fresh pineapple, like from Dole, was too expensive, so every Easter Mom would drape the ham with Grotton Canned Pineapple rings. Could this woman be related to the pineapple-canning family?

"There's a free supper every night at our temple," Christina Grotton was saying. "We all get together. It's fun."

"A lot of praying and stuff?"

"Nothing like that. No hymns, no baptisms." She touched her chest. "It's all in here."

Pua ran to the sea and stood waist high in it.

"So after the game," Larry said, "you all go back to the church..."

"Temple."

Christina arose, all legs and arms, and talked to a red-haired guy who was way too fat to play volleyball. That left Larry on the edge of her blanket, sand heaped at the borders to keep it from blowing away. The wind blew sand, paper trash, the scent of flowers and rain. It was sunny down here, but raining in the mountains. A rainbow faded, then came back brilliant.

Once, at Margate, when Mom took him to see Lucy The Elephant, they'd seen a rainbow over Atlantic City. *There's a pot of gold at the end of the rainbow, Larry,* Mom had promised him.

Why does everybody want gold? Larry asked her.

They don't mean gold nuggets, honey, they mean good things. Love, friendship and good fortune.

Funny, Larry had seen that rainbow hovering over the old rundown Atlantic City and boom, a couple of years later, casino gambling came to town. So Mom was right about rainbows.

"You're invited to the temple meal," said Christina. "It's vegetarian."

"How do I get there?" asked Larry. "I just love vegetables."

Christina drove a green, open top Range Rover. Both fenders were banged up and it was missing its rear spare tire. If you didn't know cars, you'd think this was a just a crappy jeep, but it cost more money than Larry had made last year. As they drove into the shadow of Diamond Head along a sea-cliff road, Larry shouted: "What do you do for a living?"

"I manage family properties," said Christina.

Larry was hoping she'd say: I own every canned pineapple in the world.

"What about you?" she shouted. "Where was your last job? Not the Navy?"

"Investments," Larry said.

"I thought you were an auto mechanic?"

"Then I went back to school," Larry said. "And learned how to invest full time." He shifted in his tan leather seat. "But here, I thought, I could do cars for a while, for a start and then you know..." he sniffed. "Move on to better things."

Christina's friend the red-haired fat guy sat in back and kept his yap shut. They drove through a neighborhood that made Larry want to return after dark and do entries. It looked easy. Big french doors. Lotsa good things inside, not too many dogs, lotsa bushes to hide your work. In a mellow place like Hawaii, he felt, a homeowner probably didn't own a gun. That was his big fear. Back in Jersey, they had a sick epidemic of homeowners buying guns. So who was the real criminal? Larry, or the gun-slinging homeowners?

"What kind of investments?" Christina asked.

"Oh, like property and stuff."

"Real estate," Christina said.

"Yeah. I don't like to talk about it, though. Bad luck to talk about your deals."

"If you can do real estate deals," Christina said. "You've come to the right city. You'd be wasting your time as a car mechanic."

Something told Larry to nod.

Christina turned the Rover down a jarring, dusty road. The houses along it were set back in jungle. Near the ocean, a stone house was surrounded by a wire fence. Signs were posted all along that fence. Larry had been to the Poconos once so he figured those signs would say No Hunting Private Property but they actually said: No Smoking On These Grounds.

The last house on the road was the so-called temple. It looked more like a sea shack, big and rambling and all dark cedar. The oceanfront seemed rocky, or probably that black stuff was lava. The house sat atop the lava for a nice view over the restless ocean.

A caravan of cars bounced down the pot-holed road, raising clouds of red dust. Christina opened a wooden gate on flowery grounds. A yard was paved with smooth white pebbles. Lanterns hung from a wide tree with many trunks. She touched a green statue and said: "This is Koshu, our inspiration."

Larry nodded.

"He's dead," she said.

Of course he was dead, Larry thought, you have to be dead before you get a statue. Look at Benjamin Franklin, the guy who invented electricity. Franklin's statue welcomed you to Philly, and he had become deceased, as far as Larry knew, quite a while back.

In a cookhouse worked two guys and two girls wearing turquoise robes, sweating, stirring vats of food with canoe oars.

"We take turns cooking," Christina said, as if that explained anything.

She left Larry then, and he sat on a bench. When the volleyball crowd surged through the gate, they ignored him. He did not see Pua, and began to wonder what time it was getting to be. He imagined Terry, in his dark room at the Royal, steam practically rising out of his stupid head.

Christina returned, changed from bathing suit and shift to blue-jeans and a crisp ironed shirt.

Larry jumped up and said, "Hey, is there a phone I can borrow?"

"We don't have a phone," she said.

"I'll call collect," Larry said. "I've got to call my mom, it's really important," Larry said.

"The nearest public phone," Christina said, "is at Longs Drugs up on the highway."

"Oh."

"Koshu taught that..."

Larry quit listening. He was getting hungry and the robed cooks were bringing vats of food out to the picnic tables.

Larry noticed that, like, three quarters of the people wore robes and the other half were in bathing suits. What kind of religion was this? A bathing suit religion? They were all lining up now, holding paper plates. Larry stood on tip toes to inspect the chow. A vat of rice. A tub of yellow goop. White chalky crap to drink. It made him hungry for a big greasy Number One at White House Subs back in A.C.

With extra salami.

He stared at that green statue of what's-his-name. Larry was used to a higher class religion, with angels and halos and popes and virgins. Real virgins. Not the kind you met in Jersey, like Karen. Her kind only claimed to be virgins so you'd marry them. Jersey Virgins, trying to trick innocent guys into husbandry.

And then what do you know, Karen divorces you because of Rahway. Except for that traitor Karen, Rahway wasn't such a bad deal. They had actually made a movie about Rahway, like it was Alcatraz. But they exaggerated. Larry learned more in Rahway than in nine years of Catholic School. Actually, Rahway wasn't much worse than Holy Infant, and the food in the dining room tasted about the same.

Latecomers drove up the road, in an orange VW Thing, open topped, and women jumped out of it. Pua was one of them.

As four women in bathing suits strolled up the walk, Larry opened the gate and bowed. Pua passed like she was the princess and he was the doorman. Out of the corner of his eye Larry caught Christina talking to that red-headed fat guy underneath the gigantic tree. He worried that they were talking about him so he walked over.

"You sure you don't have a phone? I was hoping to call my partner back in Philly. Collect."

"I thought you were calling your mom."

"I need to call them both, mom and my partner."

"Seriously, we have no phone," Christina said. "Koshu taught us to communicate with our hearts."

Larry began to realize that the only way to get to a pay phone was to steal a car, and he might as well choose Christina's Range Rover. Certainly you would never catch Larry driving a noisy chick machine like the VW Thing.

It was a long time ago when he and Terry had pulled the rent-a-car scam, but Larry could hot wire a car in about a minute. It required tools, though, and he did not have them. Then he got a brilliant idea. Christina had changed clothes. Where? In the temple. There was a half a chance she'd left her keys in there too.

Larry sneaked into the temple.

From the rafters hung a giant picture of a heart, with two human eyes in the center. The only light in the room glowed from that heart. There were thick green rugs beneath it. Outside, the ocean pounded fierce on lava rocks. At the back of the temple room was the painting of a man, but you could only see him from the eyebrows down. Below his picture were words in different languages, and the only ones Larry could read were:

I see!

Larry opened a door on a closet full of robes, blue jeans, bathing suits, shorts and blouses. Larry found the shift Christina had been wearing and in them, yes. Keys to the Range Rover.

Someone walked into the big room out there.

Larry went quiet. The floorboards creaked. He peeked out the crack in the door to see Pua.

"Hello?" she called.

Larry, hidden in the changing room, stood still.

Pua, in the light of Koshu's Heart, untied her bathing suit and rolled it over her cute ass. Full naked, she lay down, belly first on the rug. Did Larry hear a sob? Or was she just breathing hard? Larry loved a girl with a lot of emotion. Karen had been a religion freak, tears in her eyes whenever she mentioned Jesus, and she was wildest lay he'd ever had.

Pua stood now, gloriously naked. Hands in front of her folded, she bowed from the waist. Then she picked up her bathing suit, carried it into an open room of white tiles.

Larry heard a shower come on. He was sweating, worried about calling Terry, but wanting to see Pua naked again. He stayed quiet. After an agony of minutes, Pua appeared, wrapped in a turquoise robe.

Larry stepped into the worship room.

"Oh!" Pua said.

She lit a candle. "Don't worship in the dark," she said.

Larry's tongue was like, welded to his mouth. Some crazy kind of magic was taking over. Like his whole life had been a joke, leading to this punch line. Like everything he'd ever done was stupid except that it magically led him here, to this room, with this brown-eyed beauty. He was so mind-blown, all he could do was watch her walk out the door.

He felt flooded with warm perfumed air and bright light. He walked into the changing room and dropped the keys into Christina's shift. He felt certain he was never going to steal again.

New Larry walked out into the courtyard.

The love of his life was holding a drink in a plastic cup, and standing underneath the big tree. He knew in his heart he had found the fourth and final Mrs. Lawrence Estonophie. Would she come back and live on the Jersey Shore, fine. Would she want to stay in the islands, fine. Just as long as Larry could lay his head between those beautiful breasts every night.

On the other side of the fence, in those jungle grounds posted with No Smoking signs, an old woman was gardening in the nude. She didn't seem to care that the temple people could see her. She squatted and dug into the earth.

Pua whispered: "You know who that naked gardener is? Donna Lorris. Lorris Tobacco?" Pua pointed to his top pocket. "Big Tent cigarettes, you smoke them."

Larry's hand went to his pocket. "I'm trying to quit," he said. "This is my last pack."

"Oh, sure," said Pua, with a teasing smile.

He looked from Pua to the naked gardener to the jungle around them to the dirt road with all the houses hidden back in the bush.

"You must be new to Hawaii," Pua said. "This is Black Point. Teddy Hong Kong lives just across the way, and down that twisty jungle trail lives Bix Sanders."

Bingo!

A jungle full of rich people. Larry looked over at blond Christina, gabbing with a bunch of robed men. Now he was sure Christina was related to the pineapple fortune. Here he was barely off the airplane, and he had stumbled into a friendship with all the right people.

It took kind of a shift in his thinking though, because in South Jersey, if you had big dough, you wore lotsa jewelry, drove shiny cars, lived in a fake Italian villa and had Eagles season tickets.

"If everybody out here is so rich," Larry asked Pua, "why don't they fix the road?"

"Silly," said Pua. "They don't want to fix the road."

"Ah," Larry said, "to keep away the burglars."

"No, worse," Pua said. "The tourists.

She stuck out her hand. Larry took it, not to shake, but to hold, like he was going to kiss it. Warm and soft. God, he got a boner just taking this girl's hand.

"Lawrence Stone," he said. "My friends call me Larry."

"Pualani Long," she said. "How long have you been in the islands, Larry?"

"Just a couple of …" he gulped. "A couple of lifetimes."

Pua laughed.

Make a girl laugh, Larry figured, and you're in.

Island tour

McCabe must have been scared, because he refused to let the brothers pick him up at home. Nobody could miss the Ilikai Hotel, McCabe had told Terry. It was pastel green, towering above the yacht harbor at the edge of Waikiki. A glass elevator rose thirty stories to a rooftop restaurant.

In the hotel's circular driveway stood McCabe, good to his word, on time and with his hair combed, like any kid educated by the nuns. He stood near a gray-haired fat lady dressed up like a Hawaiian queen, in a long red muu-muu, flower leis draped around her neck. When tourists would drive up in their rental cars, she'd open the passenger door and shout: "Aloha!"

She opened the passenger door of their car, and let McCabe in.

"That's her!" Larry said. He had goose bumps. "That's the Fat Lady. I met her on the bus. She gave me the Evil Eye. She told me it was the Year of the Rooster."

"So what?" said Terry. "It's a small island. You gotta see the same people all the time."

Larry slapped McCabe on the shoulder. "You know the Fat Lady, McCabe? She said something to you, didn't she? What did she say?"

"Have a nice Hawaiian day."

"That's all?" Larry said. "She's a witch, I'm telling you. You don't know her?"

"Larry, there's almost a million people on this island. I don't know them all. I've seen her around. She's the Ilikai's greeter. Other than that ..." McCabe shrugged.

Terry drove. McCabe sat in the front seat, Larry alone in the back. He stared at the Fat Lady until she was a speck in front of a giant green hotel.

The brothers had rented a mammoth white 1979 Ford Crown Victoria, the kind of car that keeps oil refineries up at night. Terry had figured that McCabe would own a car they could borrow, because the fewer papers the brothers signed in the Islands, the better. But as Terry liked to say, the road of life is full of landmines, you gotta steer around them. So he used up an alias to rent this car.

The cops would find it abandoned someday, but by then the brothers would have said aloha to these fair islands.

"So McCabe," Terry said. "You between cars, is that it?"

"I don't drive," McCabe said.

Terry should have been looking at the traffic, but he turned his head to stare in disbelief at McCabe. He swerved and just missed a motorcycle rickshaw. "You don't drive because …?" Terry demanded.

McCabe was sweating, although the car's interior was as cool as a glass of beer.

"Medical," said McCabe. "I pass out sometimes."

"No shit?" said Terry. "What is it? Epi … eppa something?"

"Epilepsy, no." McCabe made a frightened monkey grin. "I don't want to talk about it, guys."

"Fair enough," said Terry.

And Terry was a fair man, in Larry's opinion. Tough but fair. When they were kids Terry would sometimes twist Larry's arm behind his back and say, Tell the truth Larry, I'm sick of your lies, tell the truth and I'll let you go. Then Larry would say whatever Terry wanted to hear. And Terry always let him go, with just an Indian rubber burn as punishment.

You could depend on Terry.

"So you know what?" Terry said. "We don't live in Jersey anymore."

"No?" McCabe said.

"We moved to the Sunshine state," said Larry.

"Where in Florida?" McCabe asked.

Terry glared into the mirror and said, "Nevada ain't the sunshine state, stunod."

"What is it, then?" Larry said.

"The Show-Me State. Like in, show me your cards."

"You're full of shit," Larry said.

McCabe said: "I take it you fellows haven't lived in Nevada long."

"McCabe," said Terry, "Never mind where we live."

McCabe directed Terry over a bridge and they were out of Waikiki, the traffic a bit less intense, as they drove along the palm-lined Ala Wai Canal.

"That's the Big Wahine," McCabe said, pointing toward the green hills. "She's the patron saint of Honolulu. You could make an analogy to Rio."

An allergy to Rio. Larry tossed that around in the spin-dry cycle of his mind, but it came out wet.

"You know, how Rio has Jesus," McCabe said, "with his finger sticking up."

"What finger is that? Ha ha," said Larry.

"My brother," Terry said, "the what do you call it."

"Blasphemy," said McCabe.

"My brother the blasphemy," Terry said.

"At any rate," McCabe said, "the mountains we call the Big Wahine, they look like a woman lying down."

"Hey, I see that," Larry cried.

Terry's sunglasses stared straight ahead. "I don't give a shit," he said.

McCabe tightened his seatbelt, pointed out the ramp to a freeway.

No tollbooths? What kind of freeway was this?

"Hey Lazz," Larry said. "What does aloha really mean?"

"It means shut up," said Terry.

"Fack you," said Larry.

"Everybody knows what it means," Terry said to McCabe. "Everybody but my brother."

"It means..." McCabe said...

"We know what it means," Terry snarled.

Terry drove along the back side of Diamond Head, through all the palmy ritzy neighborhoods. There was a long tense silence, and then Larry could hear Terry's cigarette-damaged throat rasping.

"So McCabe," Terry said. "You're a news reporter, right?"

"I used to be. Now I do desk work."

"Oh, a promotion!" Larry said.

"Not exactly. It's not a glamour job. I manage all the fluff: the comics, the advice columns, the horoscopes and the obituaries."

"Manage the obituaries?" said Terry. "What's to manage? People die, they get their names in the paper."

"There's more to it. For prominent people, there's pre-written obits. Like, remember when John Wayne died?"

"Crying shame," said Terry. "He was the vaulted greatness of America."

"Newspapers and wire services had his obit written years in advance, so they could do a quick update and get it out."

"So famous people," Terry said, "their deaths are what you call foreseen? Print-wise, I mean."

"Right," said McCabe.

Terry said: "So Bix Sanders, his death story is already written?"

"Sure."

"How about Uncle Sam Wing?"

McCabe gulped before he said: "Yes."

"Now that I like to hear," said Terry.

They drove in silence a while and Terry let that sink in. Then he asked: "So McCabe, how did you procreate a newspaper job anyways?"

"I applied."

"You gotta be college-trained?" Larry asked. "Or do they hire regular people?"

McCabe sighed. "Diamond Head," he informed the brothers, "is not a volcano but a cinder cone."

"See," Larry said. "It's a college boy talking."

"The actual volcano is the island itself," McCabe said. "Oahu was formed when two volcanoes met. The volcanoes are so large we can't make them out except from an airplane. We'll be driving on the lava slopes all day."

"Volcanoes?" Terry said. "They're not going to blow, are they?"

"They're shield volcanoes," McCabe said, "they don't blow."

"Neither do we," Terry said. "That's the impression we want to make on you, McCabe. This whole visit here, nobody blows their top. All is calm, like on Christmas eve. Right stunod?"

He and Larry exchanged glares.

"So the politicians," Terry said, "since you were a newsman, you must know them pretty good."

"It's a small island."

Terry said: "How do you figure it, McCabe?"

"Excuse me?"

"Million suckers in bathing suits, no casino."

"There is a plethora of gambling," McCabe said.

"A what?"

"A plethora."

"If you gotta use a word like that," Terry said, "you must be bullshitting."

"Different kinds, then. Football betting, cockfighting, illegal card rooms and God knows what else."

"Cockfighting," Terry said with his lips curled. "What is that, Chinese?"

"And Filipino."

"Like with roosters?" Larry said. "They let roosters fight?"

Terry, one hand on the wheel, whirled around. "The fuck difference does it make, roosters or hens?"

"Hens lay eggs," said Larry. "I'll bet it's the roosters that fight."

"What about it McCabe?" said Terry.

"Yes, they use roosters. They attach razor blades to their spurs."

"I could see it," Terry said.

"Roosters fighting?"

"No," Terry said. "I could see another Atlantic City out here."

"Only they'd have to call it Pacific City," Larry said.

"Ignore my fuckin' brother," Terry said.

McCabe guided them along a highway, bare cliffs on one side, choppy sea on the other. After a mile or so the view opened up. They were at the curvy edge of the island, a deep valley, houses built up and down the ridges, ocean a rich blue with the sky blending into sea on the horizon.

They passed Black Point Road, where all the rich people lived, where Larry had met Pua at a house turned into a temple. But he was going to shut up about that.

"How about some tunes on the radio?" Larry asked.

"No music," Terry said. He pointed to his head. "Headache."

"Speaking of heads, that's Koko Head," McCabe pointed out. "That big round protrusion. It's another cinder cone."

"So how well do you know this guy, Mayor-to-be Bix Sanders?" Terry asked.

"I don't know him at all," McCabe said.

"What do you hear about him?"

McCabe said: "Why do I have the feeling you guys know the answers to your questions?"

"I heard they canceled his TV show because," Larry said. "Bix was a booze hound."

"Where'd you hear that?" McCabe asked.

"I read it in the National Enquirer," Larry said.

"Read between the lines," Terry said, "they couldn't keep the son of a bitch sober long enough to shoot a scene."

At a stoplight, Terry took off his watch as if it were annoying him. It was a gold watch with an expanding band. He paid like two grand for that watch, deep discount, but it kept lousy time. You should know better than to buy a Rolex at a Boardwalk jeweler, Larry had told him, only to be given the Evil Eye.

"The other guy, Uncle Sam," Terry said. "You said you know him?"

"I covered City Council meetings a few times, so yes, I've met him, but we're hardly best friends. If you mentioned my name to him, he might remember me, or might not."

"Is he like a tough guy?"

"Not at all."

"He's soft then?"

"He's an admiralty lawyer."

"A what?"

"Law of the sea."

Terry said: "I thought the sea was what you call a free fire zone."

Larry, restless in back, kicked the front seat. He couldn't help it when these restless fits came on him. Every time they stopped at a traffic light, he wanted to fling open the door and run.

"How do you fit in, McCabe?" Terry asked.

"Fit in?"

"A guy from A.C."

McCabe had actually grown up in the suburb of Pleasantville, just across the marsh from Atlantic City. But there wasn't a Catholic high school in Pleasantville, so the McCabe children took the bus down the Black Horse Pike, over the bay and into the city.

"The Army assigned me here," McCabe claimed.

"What did you do in the Army again?" Terry asked.

"Battalion journalist. I wrote reports and news letters."

"So, during the Vietnam War," said Terry, "while I was getting shot at, you were typing in Hawaii."

McCabe shrugged. "I went where the Army sent me."

"He got a soft deal because his old man was Air Force," Larry said. "Tech sergeant. Ain't that right McCabe? He put the fix in for you."

"Nope," McCabe said. "Luck of the draw."

Terry patted McCabe's shoulder. "That's all right. So you excaped Jersey and got your degree, and you got a soft spot in the Army. I'm proud of you. You're a vaunted American. Now, tell me more about Uncle Sam Wing."

McCabe gawped, like liars do when they're coming up with their fake stories. "Sam's a snappy dresser. The TV cameras love him."

At the top of the hill, McCabe showed Terry the turn for the parking lot of Hanauma Bay. "Tread lightly," he advised the brothers. "The ground is covered in tree thorns that will poke through the soles of your sandals."

The three of them got out of the car and walked across the dusty savannah.

"Ouch!" cried Larry.

Terry threw him an elbow. "He told you, didn't he?"

Larry, hopping on one foot, removed his sandal and picked out of its sole a thorn the size of a dog's tooth.

Terry looked to McCabe for sympathy. "This is what it's like, constant misfortune, traveling with my brother."

They walked to the edge of the cliff. A switchback path down a lava cliff was clogged with people in bathing suits descending to a blue-green bay. The bay was surrounded by desert hills in a horseshoe shape. Beyond a wide beach, the clear water revealed dark shapes of clumped coral beneath. The tiny figures, no bigger than dots, were snorkelers.

"This is where Elvis made Blue Hawaii," said McCabe. "You can rent snorkels. You didn't bring bathing suits?"

Terry shook his head.

"I should have reminded you," McCabe said.

"Swimming's out," Terry said.

"My brother never learned to swim," said Larry.

"If we wanted swimming lessons," Terry said. "They got pools in Vegas."

Larry kicked at the dusty ground.

"Ready for more touring?" McCabe asked.

When they were back in the car, Terry said: "What's next, McCabe?"

"Well, we drive up the Windward Side, and the next tour stop is Chinaman's Hat. It's an island that…"

"No Chinese Hats," said Terry. "Here's what's next. Uncle Sam Wing's house."

"His house?"

"Where he lives."

"I've never been there."

"Try 6601 Lilikoi.

"We know how to get there," Larry said.

Terry drove along the highway and turned in at a prosperous, palmy subdivision, all ranch houses, in soft colors, with trimmed lawns. After Terry turned a corner, he stopped and said: "Back there, right, we just passed it. The green house, privacy fence, swimming pool in back."

McCabe turned and looked at the house.

"So let's go up for the view," Terry said. He drove up the foothills of the Windward Range, and pulled over where a stone wall curved at the cliff top. All three of them got out of the car.

They stood there. A wind blew off the ocean so strong that McCabe's hair stood straight up. Dust, cigarette butts, insects, even birds, were swept up in the fierce updraft.

Terry, at the rock wall, pointed out Uncle Sam's home and swimming pool. It was only perhaps a hundred feet from the base of the cliff. A young woman in a black bikini was sunning herself in a lounge chair poolside.

Terry nudged McCabe.

"You think you could make the shot from here?"

McCabe took a step back from the wall.

"You had to qualify, right McCabe?" Terry said. "On the firing range. At least once a year."

"I don't ..." McCabe said.

"We know guys could make this shot easy."

McCabe said: "Talk sense, Terry."

"Talk sense? I can tell you inherently what makes sense. The son-of-a-bitch down there is going to accept the generosity of our offer."

The red-faced flush of anger passed and Terry said: "He's a widower. One daughter, Claire, a student at the university. That's her down by the pool in what you call a lounging format. Uncle Sam, he's all alone now, a period of mourning for his deceased spouse."

McCabe held up his hands. "Whatever you guys want, just..."

"What's our Plan A, you ask? I'll tell what's our Plan A. Larry shut the fuck up, I'm telling this plan. Sam Wing is what you call a stickler, a hard line against casino gambling in these beautiful islands."

"Gaming," Larry said. "You're supposed to say gaming, remember?"

"Okay, gaming," Terry said with a snort. "We're issuing a patented invitation to the Desert Skies Resort, where we know all the best people, expenses paid, including the ... gaming."

"Totally comped," said Larry.

"Luxury room, limo transportation, comped liquor, although we know Sam doesn't drink much. But he likes a good steak, along with any other luxury you could mention, including female company, to ease his what you call spousal grief."

"Whores out the wazoo," explained Larry.

"The best part of Plan A," said Terry, "is Sam's last night at the roulette wheel. Big smile on his face, he drops $5000 in chips on a certain number, and lo and behold, it pays off at 35 to one."

"That's $175,000," said Larry. "We double-checked the math."

Terry shook his head. "What luck! What a week! That's like the week of a lifetime. And you know what? No, you don't know, so I'll tell you, McCabe. That's not the end. Sam would be a welcome guest at the Desert Skies, a much-preferred customer for the rest of his long and happy life."

"He'd have a lot of friends," said Larry. "He's a lawyer, right? He could end up working for Managment someday."

"Lucrative as hell," Terry said. "And housing's expensive over here. With his roulette winnings, Sam could kill his mortgage, pay his daughter's tuition, and have what you call situational spending money left over."

McCabe looked at them sideways. "How do you know how much he owes on his mortgage?"

"Management research," Terry said. "Come on," he slapped McCabe hard on the back. "Let's go to lunch."

Terry drove them past Sam's house again, and McCabe directed him toward the Pali Highway, the shortcut over the mountains to Honolulu.

"So McCabe," Terry said, harsh sun glinting off the windshield. "We're going to put you on what you call monetary retainer."

"For?"

"Because you're a guy we can trust. Right stunod?"

Larry in back, stretched, ready for nap.

Terry reached down his shirt and pulled up a sweaty tourist wallet that had been hanging from his neck.

"Five thousand," Terry said. "For a job well done."

He suspended the wallet in the air for a moment, then dropped it into McCabe's lap.

"Keep it, but don't spend it yet. The minute Uncle Sam walks through the front doors of the Desert Skies, it's all yours."

"Spend it any way you want," said Larry. "You ever made such easy money in your life?"

"What do you want in return?"

"Advice, like a consultant. See you're like the perfect situational ... what am I trying to say? You know the score back in Jersey. And you know the score here in the Islands, what could be better?"

McCabe let the wallet sit in his lap.

Terry glared into the back seat at his brother.

"Sit up, Larry, like a fucking professional, will you?"

Larry shot his brother the finger.

"It's like this," Terry said. "Globalization."

"Globalization?"

"It's the whole fucking problem in a nutshell," Terry said. "Back in the day, Management could snap his fingers..."

He snapped his own thick fingers.

"... and things happened boom boom boom."

He shook his head.

"No more," he said.

"Because of globalization," said Larry.

"Who's giving you your orders?" McCabe asked.

"That you can't ask," Terry said.

"But he's from Nevada?"

"He's from," Terry said, "wherever he wants to be from."

"We just call him Management," said Larry. "He's got places all over the world."

"And why exactly did he send you here?"

"So's we can make a difference." Terry turned to Larry. "Right, stunod? We're here to exert the Constitution as citizens in a democracy, to lure the candidates into a position of..." he sneered at Larry. "Help me out here."

"This Uncle Sam dude," Larry said.

Terry recovered and cut Larry off: "He's gotta lose."

"Wait now," McCabe said. "Are you saying some power player in Nevada sent you here to force Uncle Sam out of the race for mayor? Because if that's what you're saying, that's a criminal conspiracy."

"This McCabe's a thinker," Larry said.

"My brother's right. You are a thinker. So I know you'll think this over with the utmost of care."

McCabe touched, just touched, the wallet in his lap.

"Five thou now," Terry said. "Maybe more later."

"How exactly am I supposed to earn the money?" McCabe asked.

"Earn," Terry said. "Listen to this guy. Educated by the nuns. Honest to a fault. You always was honest,

McCabe, it's one of your beatitudes. Just be our guy," Terry clipped his shoulder. "We need a guy knows his way around the island, like you're proving to us today with this nice tour you're giving."

McCabe handed the sweaty wallet toward Terry.

Terry held a hand up.

"Yours to keep," he said. "One old friend to another. Regardless. You were the one kid was always polite to our mother."

Terry pushed away McCabe's hand, and the wallet.

"We're not taking it back," Terry said, "and that's our final promise. Let's go back to town now that our transactions are accomplished."

In a spooky silence, he drove back toward Honolulu, up a tremendous steep highway into the clouds, and down the long jungle slope into the sunshine of the city.

"Tell you one thing," Terry said. "It's diminutive, this island. You could stack like a hundred of these isles sideways into Jersey."

Waikiki came in sight, and McCabe, nervous nelly, started babbling about the old days of Holy Infant, which nuns were the worst, the awful food in the lunch room, and he finally shut up when they were again parked in the circular driveway of the Ilikai Hotel.

Larry was hoping to see the Fat Lady again, but maybe she was on the beach casting magic spells because nobody was helping the tourists out of their cars.

"Gentlemen," McCabe said, and handed the wallet toward Terry. "I'm going to return your money. I can't work for you."

"All we're asking," Terry said, "is you deliver a benign offer of a lucrative free vacation to a hard working honest politician."

"You're asking me to commit bribery."

"Who's asking?" said Terry. "We're not asking, we're giving. We come bearing gifts, just like the Wise Men. And to mix our metaphors, let me pronounce that we're not Indian givers. Are we Larry?"

"You can't insult us," Larry said.

"Irregardless," Terry said. "Now that you know what's up, you're in."

"What am I in?"

Terry clapped him on the shoulder. "You went to college, you'll find all the right words, McCabe," he said.

"We believe in you," Larry said.

McCabe just sat there, silent, and it took a moment for Larry to realize what had happened.

"Holy fack!" said Larry. "He passed out."

He shook McCabe by the shoulder. "Wake up, McCabe!"

Officer Shimada

No night is so black that it brings true darkness to Waikiki. Lazarus Patrick McCabe stood at the foot of the harsh-lit, shaky wooden staircase that led up to David Shimada's apartment. The termite-eaten complex where David rented had been built as emergency housing after Pearl Harbor. It now rotted in the shadows between two gleaming high-rise hotels, the Ilikai and the Hilton Hawaiian Village. The property would have been re-developed to high rises long ago, but it was encumbered by thirty-four lawsuits.

David had rented the only second-floor apartment. All the ground-floor units had been converted to tourist retail, and were collectively called Pirate's Path. The shops were bright now, occupied by vendors of: coconuts with pre-inserted straws, ten-for-a-dollar postcards, coral jewelry, aloha shirts made in China, throw-away cameras, time-sharing schemes, straw beach mats, boogie boards, sun-tan lotion, machine-carved tiki gods, luau tickets, pineapple-on-a-stick, sunset dinner cruises, puka shell necklaces and his-and-her matching bathing suits. The gaudiest booth sold tickets (two *free* Rum Volcanoes included!) to the Teddy Hong Kong show.

Even at night, especially at night, Pirate's Path glowed with false light and was mobbed with sunburned bargain seekers in their best aloha-wear. McCabe, who dreaded being mistaken for a tourist, owned exactly one aloha shirt, and reserved its wear for weddings. And he went to a lot of them. Everybody, it seemed, was married but him.

He admired David's dark blue 1969 GTO, parked under the stairway and gleaming with the reflection of the shops' lights. He tucked a six-pack of Anchor Steam, and a manila envelope, under his arms and climbed the shaky stairway.

David's housing situation was a disturbing reflection of island realities. Pop Shimada owned a home on the Big Wahine. But doctors and lawyers, Californians and foreigners had bid up Big Wahine real estate, and only the elite could buy there now. David, his wife and daughter had been priced out, way out, and had bought a cheaply built, but expensive, townhouse on what used to be a sugar plantation. His wife had thrown him out, and now David, despite a good paycheck from the HPD, was living like a surf bum.

McCabe knocked on the door and held up the beer as his opening gambit.

David Shimada was McCabe's age, 32, a short, body-builder of a man with a military crew-cut. He wore a wrinkled green polo shirt and stringy cutoff blue-jeans.

"McCabe in Waikiki?" Shimada asked.

"I'm tracking down an old Army buddy. Obsessed with the maintenance of a hot-rod he bought in his youth."

"Never seen the guy, officer." Shimada stepped back and let the door open. "Anchor Steam? I thought you were off beer?"

David's front room was spare: a futon fold-down, a battered coffee table, a straw floor mat, a deck chair, two pole lamps. On the wall was spread a huge map of the mainland United States, with a red crayon path that veered from sea to sea.

McCabe sat at the futon while Shimada ducked into the kitchen. Even from this shabby apartment, the view would once have been the magnificent outline of the Big Wahine, the lights of civilization crawling over her belly. You could glimpse it still, but through the crude steel skeletons of rising condos.

"How's Sharon?" McCabe was almost afraid to ask.

David shrugged.

"Rachel?"

"Her teachers send her home with nasty notes."

"Chip off the old block," said McCabe. He nodded toward the big map.

"You going to make that trip?"

"Someday," Shimada said. His red crayon marks traced the route: Los Angeles, backward along Route 66 to Chicago, down the Mississippi to New Orleans, straight east to St. Augustine, up the coast to the rocky shores of Maine.

"Still determined to do it in the Goat?"

"Eight hundred bucks to ship it to Long Beach," said Shimada. "Then sell it in Boston and fly home."

"You'll do it some day, I know you will."

"With Rachel, when she graduates grammar school," David said. "I might as well introduce her to the Mainland. By the time she grows up, none of us will be able to afford to live here."

McCabe had known David for more than a decade now. They'd met as soldiers in the Tropic Lightning Division. Both had lucky assignments. David was the C.O's driver, and so spent a lot of time hanging around HQ.

David had a love-hate relationship with his home island. He felt trapped here, on the world's most remote land mass. What he wanted for his daughter was the choice to stay or leave. His plan was to get her into Berkeley, let her experience the Mainland, and then choose whether to return. Maybe he too would live in California upon retirement.

Beer in hand, David brought out a kitchen chair, turned it backward, sat in it.

"David," McCabe said, "this is kind of a business call."

"Shoot."

"Funny you chose the word *shoot*."

McCabe opened the manila envelope and laid on the coffee table a glossy 5x9 color photo. It showed a young, skinny man with dark hair in a butch cut. He had big brown eyes, wore a t-shirt. A white plumeria lei hung around his neck. He was kissing one of the college girls who was paid to dance the hula the airport.

"You've probably never seen this man," he said.

Shimada shrugged.

Hundreds of these photos were posted every day at Pirate's Path, in the expectation that tourists would purchase them as souvenirs.

"He's got a brother," McCabe said. "Older, heavier, with a cold-eyed stare. Apparently the brother didn't kiss the hula girls."

"So?" Shimada sipped Anchor Steam.

"Big brother's name is Terry Estonophie. Kissy face is Larry."

"You know them."

"They're from Atlantic City."

"I always wondered what Atlantic City was like."

"Ignorance," McCabe said, "is bliss. When you make your grand journey, don't be like George Washington."

"Eh?"

"Don't cross the Delaware. Look, in high school the brothers were the chief troublemakers. Larry dropped out of school and ended up in prison. Terry graduated to the College of Mobster Knowledge."

"It's no crime to visit Hawaii."

McCabe tapped the photo.

"This is no surfing safari. They're staying at the Royal. You know Mango at the bell desk, right? I asked Mango and he said Terry checked in, under the name Stone. The younger brother is not registered, but hangs out, probably sleeps there. They order room service, rarely go out, never have female visitors."

"So, a business trip."

"Exactly."

"I don't have much to eat," David said. "Kim Chee? Water? Juice?"

"What brand of juice?"

"Grotton."

"Water. I'm boycotting Grotton products."

Boycotts of Grotton products erupted every few months in Hawaii. The Grotton family owned vast swaths of land on all four main Hawaiian islands. They had arm-twisted the Legislature into cutting taxes on agricultural land to an absurdly low level. Competing with Dole and Libby in the fresh fruit market was far too much trouble for Grotton. So they auctioned off all their "U.S. Fancy" and "No. 1" grade pineapples, and kept the bruised, sunburnt, and insect-damaged fruit for canning and juicing.

But pineapples had become a sideshow in the Grotton circus. The company now made its fortune in real estate. Their strategy was simple: They never sold their ag land, but held it virtually tax-free, developing housing tracts and resort complexes as the economy boomed. All their developments were leasehold, with the land reverting to Grotton after 99 years.

David walked into the kitchen and returned with a jar of kim chee, two bowls of cold white rice, and a glass of ice water. He handed the water, the kim chee, a bowl of rice and a pair of chopsticks to McCabe.

"Warm kim chee?" McCabe said.

"In Korea they bury this stuff for a year. You think it needs refrigeration?"

"You're the one," McCabe said. "who'll have to explain my carcass to your brethren in blue." He picked out a lump of pickled bok choy.

In a normal place, two friends might go out for a drink or cup of coffee, but Waikiki was not a normal place. David's apartment was indeed surrounded by

restaurants, but they charged prices no sensible local
would pay.

"How long did you live in Jersey?" David asked.

"As long as I lived anywhere, except for the
Islands. Six years. I'm not claiming the brothers are
Mafia. For every genuine Mafioso in New Jersey, there
are a thousand pretenders."

He passed the jar of kim chee to Shimada.

"What exactly are they doing in my islands?" David
asked.

"They've taken an interest in the fortunes of Uncle
Sam Wing."

"I'm surprised anybody from Jersey knows who
Sam is."

"The brothers reek of connections to Las Vegas
nowadays. And what do Las Vegas and Atlantic City have
in common?"

"Estonophie," Shimada said. "What kind of name
is that?"

McCabe shrugged.

A city bus roared down Ala Moana, nullifying all
conversation. When it passed, McCabe said: "The last
time I saw these brothers was during the commission of a
criminal act."

"You going to tell me?"

"It involved rental cars. They milked that scam for
a long time, were caught, but never prosecuted. Terry is
the muscle, Larry is the con-man. Their mother was one
of those crazy people who never left the house.
Sometimes we would glimpse her face at the curtain, like
a ghost. Papa Estonophie was named Tiny, which meant
of course that he was gigantic in girth. He'd sit in front of
his emporium all day with a cigar in his mouth. Then at

night he drank himself into a stupor at the Knights of
Columbus. His shop was a one-room shotgun shack on
Mediterranean Avenue. All the Monopoly streets are in
Atlantic City, you know that, right? And yes,
Mediterranean is actually the cheapest street in town.
Tiny's store sold general merchandise, you know, cartons
of cigarettes, TVs, stereos, toothpaste."

"Whatever the hijackers brought in."

"Right. Containerized shipping was invented in
New Jersey. Can you guess why? Too much merchandise
disappearing from the docks. The old man died of a
gunshot wound, by the way, a year after Terry got out of
high school. Tiny Estonophie was shot in the gut, and left
in an alley all night to writhe in agony. His death amused
the local police. No shooter was so much as accused."

"Nice," Shimada said.

"There are people who wonder if it was Terry who
shot his father."

"Nicer yet," Shimada said.

"Atlantic City," McCabe said. "was even more
dreadful before the casinos."

"All this time I thought you grew up in ..."

"Pleasantville, across the bay. But we attended the
same Catholic school. Terry was suspended in his senior
year, after knocking out some boy's teeth. Larry dropped
out after his second suspension. He picked the lock on
the church poor box. He claimed it was his money
because he was poor."

"You haven't told me what they're doing here."

"David, I've got a favor to ask."

"Be my guest."

"You're tight with the Chief. Is there any way you
could suggest permit approval?"

"Carry permit?"

McCabe nodded.

Gun laws were strictly enforced in Honolulu, and Halawa Jail was full of mugs who'd been nabbed carrying hot iron. Only the Chief of Police could issue a permit to carry a weapon, and he guarded those permits like they were his first born son. David was an intelligence officer who worked directly for Police Chief Abraham Abreu. If anyone could get McCabe a concealed-carry permit, it was David.

"I don't know," David said. "That's a tough one. It's been years."

He took a thoughtful sip of beer.

"McCabe, my father always warned me: The nail that sticks up gets hammered down. It was good advice. Some of the guys in my Academy class are still on patrol. I was out of uniform after seventeen months. You know why? Because power is a reality. Every time I saw somebody wearing brass, I used my ears instead of my mouth. What you want a gun for anyway?"

"I'm in trouble. The brothers want to enlist me in a scheme to bribe Uncle Sam Wing. They want to buy him out of the mayor's race."

David juggled the empty beer bottle hand to hand. "Dare I ask?"

"You once pointed out that all the new hotels in Waikiki were built with casino-style lobbies. Lobbies that, if not for gambling, would be a waste of expensive real estate. It was like they were preparing for the era of slot-machine aloha. I think that era is about to arrive."

David set the beer bottle at his bare feet. "Sam Wing out, Bix Sanders in," he said. He wandered to the windows, looked out at the night traffic of Waikiki, the tour buses, the rickshaws, the rental cars, the Jitneys, the motor scooters. "Just what we need, casinos."

"I know."

"What kind of island will this be when our kids grow up?"

A car horn blared.

"That's why I want Rachel to have mainland options," David said. "Casino gambling, death sentence for us regular folks."

"It's already a madhouse down here."

"Okay," David said. "It's starting to make sense. Bix. The rumors. Reckless gambling, drinking. Maybe Vegas has a hook into the star of a canceled TV series. He wouldn't be the first guy to gamble away a fortune."

He whirled on McCabe.

"Why you?"

"McGuire Air Base was my pop's last assignment. My sisters settled in south Jersey. Three of them. Seven nieces and nephews altogether."

"And?"

"I'm the one guy in the Islands who knows how vicious Terry is. There are hundreds of millions of dollars at stake, David. For that kind of coin, Terry's employers wouldn't hesitate to … They don't actually have to do anything to my sisters. The threat alone …"

David opened another Anchor Steam. "So you've gotta?"

"I've got to do something."

"Blow town. Go into hiding. Molokai. The Big Island. Better yet, the Mainland. How about Alaska?"

"There's still the problem of my sisters," said McCabe, feeling shaky, wishing his disease would permit him a relaxing beer. "And Reiko won't leave Oahu. She's been to the mainland. She doesn't like it one bit. She feels out of place there."

David stared at his map, silent.

McCabe became aware of the zooming traffic, the construction noise, condos going up even in the dark. He inhaled the odor of hot asphalt, the whiff of coconut oil, the salty ocean, heard the rustling of palms, a steel guitar tune, the babble of bargaining tourists below.

David broke the spell. "They haven't threatened you?"

"They paid me. They made me take the money. Five thou."

"Wrap it up, plastic bag. Put it in safe deposit. Don't spend even one dollar. Evidence. You lack criminal intent. If I were you, I'd see Porky Hashimoto."

"Why Porky?"

"Police protection won't work, that you know, right? Even if the Chief signed a carry permit for you, a gun would do you no good. You can't do one-man battle with the Vegas mob. Even if you're strapped with a magnum, they have the element of surprise and your motor skills will desert you just when you need them most." David held up one finger. "But Porky ..."

"Hasn't he been disbarred?"

"That fell through," David said. "The usual skullduggery. No matter, you don't need legal advice, you need illegal advice."

"There's gotta be a better..."

"Porky's the Master of Darkness and better yet, an ally of Sam Wing."

"I don't know, David."

"You can stall these Jersey guys a couple of days?

"Maybe."

"You don't need a gun. You need Porky."

Pearl Harbor

Terry pounded on McCabe's door. Number 7 right? Thump, thump, thump. Across the street at the Kaza School, kids chanted some foreign prayer. It ended with them shouting: "I see."

Thump, thump, thump.

"McCabe!"

No answer, but door Number 8 opened. The nurse poked her ponytailed head out. "Can I help you?"

"Oh, good morning, sorry to disturb you," Terry said. He used the gentleman's tone Mom had instructed him to employ when he sought a lady's favor. *Ask nice, Terrance, and you'll always get what you want.*

"Does Lazarus happen to be around the premises?"

The nurse shook her head. She was not dressed like a nurse, not this early, eight o'clock in the morning. She wore red shorts and a white halter top that exposed her belly. She was barefoot. Didn't any of these island people own a decent pair of shoes?

"Have you any idea where I might facilitate Mister McCabe?" Terry said. "I have an appointment."

McCabe's voice leaked out of his cranked-shut kitchen windows.

"I'm here."

Just what I wanted, Terry said to himself. McCabe, cowering.

"Give me a minute," said McCabe.

"It's a lovely morning you have here," Terry said. "I congratulate you on your splendid weather."

"Me?" asked the nurse.

"I take it you're enjoying a day off from your laborious medical efforts," Terry said.

"Oh no, we go in at three," she said.

"Perhaps you would care to join our previously scheduled excursion."

The sound of vomiting came from McCabe's apartment.

"Excuse me," said the nurse, and barged into Number 7. Terry followed, waited in the living room while the nurse, in the bathroom, fussed over McCabe.

Life was a road full of landmines, and the nurse was just another one. Now she could identify Terry to the cops, so she was in. Terry would have preferred to leave her out, her being an unpredictable female and all. But the more he pondered the new equation, the more he liked it. Adding her was a risk, but McCabe would feel the need to protect her, and it would maybe give some urgency to his response, which so far had been, you could say hesitational.

Terry heard McCabe furiously brushing his teeth, and then he appeared at the bathroom door.

"Something you ate?" Terry asked. "Did you consumate some of that, what you call, notorious raw fish. What do you call that?"

"I'm good to go now," said McCabe. "Bit of a nervous stomach I guess."

"Nothing to be nerved up about," Terry said. "I didn't catch your girl's name.

"Reiko," said McCabe. "She's got to stay here."

"What is she, a dog? She can't make up her own mind?"

"We're coming along," Reiko said.

"We?" asked Terry. "You and whom else?"

"When she says *we*, she means *I*," McCabe said. "It's a small-town, local kind of thing, Terry."

"Good," Terry said. "As it occurs, I prefer feminine accompaniment. Besides, your nurse here might provide what you call historic prospective, and you never know, somebody might get hurt out there, and need the medical profession. You're of the Japanese persuasion, I take it?"

"The grandparents came from Okinawa," Reiko said.

"Same thing, if my geographical terminology is correct."

Reiko shook her head. "No."

"All the same," Terry said. "Let's go."

He put a friendly arm around Reiko's shoulder. "We'll return in plenty of time for you to practice your healing arts."

Terry drove the Crown Victoria. McCabe sat in front, his girl in back. She was the annoying kind who hums. McCabe was a heavy breather. The tires sang on the concrete, the sun glared off the tinted windows, the car's air conditioning rasped and rattled. No conversation? That was okay with Terry. Your prototypical victim was more easily indimidated when deprived of verbal relief.

Terry had plotted the route on a Chevron map in heavy pencil and he followed it perfect, because he was a pro and needed no navigational assistance from a college wimp. Past the big rust-colored football stadium and, zam-bam, not one single bad turn prior to arrival at the Pearl Harbor Memorials.

Terry reached for the glove-box and removed an expensive camera. He hung it around his neck by a red strap. It was a German camera, since he would never insult the honored dead by bringing a Japanese-made device to these sacred premises. "I promised my Uncle Richie I would take a picture," he said. "My father's brother. He was one of the what you call hero generation."

Leading them into a museum, Terry bulled past the exhibits, and obtained the tickets, which to his surprise were issued at no cost, except to the American taxpayer. Government generosity he found irritating, because the truth was, except for these tickets, he had never taken a freebie from Uncle Sap, while paying mandatory taxes so that every lazy slob in America could get what you call largesse.

Now where was Larry? And would he dress with respect to the Drowned Dead?

"Smile!" Terry said, and snapped a picture of McCabe and his girl near some kind of out-dated bomber plane. Its nose was stuck way up in the air, which reminded Terry of a certain fellow in Vegas. Terry had smooth-talked Management, hiding from him the pertinent fact of Larry coming along as half-assed partner. And this was the thanks Terry got, Larry the no show, probably in bed with some dope-smoking babe.

He checked his gold Rolex. The second hand was what you call spastic. He'd have to take this watch in for a tune-up. "My brother has been unceremoniously delayed," he said, handing a ticket to McCabe and the girl.

But here was the first of the day's landmines. Terry had not imagined that the Arizona Memorial was reached by boat. The doomed battleship had been anchored on Pearl Harbor Day, correct? So you should just walk the plank to get there, but no, it was across a half mile of treacherous green water.

There was no backing out now. Terry was the last to step on the launch because, to be honest, he had yet to overcome his one remaining personal weakness. It wasn't the crowd of tourists that made him feel dizzy and faint, but the launch bobbing on the water of Pearl Harbor.

It took Terry back, and this was no volunteer tour. No longer was he standing in Hawaii's bright sunshine. Now in his churning mind, everything was some shade of brown. It was hot rain, a hundred degrees. His jeep was in a jam at a hectic ferry dock at the Mekong River crossing. All around him were gooks on cyclos, market ladies holding chickens upside down, treacherous ARVN soldiers, old men huddling under cheap plastic ponchos, and a hundred school children, kids with golden skin, black hair, wearing drenched white blouses over blue trousers and skirts. What do you know, Catholic school, the nuns rapping knuckles even in this uncivilized half of the world.

You had to watch the children, though, because the most innocent-looking kid might drop a grenade in your jeep and run.

After seven months in-country, this was Terry's first convoy as road master. He'd been given the bump to Acting Jack, which was Buck Sergeant, but without the higher pay. The gook civilians were pissed that they had to make way for Terry's convoy, but let them bitch and moan, for Terry didn't speak the language. Army trucks had priority. Terry's jeep led the convoy onto the ferry and maybe, he almost had to admit it now, they had overloaded. He had argued with the ferry captain. *Goddamn you GI* was the only English the old man spoke. But the last two trucks, filled with PX cigarettes, they had jammed on, even though the rear wheels loomed a few inches over the ferry's steel plate edge.

But you can't leave trucks behind, that was what you call the interminable rule of convoys.

Halfway across the wide Mekong, Terry remembered seeing a heavy puff of stinky smoke from the ferry's diesel stack, and then nightmare. He didn't see what actually happened but only what you could call the hallucinations of his cranial mind. He was sitting up in his jeep, clinging to the steering wheel, when the ferry swamped and rolled, sickening, into the wide brown river. The ferry's hot diesel engine hit the water with horrible hiss and roar.

No way could he swim. How he came to the surface was hugging a bale of straw. Gooks and GIs drowned together, but that was a fact he learned in what

you call mental retrospect. In the river he clung to the
straw bale. He floated in a frightening strong current he
could not resist. Where was he being swept off to? South
China Sea. He pictured himself swept out into the
horrible lonesome ocean, miles deep, hopefully you
would be dead before the sharks found you.

But God was listening to Terry chant the Hail
Mary through shivering lips, because his bale got tangled
in a big float of lillypads and he was rescued.
Embarrassing, but it was two gook fishermen in a sampan
that fished him out.

And that was his last convoy. The Army gave him
what you call a medicinal profile. Meaning he was a
psychic case, in their wrong but professional opinion. He
was pronounced no longer fit to drive convoy. They took
away his Acting Jack stripe and his forty-five. They gave
him the humiliation task of Barracks Orderly, B.O. as the
guys called it. Terry stayed behind to guard the TVs and
stereos while the boys went adventuring. Every convoy
was partly a scam, since some cargo never made it
through. Just like in Jersey! That cargo was sold to fund
what you could call a celibate of victory. So every convoy
ended with a party at Can Tho, steaks on the grill, beer in
the ice bucket.

Terry, on profile, alone in the barracks, could not
drink enough beer to kill the bad feeling he got from
missing the party.

So now! Terry, on the launch crossing the
treacherous Pearl Harbor, gripped the stainless steel rail.
He leaned over to hide what you call his facial emotions
from McCabe and the nurse.

Terry felt only a little better when they got to the
Arizona Memorial, since that too was surrounded by

treacherous water. Hawaii's ocean was sparkling clear, but not at Pearl Harbor. Down there in the fishy murk, 1177 good Americans had suffered the fate Terry barely escaped. What incensed him now was the Japanese tourists walking all over this sacred spot. Taking pictures of one another. With Japanese cameras. Who won the war anyway, America or the goddamn Japanese?

It infuriated him, their smiling. The Trade Winds blowing the ladies' dresses, the men chattering and pointing. When they got home to Tokyo, they'd show their photos, brag of their conquests: look, here's what we did to those dumb Americans on the Day of Infantry.

"I don't think you should take it personal," Terry said to Rei.

"What's that?"

"I don't blame you for Pearl Harbor," Terry said. "It's forgiven, you know, since you didn't have no part of history."

"Pardon?"

"I mean," Terry said, "what kind of empathy feeling do you get, looking down at what your people did to American soldiers."

"Terry," McCabe said. "Rei's father is an American. He fought in the United States Army in World War II. In Italy. He's got a Bronze Star and a Purple Heart. He's an American hero."

Terry stared at Rei and thought: Maybe bullshit. Japan and Italy. Hmm. Whose side was Italy on, anyway? But just in case, you cannot insult an American veteran, no matter what stripe. He supposed there was the stern possibility of this girl's father having slipped into the U.S. Army in those desperado days. If so…

He saluted.

"Then respect to your ancestry," he said. "But these camera swinging Tokyos …" he pointed to the crowd of tourists, "got no business here. Sneak attack."

"It would have been better with 24-hour notice?" McCabe said.

"Don't be a wise guy, McCabe." He fixed a look on Reiko. "In school this guy always had the smart-mouth answer."

McCabe began reading a plaque and one of the Japanese tourists asked him questions, pointing off toward the mountains.

Terry blocked Rei into one corner of the pure white memorial.

"You are in a position to do me a favor of an unforgettable nature."

"Oh?"

"Your boyfriend is in a historical precedent."

"How so?"

"The details are forthcoming. Needless to say, the feminine influence is what you could call a derisive factor. See…" Terry used the soft pussy-cat tone … "in case you haven't noticed, McCabe is not what you call… of the heroic mentality. Not to malign his characters, but sometimes, well to use a baseball metaphor, when it's his turn at the plate, he's afraid to swing the bat. So he stands there in fear and gets struck out. Gabeesh?"

Her eyes began a panic search for McCabe.

"We just need a small favor from him. He knows what to do but he is putting it off by procrastinating. Anything you can provide him, like mental fortitude, we would appreciate."

He offered her a smoke from his pack of Big Tents.

"There's no smoking here," said Rei.

Terry lit up with his First Cav lighter. "So if I'm calculating with any accuracy," he said, "it would seem you leave work at between eleven and midnight."

Rei nodded.

"That can be a dangerous hour. Aren't you afraid of what you call beasts lurking in the night?"

"There's a security guard in the parking lot," said Rei.

"Old, fat guy with white hair, right? Smokes Marlboros. Reads comic books to keep himself busy."

Rei stared at him, this time with the look he wanted, respect.

"Aside from your own personal safety," Terry said as McCabe approached. "Did you ever think in horror, that someday your boyfriend might end up in your emergency room?"

On the launch ride to shore, Terry actually felt good enough to let go of the rail. He wasn't going to drown today after all. The approach of solid ground calmed him. When they stepped off onto a pebbled path he said: "I'm going to let you two lovebirds take a taxi home. I have business on this side of the island."

He handed McCabe a hundred dollar bill.

"You really have to take it. I would be insulted in a terrible fashion. What kind of mind-numbing host would I be, deploying my guests miles from their domicile?"

McCabe shook his head, kept his hands in his trouser pockets.

Terry stuffed the bill in between McCabe's shirt and sweaty chest.

"We'll be in touch," Terry said. "Within 48 hours, I assume. Goodbye and let me say, there's nothing so welcome as camaraderie."

Terry hopped into the Crown Victoria, which seemed like a hundred twenty degrees inside. Down with the windows, in with the breeze, he was so glad to be on land again. How anybody could live on this rock, water in every direction, he could never figure. Atlantic City, too, was an island, but once you crossed the Black Horse Pike, you had 3000 miles of solid American ground west of you.

He drove away, a last glance in the rearview at McCabe and Reiko. He felt a genuine progress had been made, sufficient. The original plan was to let McCabe know that his sisters back in Jersey were vulnerable. That was only backup now, because they had stumbled into the fortunate situation of McCabe having a next-door girlfriend. And in Terry's reading, the little nurse went from wary to terrified after only one hour in his company. This was the effect he was after. He wished her no harm, especially if she really was a Bronze Star daughter. Hurt he didn't need. Hurt was, you could call it unprofessional. Hurt only happened when fear failed, and Terry was determined that fear would not fail.

He wished McCabe no harm either. All these people needed to learn was to cooperate. There are certain people, like Vegas Management, determined to get their way, you could call them generals in an Invisible Army. Terry was like a captain, bucking for major. Would he ever achieve generalship? Not likely. But honorable retirement, with a fine pension, nice house out in the sunny desert, certain privileges, that he could aspire to.

The wonderful Nevada desert. Far from any treacherous ocean.

So he felt good, driving back along the H-1. Message of fear sent to both McCabe and Nurse. Could they miss the metaphor of Pearl Harbor? No. They were college groomed. They would understand: This could be your personal Pearl Harbor, so let's not have no sneak attack. Devastation could follow unless you go with the plan. Your personal battleship could be sunk into the waves. That was all he tried to accomplish today, and he lit a Big Tent cigarette as a reward, using the gold-plated lighter he had purchased at the Pacex, oh, more than a decade in past years.

Purchased. He was no thief, like some people he could mention. Larry would have stolen this lighter because he had no personal rectitude whatsoever. He stole from the Church, he'd steal from the Army. Larry. AWOL. Good thing the kid was too young for the draft, he would have been ruined by Basic Training.

Me, get out of bed, Sarge?

Terry laughed imagining Larry vs. drill sergeant.

When he pulled up at the Tiki Torch Hotel, their pathetic symbol of gas-fired torches burned even in daylight. Sitting in rusty metal chairs, wasted men and women, welfare losers in a hotel too dirty for tourists.

The ground floor had been taken over by businesses. Post-cards and t-shirts, and even a travel agent. Pathetic, none of these businesses had even a gawker. The travel agent in particular struck Terry as worthless because here you were in vacation paradise, where did you need to go? The clerk of this motel was a tall, skinny, curly-haired Hawaiian guy. He struck Terry right away as a swish. It wasn't no great piece of detective work either, since the guy wore a white shirt with epaulets and a skirt. A skirt on a man!

Terry couldn't help but gawk at this skirt-wearing man, so he tried to disguise his curiosity. He pretended to be interested in a rack of brochures. They were waving like flags in the breeze, because this little office was practically out in the open.

"Are you interested in time-sharing, sir?" asked the skirt-man.

"What do you call that, not a skirt, a…"

"A lava-lava, sir. It's a Hawaiian tradition, much like a kilt. I see you're interested in time shares, and I have several wonderful opportunities available."

Carl was this man's name, a gold bar pinned to his shirt announced it.

"What does anybody want a time share for?"

"Well, sir, instead of renting, you own. You come back every year to the same place. Pride of ownership." He leaned over the desk like he was telling a secret. "And then you sell for a profit."

"Little guy, 206, crewcut, brown eyes, he been around this morning?"

"Oh, you mean Larry. He's a stitch, isn't he? I haven't seen him all morning."

"Figures," Terry said.

He climbed to the second floor and pounded on the middle door. Sleepy Larry opened. In white underwear. Blinking.

"Eight a.m. Pearl Harbor," Terry said. "Remember?"

He forgave his brother. The kid was not up to snuff, which actually, made Terry feel more proud of his own self. It was Terry who had the discipline. *Why can't you be more like your big brother?* Mom used to scold Larry. But every time she said that, Larry just acted up worse, like baby brothers always did, trying to squeeze some love out of Mom.

It was Terry, first born, who had the main claim on Mom's heart. Even though she tried to hide it, Terry could see the sparkle of pride in her eyes. *My he-man,* she said, especially on those nights when Dad came home drunk.

And then came the premier night of their family life, when Dad slapped Mom and Terry threw him out of the house. Actually threw. Down the stairs and into the mud. On Easter Sunday night.

"Come on in," Larry said and opened the door. "I had them spray for roaches. Carl, downstairs, you met him? He's my friend. He told me a lot of fun stuff about the history of this place."

"You're talking about the guy in the skirt? Larry, we're not here to make friends, especially with a swish. And we're not here to learn history. Or get a fucking sun tan."

Terry stepped in and closed the door. It smelled like a chemical factory in there. Plus Terry could smell the rotten meat stink from the butcher shop below. The back of the room was not solid but a wall of jalousie windows that Larry had cranked open. His view was a greasy shop that rented motor scooters.

Larry sniffed. "You been sweating?" he asked Terry. "You kind of stink."

"What? I'm offensive?"

Larry held his nose. "B.O."

Terry lifted one arm and sniffed his arm pit. "I don't smell nothing."

"Pee-yew," Larry said. "Are you kidding? You smell like goat piss."

"It's nothing verifiable," said Terry.

"My nose verifies it."

"I'm taking a shower immediate," Terry said. "You. Go to the Royal. Fetch my red shirt and black trousers, dark socks and underwear. And my deodorant."

Terry rushed into the bathroom and slammed the door.

Larry whistled and palmed a big red key. He heard the pipes lurch as the shower came on. He had pulled this kind of trick before, to distract Terry from his righteous anger. Terry smelled of nothing but Old Spice cologne. However, the thought that he might smell offensive always shook him up.

Larry passed the front desk with a wave at Carl, hopped on a white Honda motor scooter. Carl was a cool guy, even if he did wear a skirt. It was Carl who had first clued him in to Captain Dudoit.

Larry had rented this scooter on the sly, it was like, freedom from his brother. Plus it was a blast to weave through Waikiki traffic. Larry felt he had outsmarted Terry. Now there would be no fight over Larry's failure to show up at Pearl Harbor. Larry didn't want to tour no underwater museum at practically sunrise, plus he was afraid, all them dead sailors, Pearl Harbor would be lousy with ghosts. Terry didn't believe in ghosts but Larry had felt their spooky presence lots of times.

Terry would be grateful when he stepped out of the shower. He'd be full of thanksgiving when Larry showed up with fresh clothing and a couple of Burger King cheeseburgers. That would give Terry a win because he insisted Burger King was superior to Larry's choice, McDonald's. Larry was like a man of the people and a Big Mac was good enough for him. He didn't need no royal hamburger with a cardboard crown.

No, Terry didn't stink, he was fussy clean always. Terry had the brawn but Larry had the brains. Larry weaved past Waikiki's sunny traffic jams, thinking that sometimes he could put a collar on his brother and walk him like a dog.

Mynah Bird Beach

8

"I've never held a real job," Pua said.

She sighed. She looked past Larry to the volleyball game on the beach. It was just sunset. Four strong young guys were playing, and she knew every one of them. The problem with this island was, everybody knew everybody. Once people made up their mind about you, they stuck a label on you that would never peel off. Her label: Daughter of A Swindler. It wasn't true! It wasn't her dad's fault, he was only trying to make everybody happy.

"I just look after Dad," she said. "That's my job. My brothers," she wrinkled her nose, "took off for the Mainland."

Larry Estonophie was holding her hands over a beer-sticky table cloth. They were at the Mynah Bird, a beach bar set like a grass shack between the Hawaiian Village and Ilikai hotels, at the last curving elbow of

Waikiki Beach. The Mynah Bird had serving booze and gossip since the steamship era. Although, or perhaps because, it was far from the Capitol, it had become a politician's hangout. Here, since the days of the monarchy and the sugar barons, the deals had been cut that turned Waikiki from the King's duck pond into a world-famous resort.

On stage above the bar, a clump of musicians, all in red-and-white striped shirts, were assembled into a Dixieland band. One-Lung Pete, the famous bartender, who'd appeared on many episodes of *Danger, Hawaii,* was tending bar, huffing and gasping to keep up, pouring sloppy pitchers of cheap beer. The banjo player was scraping away at a tinny solo.

"Do you or don't you?" Larry asked.

"Do I or don't I?" Had Pua been missing parts of conversations again? It happened on this medication.

"Smoke marijuana," Larry said.

She shook her head. She sipped ginger ale.

"Me neither," Larry said. The banjo solo ended, the band went into full swing, and Larry had to shout.

"My friend asked me to bring him back some Maui Wowee."

"I'm not into drugs," shouted Pua.

"Me neither," Larry shouted. "I was just thinking about my friend. He's never smoked any Maui Wowee."

"Oh look," Pua said.

At the palmy entrance to the beer hall appeared a tall familiar man.

"That's Bix Sanders!" Pua squeaked.

If there was one face from Hawaii that people all over the world knew, it was Bix Sanders. Larry and half the audience rose from their seats for a better look.

"Who's that with him?" he shouted to Pua, but the music faded and he said at normal volume. "That's not his wife."

Pua nodded. "It sure is."

Bix Sanders, he of the ruggedly handsome, acne-pitted face, was big in every way. Six foot four, wide at the shoulders, he moved like a dancer. The woman at his side was a dumpy five-foot-three, with mousy gray hair cut in a pageboy. Together, they looked like James Bond holding hands with a retired library clerk.

"She keeps him sober," Pua said.

"You know them?"

"My dad," she said, "knows everybody. You don't know how popular my dad was before things went sour. We've been over to the Sanders compound. Not in the house, just in his backyard for luau. You know where he lives, out at Black Point."

Larry stared into Pua's eyes. She, frightened by his intensity, looked down into the bubbles of her soft drink. Pua allowed him to massage her hands. His felt grubby and soft. She wondered what kind of work he did. He dressed in an aloha shirt, but had it buttoned up, as if he thought it needed a tie. He was a little guy, and she had never dated any man smaller than she was. But he seemed like a funny guy, and had such soft, beautiful eyes.

Pua gawked as Bix and his sobering wife were escorted to a table near the stage. The musicians stood around, hot and exhausted, while the trumpet player was slurring the same jokes he told every Sunday, too loud, and into the buzzing microphone. He got away with the same jokes because on Sundays the crowd was mostly beer-blasted mainlanders, who in their ignorance saw the

Mynah Bird as just another tourist tavern with a view of Diamond Head.

"I hope Bix doesn't start drinking," Pua said. "He's not ordering beer, is he? It always starts with beer." She sat back and said: "He could be our next mayor."

"Bix?"

"Anyway, dad's a friend of the old governor. I mean the governor who's quitting."

"Really, your dad knows the governor?"

"So do I," she said. "It's a small island. There's a million people here but sometimes it seems like a village."

"There's something about Hawaii," Larry said, "I can't really put it..."

"It's just me and Dad," Pua said. "My mom died a long time ago."

"My mom too," Larry said. "You know, I wasn't there at the hospital, when she died, I mean I was there but I went downstairs for coffee and that's, when ..."

His lips twitched as he told that lie. Actually, he'd ducked over to the Boardwalk for a couple of beers.

But Pua interpreted that twitch as a sign of grief. She decided that a boy who grieved his mother, who was sorry he'd missed the moment of her passing, had a warm heart.

"You came all the way here by yourself?"

"With my brother. He's you know like an intellectual. Museums and stuff."

"So what kind of things do you like?"

Larry looked over the crowded room. Then he stared at Pua, then at her breasts, and dropped his gaze to the table.

"Go on tell me," Pua said. "You know, in Hawaii, we're very honest."

"I can't say it," Larry said.

"Come on, you're no fun."

"I love you."

He said it loud to be heard over the music, but it came out during a pause in the song, and it was like Larry had screamed those words to all of Waikiki.

Pua knocked over her ginger ale. The band started up a ragtime number. She pushed away from the table, put her hands to her face and ran for the exit.

She stood breathing rapid, where a stone wall met the beach. The volleyball players were straggling toward the parking lot. The sun was all the way down and here was the magic moment, neither day nor night.

Calm down calm down she said to herself. She fingered the Koshu Kaza medallion that hung from her neck, the heart with two eyes. She muttered the magic words: *"I see."* And what did she see when she followed Koshu's dictum and tried to look calmly and truly?

A young stud naked but for a lava-lava ran along the sidewalk, lighting tiki torches. The pulse of an unseen Hawaiian drummer competed with the Dixieland jazz flowing out of the Mynah Bird. No one was threatening her, so why did her chest feel tight? Her breathing was raspy. Her face burned on fire. She was having her first heart attack, she was sure of it.

Kapuna, the Ilikai Hotel's doorwoman, dressed in muu-muu and red feather cape, performed her last task of the evening, and appeared on the beach facing the ocean. She blew a long note from a conch shell, without which, Hawaiian legend said, the sun could not properly set.

Larry was behind her.

"I upset you," he said. He put a hand on her arm and she jerked it away. She suddenly felt like she was freezing, teeth chattering, knees quivering.

"No!" she shouted when he put his arm around her. "Don't say you love me, never never say you love me."

"Okay okay," he held his hands up.

Pua dug into her purse for a prescription bottle, opened it with two shaking hands, turned her back to Larry, put two tiny white pills on her tongue and tried to swallow. Her mouth was too dry, they wouldn't go down.

"Juice, please get me some juice or soda or something," she cried. Larry backed away. He said something she didn't catch; her ears were ringing and she felt dizzy.

Larry ran for the Mynah Bird.

Pua caught a long deep breath. She spit the pills out into her palm. She walked toward the sea, the sand cool on her bare feet. She leaned against the trunk of a curved coco palm. Across the sand, a dinner-sail catamaran was tying up at the dock. She could hear the rhythm of the ocean waves. She turned and looked toward the Mynah Bird, suddenly afraid she would never see tourist Larry again.

Men had said they had loved before, but never with such a soft beautiful honest glow in their eyes.

Was it really too much to hope for, a good man who'd stick with her? She let herself slide to the base of the tree until she was sitting. Who could love a fat ugly stupid dark-skinned girl like her?

She was wearing white capri pants and a red-and-orange striped blouse and she had kicked her shoes away and right now she wished she could tear her clothes off and plunge into the ocean. Clean and pure, without anybody seeing her, without anybody caring, without lust or shame, just her, Pualani Long, naked like a baby in the ocean she loved.

Suddenly Tourist Larry was kneeling beside her, casting a long shadow on the torchlit sand. He offered her a can of Grotton Pineapple juice.

"I feel better now," she said, hand on her chest.

The two pills had turned in her sweating hands into milky spatters. She wiped the white residue off her hands using sand. She was mighty thirsty though, and gulped the juice.

"I'm sorry," Larry said. "I made you feel bad."

He lay one hand gently atop hers.

"Please don't touch me right now," Pua said. "I get emotional."

Larry sat across from her. The torch light turned his face a flickering orange. He had his arms around his knees and he looked like a boy-god rising from the darkening ocean.

"Do you know what it means to love a person?" Pua said.

Larry looked down at the sand.

"It means terrible things. It means..." she began crying, then sobbing then bawling. She put her knees up, head in her arms, and let it come. Her body was wracked with sobs. She even frightened herself, making a horrible sound, a braying, and deep, deep breaths. She prayed to Koshu, prayed for pure vision, prayed that when she opened her eyes she might truly see. When she recovered herself, and opened her eyes, she felt better, and Tourist Larry was gone.

Which she had known all along. She was like a flower, men were like bees, buzzing in for a landing, then taking off. Flower was her name, Pua, and Dad had well named her.

It was all right. She had been rejected by handsomer men. Larry was just another tourist.

Pua arose, dusted sand off her legs, turned around and there stood Larry, with her leather sandals dangling from one hand.

"I went to get your shoes," he said.

Arm in arm they walked through the open grounds of the Ilikai Hotel, with its shuttered shops disguised to look like Port Honolulu in the whaling days, all fountains, palm groves and water falling from a gigantic carved Tiki God.

Crazy, but to Pua hotel grounds were the most romantic places in Hawaii. They were a fantasy, a relief from the relentless city. Yes, there were nicer, more natural places up there in the mountains, but that was all forbidden Grotton family land.

Larry knew when to be quiet, and she liked a man who knew that. She stopped him by the Tiki God, whose mouth was spouting water. She ran a hand over Larry's dark brushy hair.

"That's such a cute haircut on you," she said.

Larry tugged on her arm and asked: "Do you know that lady?"

"Which one?"

He pointed to the hotel's doorwoman, a chubby grandma dressed in a muu-muu. She had removed her red feather cape and folded it over her arm. She was heaving herself into an open-top Jeep, driven it by her gray-haired husband.

"Kapuna," Pua said. "I don't know her last name. She's worked here a lifetime, before these hotels even. Rumor is, she was a paid lady back in the old times."

"Paid lady?"

"Yes, you know, don't make me say it, it's embarrassing. Paid by soldiers, you know, for love, during the War."

"You mean Pearl Harbor, that war?"

Pua nodded. "Ever since I was a little girl, I came to this beach for the sunset. We lived just on the other side of the canal when my family was broke. Ever since I can remember, Tutu Kapuna was here to blow the conch shell at sunset."

"She's a witch," Larry said. "I saw her on the bus coming in from the airport. She told me I was a Rooster and she was a Rat and she said I was going to be very, very lucky in the Islands."

"Rats are tricky," said Pua. "You have to really be careful when dealing with a Rat."

The Jeep with Tutu Kapuna in it joined the river of tail lights on Ala Moana Boulevard.

Larry squared around, took both Pua's hands, and gave her his best sincere look that really did come from his heart.

"Is it okay if I just kind of like you?" he asked.

Bobbo's Jungle

Lazarus Patrick McCabe lived car free, which meant he mooched rides from his girlfriend. Reiko, a thrifty, practical soul, who drove a humble 1978 Volkswagen Beetle. It was bright yellow, with just the beginnings of ocean-air rust eating at the wheel wells. Rei drove up the Pali Highway to the crest of the mountains, while McCabe in the passenger seat, chewed his nails.

The back seats were crammed with Rei's luggage.

They coasted down the steep slope, and the view through the windshield was the same one you'd get if you were flying: The hook-shaped Kaneohe Bay, the sheer Pali cliffs, the lush but orderly suburbs. The drop was so steep, it almost seemed Rei could land her Beetle on the runway of the Marine airbase.

"You're sure, McCabe?" Rei asked.

"He's stoned night and day," McCabe said. "He'll hardly notice you."

"That's not an answer."

"He was enthusiastic."

"Why?"

"We're friends," McCabe said. "Think of it as a vacation, Rei."

Rei's lips quivered. "Until the police raid."

"He doesn't grow enough weed for the cops to care," McCabe said. "They all know him anyway. Bobbo's harmless." He touched her cheek, gently. He loved this woman, though she was difficult. She was an ER nurse, and so tough and skeptical. She spent much of her time dealing with the results of peoples' reckless decisions.

But she was also naïve enough to convert to Koshu-Kaza.

"The Jersey boys will be gone in a week," McCabe said.

"Hmmph," said Rei.

"You'll be going from a one-bedroom apartment in Makiki to a Windward estate. That's bad?"

"You see those suitcases in back?" Rei asked. "That means, McCabe ... that means we're already convinced."

McCabe liked to talk and Rei preferred to listen, so their life together was like a jigsaw puzzle that fit perfectly. For reasons McCabe could not fathom, she was in love with him, tolerant of his faults, by turns amused and exasperated by his carelessness and lack of ambition. Their relationship hinged on two conditions: that McCabe hold some kind of job, and that they live on Oahu for the rest of their lives.

So they drove in silent mutual understanding until they reached the main highway, and then McCabe directed Rei down smaller and smaller roads until the VW was raising dust on a dirt lane. They turned along a driveway lined with coconut palms and stopped at an unpainted ramshackle house.

Chickens scattered at their approach.

The house had a rusty tin roof half covered with palm fronds. A massive garage in the jungle shade held the skeletons of old cars. On a rickety, palm-shaded porch sat Bobbo Burns, tilted back in a wooden chair, yellow legal pad on his lap, pencil in hand.

"The living legend," said McCabe, and leaped out of the car. He beckoned to Rei. She wore long tweed trousers and a dowdy green blouse, a woman who could look sexy but chose not to.

"Rei Nakamoto," McCabe said. "Meet Bobbo Burns."

Bobbo was a skinny, ghost-gray fellow of perhaps 60 years who avoided sun and lived in the shade. He had a long gray pony tail kept in a simple rubber band. His clothes looked like the pickings of second hand shop, and a worn leather vest did nothing to upgrade his attire. At his feet was a bottle of rum and a hen who squawked and ruffled her feathers at McCabe's approach.

Bobbo, gentleman, crushed an unfiltered cigarette in a tin can ashtray, bowed, took Rei's hand and brushed it with his lips.

"Enchante," said Bobbo.

Rei giggled.

"You'll need help with your bags." Bobbo rang a cowbell that hung from the rafters. "Marly! Marlene!"

Bobbo sipped from a cocktail glass and said, "My daughter won't let me lift a finger." He patted his chest. "The ticker."

Around the corner appeared a husky woman who, it seemed, could not possibly be the daughter of this pony-tailed gray ghost. She was fit and strong, maybe thirty years old, with a copper complexion, dark eyes and short hair.

"Marly will show you to your accommodations," Bobbo told Rei. "While McCabe and I ..." he lifted his cocktail glass, "have a drink."

Rei and Marly drove the VW deeper into the jungle and when they had disappeared, a flock of motley chickens eased out of hiding, pecked at insects freshly uncovered in the tire tracks.

"So what is this about, McCabe?" Bobbo asked. "What couldn't you say on the phone?"

From a galvanized ice bucket he lifted a small can of Grotton pineapple juice, popped the lid, and handed it to McCabe. McCabe took a position opposite Bobbo's wooden throne, and leaned on splintery porch rails.

"I appreciate it, Bobbo."

"Nonsense," said Bobbo. "Appreciation is for freshman art students. What you mean to say is: You now owe me a favor."

"I do."

"Good, I'll call it in some day." He lit a cigarette. "Soon. How is the old battle axe?"

"Still battling," McCabe said.

McCabe and Bobbo had become allies because they were newsroom outcasts. Norma Keeper, editor of the Honolulu Record, loathed them both, but for different reasons. Bobbo, however, had the much better deal. He hadn't appeared in the newsroom for the last four years. He wrote his column, *Surrounded by Water,* and faxed it in every night for the next day's Page Three. It consisted mostly of political and celebrity gossip, Bobbo having a lifetime of sources all over town. Every column ended with a paragraph or two under the heading: *When Waikiki Was A Duck Pond,* in which he waxed sentimental about the good old days.

Mrs. Keeper hated Bobbo because his every column embarrassed, denigrated, insulted or vilified at least one important public figure. However, every time Bobbo went on vacation, circulation dropped. And for decades, Mahalo Department Stores had faithfully bought an expensive ad that took up the whole page next to Bobbo's column.

McCabe's deal was different. Because of the Newspaper Guild, Mrs. Keeper couldn't fire him, although she wanted to. He'd embarrassed the newspaper by falling asleep during a press conference with the Governor. TV stations, desperate for content, broadcast this non-event on the five o'clock news. That footage had become legendary in local journalism circles: A sleeping reporter for the Honolulu Record, notebook in his lap, his fellow reporters howling with laughter, a twisted smile on the normally stoic face of Governor Arno Lee.

McCabe and the Newspaper Guild had presented his defense: a doctor backed them up, too. Narcolepsy. McCabe's job was saved, but he'd had to surrender his driver's license. And Mrs. Keeper had demoted him to desk duty as writer of obituaries and horoscopes.

"Mrs. Keeper keeps asking after your health," McCabe said.

"I'll bet," said Bobbo and sucked down smoke. "The day I keel over, she'll buy sushi for the newsroom."

"Seriously, Bobbo, it's going from bad to worse at the Record."

"The decline of civilization," Bobbo said. "I predicted it long ago." He sighed. "When I announce, officially, for mayor, they'll suspend my column. But not my paycheck. Thereafter, I will inhabit the best of all worlds."

McCabe had heard Bobbo threaten to run for Mayor many times, and he dismissed it now, but with a shudder of foreboding.

Bobbo leaned over the porch, as if he were a captain of a leaky ship, scanning the horizon for a port.

"McCabe, what have you gotten yourself into?"

"As I told you on the phone, I was minding my own business when there was a knock on the door."

"Isn't that the way," said Bobbo.

"I can't get Rei mixed up in this. They saw her coming out of my apartment, and they roped her in."

Bobbo glared at the cigarette as if he had found something disgusting trapped in his fingers, and flung it overboard into the dust. "Personally, I wouldn't mind a painless death. A bullet in the head, McCabe, how bad could that be?"

"Reiko will not leave this island," McCabe said. "Not now, not ever. I'm sweet on her, Bobbo. She's The One. I know you think it's foolish, romantic and banal, but I want to marry her. Sure, we'll end up in some townhouse in Mililani, with two squalling keikis and an impossible mortgage. But Bobbo, you're nobody in these Islands if you're not family. I spent my youth being dragged around the world, always the outsider. Aviano.

Elmendorf. Thule, Anderson. McGuire. I don't really belong anywhere. I'm trying to make a home here. Where else have I got?"

"I don't see a ring on your finger."

"Rei's father has forbidden her to date haoles, never mind marry one. He's a very traditional man. He's also deathly sick. If we were to get married, she's afraid it might kill him."

"So you're waiting for her old man to kick off."

"Essentially."

Bobbo sipped his rum-pineapple drink.

"Well, Marilyn's at Berkeley. I don't know when she'll be back, maybe at the end of the semester, so your girl can stay in Marilyn's cottage indefinitely ..." he shrugged. "I guess."

"Rei's an ER nurse, Bobbo."

"Are you suggesting that at my decrepit age I might need medical assistance?"

"I'm saying she's a practical, helpful, kind, highly-skilled, well-balanced person. She won't be any trouble here."

Bobbo walked off the porch, scattered feed for the chickens.

"So let's talk politics, McCabe," he said. "Did you know I never killed a chicken in my life? Don't have the heart to do it. My chickens die of old age, or mongoose attack. Sometimes they're driven from the flock, the rooster decides he doesn't like them. Much as you and I were driven from the newsroom by Mrs. Keeper, the Female Rooster."

"It's simple, Bobbo, these guys want casino gambling and Sam Wing stands in the way. They're willing to spend a relative pittance to lure him out of the picture, and they gain a hundred million in slot machine profits. Great return on investment."

"And if Sam won't bite?"

"That's the question."

"No, the question for you, McCabe, is how to avoid prosecution for criminal conspiracy."

"I'm in under threat, Bobbo."

"However if you so testify, you'll need term life insurance in the worst possible way."

McCabe, hands in pockets, paced the porch.

Bobbo said: "I hear the Kamchatka Peninsula is lovely this time of year."

"Even if Reiko and I went into hiding, that wouldn't solve the problem. I have three sisters, and nieces and nephews all over South Jersey. The brothers chose me as a messenger precisely because I'm the one guy in the islands who knows what damage they can do."

"And so you're here for advice," said Bobbo.

"HPD can't help me."

"I wouldn't dream of suggesting the boys in blue," Bobbo said. "They're good at uprooting harmless plants, and breaking up drunken brawls on Kalakaua Avenue, but not much else."

He scattered chicken feed, and the hens ran up squawking. "My daughters won't let me eat the eggs. Bad for the ticker. So why do I keep these birds?"

He looked up. "I suppose I admire birds," he said. "All kinds of birds. Even these dumb flightless clucks. When I was young and just out of the Navy, I used to sit at the Duck Pond …" he brought himself back to the present, it seemed, by lighting a Big Tent cigarette. "Oh Hell. Your problem, McCabe, has only one solution."

"And that is?"

"Porky. Hashimoto."

"You're not the first to suggest that. I've never met Porky. Maybe because I'm not a criminal."

"Ah, but he is."

"He's about to be disbarred."

"All the better," said Bobbo. "They disbarred me from the newsroom, and did you ever wonder why? It's because I had a peek behind the curtain. I had to be banned. I had seen forbidden things, had rung the bell of truth… Porky, too, has seen behind the curtain, and so he's been banished by the legal establishment. Porky Hashimoto. I daresay when you paint your picture for him, it won't be on the canvas of ignorance."

"What?"

"Oh, he'll probably know the story before you tell it to him. No man is omniscient, McCabe, but the rumors about Porky do make you wonder."

McCabe watched the rooster charge the hens. Rei walked up the drive, having changed into shorts. The rooster made a run at Rei, bullied her off the path.

Did the bullies always win? McCabe asked himself.

Was every year the Year of the Rooster?

Macadamia Nuts

10

McCabe waited in the Green Room. It was painted in the drab shades of American cash. The main feature of the room was a long, conference table, of polished wood, bare except for a legal pad and a crystal bowl overflowing with macadamia nuts. The windows framed the brilliantly white State Capitol.

Outside those windows, a bare-chested young man, dressed in ragged shorts, shinnied up a coconut tree. His only climbing aid was a canvas safety belt. As he reached the treetop he hacked at fronds and coconuts with a machete. Thunk thunk, the heavy nuts plopped to the ground. The fronds floated after them like wounded eagles.

Porky Hashimoto barged through a double door and sat before the bowl of nuts. Porky, true to his nickname, was a short, rotund man with tiny eyeglasses and a carelessly-shaved face that clashed with his magnificent pinstriped suit.

He fiddled with the bowl of nuts, popped one, into his mouth.

"L.P. McCabe," Porky said, chewing. "Has that byline graced Page One recently? If so, it has escaped my notice."

"May I sit?" McCabe asked.

"It's a matter of supreme indifference to me," Porky said.

McCabe rolled out a plush chair and sat across from him.

"Do I hear every rumor that circulates in this town, McCabe? Sometimes it seems so. Last I heard you had fallen into disfavor with Mrs. Norma Keeper, editor, cocktail circuit gadfly, and keeper of the journalistic flame."

"I wouldn't say that."

"What would you say? And I remind you, McCabe, that labor law is hardly my specialty. The Newspaper Guild is served by marginally competent attorneys, I'm sure."

"It's a medical ..." said McCabe.

Porky held up a hand. "Ah, yes. How could I forget? I assumed you would skulk away from our fair islands following your televised humiliation." He picked up a macadamia nut, examined it as if it were a globe of the world. . "Humiliation. Was there ever a concept so sweet? What Herculean tasks are you currently undertaking at that bastion of journalism, that mighty defender of the First Amendment?"

"Desk work," said McCabe. "Writing obits, editing the horoscope and advice columns."

"I'm sure such strenuous tasks require your full concentration. And what crisis brings you to Royce Hashimoto Associates today?"

"That's the tricky part," said McCabe.

Porky shrugged. "I'm not omniscient, McCabe, despite all you may have heard."

"That's exactly what I heard. Omniscient."

"Do I have well-placed sources, McCabe? What kind of attorney would I be without good intelligence? I would be like a blind-folded fighter pilot in shrapnel-filled skies."

"Let me guess. Your sources are One-Lung Pete at the Mynah Bird, Mango at the Royal, and Kapuna at the Ilikai."

"You've named gossip column sources, McCabe. Would a serious legal entity bother collecting Waikiki gossip?"

"Okay, let me lay it out. Governor Lee's wife gets cancer, and he resigns mid-term. Mayor Riley has been eyeing the Governor's office for years, and this is his chance to move up."

"McCabe, you are paying $300 an hour to relate to me things every bus driver knows."

"All right, well, that leaves two viable Democrats to replace Riley as mayor: Bix Sanders and Sam Wing. If what I hear around the newsroom is true, you are politically connected to the Wing campaign."

"You must hear a great many dubious stories around the newsroom. Far too many of them find their way into print. However, nothing warms a libel attorney's heart like a careless journalist."

"So a few days after Governor Lee resigns, I get a visit from certain fellows I knew in my boyhood, back in

New Jersey. And they have a kind of a stunning proposition for me."

"I'm waiting."

"They want to get to Sam through me, and offer him a bribe to quit the race just before the election."

Porky pushed his chair back and thump thump, plopped his feet, in cowboy boots, on the table.

"McCabe, I take it you noticed that young man out there trimming the coconut trees? He may look like he's posing for a post card, but I assure you he is a bonded and insured employee of the City and County of Honolulu. Why do I mention this, McCabe? Because, prior to lawsuits initiated by Royce Hashimoto Associates, this city was a veritable free fire zone of falling coconuts. Five or six tourists every year would be seriously injured, occasionally killed, by falling nuts. Our firm made a minor specialty of suing on the tourists' behalf. Since the city attorneys fear the humiliation we would inflict upon them in the courtroom, the settlements were enormous. Humiliation, McCabe, can be a very profitable game.

"Eventually the City decided it was cheaper to hire tree trimmers than to constantly pay damages. So you see, McCabe, right out that window is evidence of the benefits Royce Hashimoto Associates has bestowed on our society. Otherwise unemployable local men now have jobs climbing trees. And somewhere in Saskatchewan, a sunburned Canadian is snowshoeing through the woods, unaware that he owes his longevity to Royce Hashimoto Associates."

He turned and picked up a phone on the bookshelf behind him.

"Missy!" he barked, and then hung up. He said to McCabe: "I require a witness."

He pushed the bowl of macadamia nuts across the table toward, but not really to, McCabe. "Healthy fats!" he proclaimed.

The door opened and in walked a skinny young woman in a dull dress that hung shapeless off her.

"I believe you know Mr. McCabe?"

Looking at the floor, she nodded.

Missy Kailani had worked as a news clerk at The Record years ago, until derailed by pregnancy and a footloose boyfriend. Missy was remarkable for her utter lack of self esteem. As far as McCabe could recall, she never looked anyone directly in the eyes, and never said a word about herself.

"Miss Kailani is my paralegal, a notary in the State of Hawaii, and she will serve as my witness. Mr. McCabe, kindly repeat the story as you have told it to me."

McCabe told his story as Missy took notes

"Conspiracy and felony bribery," Porky said, "at the bare minimum. As an officer of the court, I cannot be party to criminal activity. So I am advising Mr. McCabe of the danger of violating federal election and conspiracy laws, and that he should present his unproven allegations, paranoid fantasies and baseless innuendos to federal authorities, to wit and specifically, the Federal Bureau of Investigation."

Missy wrote furiously on a legal pad. When finished, she stared at the floor.

"Thank you, Miss Kailani."

When she'd made her silent exit, Porky said: "Some day I'm going to give that girl a raise. Have these New Jersey men made threats?"

"I'm not going to the FBI. At worst they'd hang me out to dry, at best they'd put me in witness protection and I'd end up in Fairbanks."

"What exactly is the Jersey offer?"

"A hundred seventy five grand and an endless trip to the Vegas salad bar."

"You have an amusing if pedestrian wit, McCabe. Doubtless the Record's dreary pages could use a touch of your comic talents. But at Royce Hashimoto Associates, we prefer accuracy and detail."

"Okay, an annual comped trip, plus he'd be put on retainer by the Desert Skies Gaming Corporation."

"And what is the timetable for your offer?"

"I haven't figured out how to approach Sam. But the Jersey boys are antsy."

"Hmm," said Porky. "Does this offer make financial sense? No it does not."

"How so?"

"Is there a salary differential between the Council Chairman and the Mayor? Indeed there is, and it amounts to roughly $40,000 per year. The mayor is limited to two four year terms, but 8 times $40,000 amounts to $320,000. They are offering Uncle Sam a negative-value proposition."

He took his cowboy boots off the table, paced in front of the windows.

"And does this calculation take into consideration a mayor's other, shall we say discretionary, financial opportunities? No it does not."

"It's not really an offer, it's kind of a demand."

"I see," said Porky, and shoved his hands into his pockets. He shed his jacket, revealing red suspenders and perfectly fitted shirt. This was a man with not one but several Hong Kong tailors.

"How do you propose to deliver this demand, McCabe?"

"That's where I thought you could help me."

Porky put his hands up, as if trying to halt a mad, runaway driver. "Do I empathize with your plight, McCabe? On a strictly humanitarian basis, most assuredly. Sam Wing is not a client of mine. If he was, we certainly would not be enjoying this, or indeed any, conversation. However, Councilman Wing and I are political sympaticos. I assure you that Sam is quite serious about being Mayor and beyond that, he has ambitions for the big chair at the Capitol. Bix Sanders is eminently beatable, and this city is rife with rumors of his drinking and gambling binges. Even the hint that Bix is involved in a Las Vegas coup would seriously wound his candidacy."

Porky shrugged.

"So what advice can I possibly offer you, McCabe? You refuse to trust the authorities. And I can't very well advise you to commit a crime."

"I've talked to a friend in the HPD."

Porky raised one eyebrow. "And how is David Shimada? He's embarking on a contentious divorce, I understand."

"He's been thrown out of the house, I know that."

"They say only the attorneys win in these nasty divorce cases," Porky intoned, shaking his head as if the very notion of divorce was breaking his heart. "I knew David's wife in high school. She was a particularly unpleasant young woman. Was she attractive? Devastatingly so. But also demanding and haughty. Before the tragic passage of no-fault divorce laws, their mutual claims of cruelty and neglect would be laid out in intimate detail for every cheap barrister … But I digress. What was Officer Shimada's reaction upon learning of this conspiracy?"

"He, well, he referred me here."

"What, then, would be your theoretical timetable for making this ill-advised, insulting and illegal offer to Councilman Wing?"

"Next day or two."

"Give me twenty-four hours to formulate a strategy, McCabe. Do I expect to revisit this matter with you? Yes I do, on Thursday, at two p.m. sharp, at the last picnic table, at the Ewa end of Ala Moana Park."

He nudged the bowl. "Why don't you have a nut, McCabe?"

Ancient romance

11

Larry Estonophie, lying on one elbow, lazed on Pua's back steps. This girl's backyard was a Jersey guy's tropical fantasy. Palm trees grew out of a neat-cut lawn, surrounded by flowery hedges. Coconuts lay on the lawn, free food delivered by God himself. Larry roused himself and kicked a coconut like it was soccer ball.

Hawaii 1, Jersey zip.

Pua appeared on the porch, carrying a tray that held two tall glasses of pineapple juice and a bowl of ice cubes. She descended the steps graceful like a dancer. She brought the tray, ice cubes rattling, to a white iron table that was set in the shade of a pine tree.

Pine trees in Hawaii, Larry would have never guessed it. It reminded him of the Jersey Pine Barrens, where Ronnie Zack, who stole the wrong guy's car, had come to his final and well-deserved rest. His poor mother! She still believed Ronnie was going to come home someday.

Larry took a seat in a white iron chair, sipped tea, purred like a cat. "I guess you're used to this. I mean, it's your backyard, but to me ..."

He shook his head. It was just too awesome. These people didn't know what a paradise they had.

"Where I grew up," he sipped tea, "our backyard was a dirt lot with broken glass. It was green glass, sort of like a Jersey lawn." He guffawed. "Broken wine bottles. Our house was behind a liquor store." He shrugged. "Then they knocked it all down. Where our house used to be, now it's a casino parking ramp. If you ever go to Atlantic City, park your own car. Never trust the valet."

Pua wasn't really charmed by his Jersey stories, he could tell. He had to find something this babe liked to talk about. He thought over topics he knew well: Football, prison, locksmithing and cars. He figured cars as his best bet, but when he looked up to ask about her VW Thing he was stopped by the intensity of her eyes. She was just staring, with like liquid eyes, and then she looked down at her lap.

"You are funny," Pua said. "I like you."

"Me, I'm funny?" Larry said.

Pua laughed and sipped at her juice. She smoothed her striped overalls over her thighs and Larry watched that motion with a warm feeling.

"What's funny about me?"

"You're really non-Hawaiian."

"I'm what?"

"You're not like island guys at all."

"Is that bad?"

Larry leaned forward in the chair, pulled up a handful of grass, scattered the blades into the breeze. "Some day," he said, "I want a backyard with grass." He looked Pua over, uh, he was sick with love. He had to keep talking or he would leap over the table and throw a lip-lock on her.

But did she understand that *backyard with grass* could have two meanings? His clever word-play, like, slipped past her.

"So," he said, "you grew up in this house?"

She nodded.

"In the early days we lived along that stinky canal, you know, the Ala Wai, the one in Waikiki? But then you know, statehood, and everybody in real estate made plenty *kala*. That's Hawaiian for money."

Larry focused on the blue tattoo on her arm, a simple cross. It was crude, like the tattoos guys give themselves in prison.

"Are you a Christian lady?" he asked.

"I used to be. I converted."

"To what do you call it?"

"Kaza. Koshu Kaza."

"What does that mean in English?"

"Koshu means welcome and kaza means fate."

"Wow," Larry said and whistled. "You people don't have Jesus, Mary and Joseph? That's too strange of a religion for me."

He sipped pineapple juice and asked: "Did you go to college and all?"

He had never visited a college campus, and could only envision one dimly. Surf pounded in the background of his imaginary Hawaiian college. Palm trees swayed. Steel guitars played, hula girls danced.

Pua, biting her lip, shook her head.

"No college for me neither," Larry said. "I was like recruited by a couple of the better schools, but I had to turn them down." He stared at the grass between his feet and said, "Can I tell you something?" Then he looked into Pua's warm eyes. "It's like really strange. You'll think I'm crazy."

"No I won't."

"I've never told this to anybody, not even my brother."

When she tilted the glass back for a drink, Larry saw the slash marks on her wrist. He knew what they meant. How desperate this chick must have felt when she drew the blade across her wrists and watched that first blood spurt out. She'd wounded herself, she'd known that bottomless misery, like Larry had felt in prison, so he decided to trust her.

Larry sat straight up in the chair. He folded his hands in front of him on the table. "When I got off the plane here," he said. "I had a really weird thing happen to me."

Suddenly he couldn't look at Pua. He stared at the white siding of her house, the water spigot rising from the lawn, her bedroom window, reflecting a palm tree.

He sucked down a big breath for courage.

"I looked up at those mountains, and it was like, yo, I swear to god, I've been here before. You know. The Big Wahine, it was like I'd seen her before, too. Everything seemed, like, weirdly familiar."

He glanced at Pua. She was serious, not laughing as he'd feared.

"I mean, I'm strictly from Jersey, right? What do I know about the Hawaiian islands? But everything seemed like, no surprise. It was like I knew my way around. I'm asking myself, how could this be? It was like I had lived here before."

He tilted his chair back. He looked at the brilliant blue sky, which was home to the Big Catholic. Larry Estonophie had a deep respect for the Big Catholic. He was like an absent father who, unless you behaved, He might come home from the K of C and whip the shit out of you. The Big Catholic was a mean bastard with a long memory and a flash temper. Didn't He like, piss all over Noah for forty days and forty nights? Larry knew he would have to pay the Big Catholic back for every one of his bad deeds and lies someday, but you had an eternity to do it, which meant you could space out the punishments, couple of thousand years of easy living, and then a few lashes of the whip and you were off for centuries of fun.

And he was paying down some Purgatory time now by telling this chick the truth. Help me Big Catholic, Larry said to himself, and make this beautiful girl believe the honest words coming out of my mouth.

"Did you ever," he said, "think like, maybe you've lived another lifetime?"

A light came into Pua's eyes. "I might have been a Hawaiian queen once," she said. She shrugged. "That's what a fortune teller told me."

She perked up. "You've met her. Kapuna. The heavy lady who blows the conch at sunset. She tells fortunes."

"Wow." Larry sat back to think that over. "You know, I'm staying down in Waikiki, and there's all these street names, Kalakaua, Kuhio, Ala Moana. But my hotel's on like Doo-Doo-It Lane. That don't sound Hawaiian to me."

"Well, silly, Long, doesn't seem like a Hawaiian name either, does it?"

"So I ask Carl, the desk clerk, and he said, the street was named after a sea captain in ancient times. And that started me thinking, you know, why did Hawaii seem so familiar and, well maybe it's because I sailed here in the olden days."

"It's pronounced Doo-dwa. Doo-dwa Lane."

She'd missed the point but Larry felt that maybe it was just too weird for her, this idea of reincarnation. He gave up. He'd explain it when they knew each other better. He rattled the ice cubes in the pale remainder of juice. He kicked his shoes off. Oh, he could get real comfortable here. And wouldn't it be great if he could get his hands on some of that good Hawaiian weed? That would have to wait until after mission accomplished, though, because Terry had warned him not to risk getting arrested on a dope charge.

How old was this chick's father? Would she like, be inheriting the house soon?

Speaking of soon, Terry would be having a fit, looking all over for him. He flashed on the angry face of his brother. Fack him. Let him be pissed.

Pua carried the glasses back up the stairs for a refill, and Larry, hearing the cry of parrots, invisible in the trees, began to think even harder. The magnetic attraction he had to Pua. The feeling he had been in Hawaii before. Maybe this was like an ancient romance. Maybe way back in eighteen-something he was a sailor who came ashore and met a gorgeous Hawaiian princess. They fell madly in love but the evil king her father wouldn't let them marry

because the sailor was too lowly. Now they were back to
finish their romance, a hundred years later. It was just
possible. What else could explain the deep deep feelings
running through him right now?

Pua sat on the porch next to him and said, "You're
so sunburned."

"I was surfing."

"You surf?"

"Oh yeah."

"Why didn't you tell me?"

"I just learned today."

"Oh you. You can't learn surfing in one day."

"You can if you lived here before."

She laughed.

"Do you believe in ghosts?" Larry asked.

"Maybe," said Pua.

"I do, definitely," said Larry.

He kissed her. Wow she was hot. He had never felt
so strongly about a girl, not since Karen, hey, it was
frightening. It was wonderful, too. When he kissed her,
he got a jolt of love for Pua, and at the same time, fear of
Terry.

The Cherry Girl

12

If Terry knew his brother, the dumbinutive bastard was in a strip joint. Two of Larry's three ex-wives had been dancers in a strip joint. The exception was Karen. He met her in a casino. Larry was a sucker for a horny babe. They were going to be his, what you call demise, that was the word. Or, if you needed nine letters, ruination.

Terry stepped into the Royal Hawaiian's lobby and the butler, or whatever that guy was called, whistled for a cab. The butler wore an aloha shirt with the name MANGO pinned to it. What kind of horseshit name was Mango? With the job he had, five will get you ten he was a swish. Mango stood waving at cabs like he was conducting a sympathy orchestra. Except it was outdoors at night with floodlit palm trees to make it look suspiciously tropical.

Terry tipped Mango $2, settled into a cab and told the driver, "I'm in the mood to watch a naked girl remove her clothing."

It was awkward, since the driver was a broad. And not the kind you would care to see naked. She was a *faccia brute*, as they said in Jersey.

Ugly face. She scowled and grumbled: "There are several places I could take you."

"I would purposefully transit from one to the other," Terry said. "What do you call. Circum-perambulation. You could enjoy gainful employment all evening, with a beneficial tip at the end."

"Whoopee," said the broad, sneaky, so you could barely hear her.

Terry glanced at the license underneath the meter. Prudence Yamanaki, it said.

"Prudence," Terry said. "You could dress more stylistic. Put more makeup on that pretty face, you'd fetch higher gratitudes."

"Is that so?" Prudence said, but Terry could tell she wasn't buying it.

When they were free of the bad traffic, Terry sat back and looked at the city rushing by. Honolulu was a boring city in terms of, not much neon. Little cinderblock apartment buildings. Crappy little stores that reminded him of his dad's joint, Tiny's Variety. This was a city in which excitement was some drunk crooning into a microphone while wearing flowers around his neck.

In Jersey, you got bored, you drove to Philly. From Honolulu you could only drive to Davy Jones' Locker. These Island people had no what you call subculture, that was the problem.

"I know all the cabbie hoodwinks," Terry told Prudence. "Like the circle route, I'm acutely aware of that one."

She glared into the mirror.

He said: "Where we going? You mean to tell me there's no girlie extablishments in Waikiki?"

"They're mostly on Hotel Street, downtown. Where the banks and insurance companies are. Unless you want to go to Pearl City, that's forty bucks one way."

"Why should I pay forty bucks to be conveyed to this Pearl City?"

"Sailors. Bad girls."

"Sailors?" said Terry. "Not me, I'm a thousand percent man, missy. I'm seeking genuine feminine females. No pretenders, no contenders, no girls with lumps in their underwear, if you get my mental drift."

"There's a hostess bar near the police station. I'll take you there first. It's the wildest one, too. It's called the Cherry Girl."

"What's the main eventuality?"

"Nude waitresses."

He could envision Larry in a corner, with each monkey arm around a naked girl.

The Cherry Girl was nothing on the outside. A dark shack, no windows, coulda been a warehouse. Nondescript is how he would describe it. Terry walked in and looked around, it was too early for the dancers' incendiary acts. It was almost too early for customers, just a few stooges who looked like construction workers. So! They had them here too. Union hard hats with no-show jobs who hung in taverns. Maybe he should have loosened his tie and left his suit-jacket in the cab, to fit in with the blue collar crowd. He glanced out the window, good, Prudence was waiting for him.

What kind of cabbie name was Prudence? Did her father think, upon the occasion of her birthing, I'll name my daughter Prudence, she'll grow up fat and ugly and drive perverts around in a filthy cab? No, of course not. Her father thought, I've got a baby rogue scholar here who'll grow up to inculcate cancer, a world hero with the Pulitzer Prize. So the lesson Terry took from this lineup of thought was, nobody knows the future of a crystal ball.

The bar was shaped like an L and when he walked around the corner, boom, no Larry. Row of empty red booths. Some naked babe pussyfooted up behind him, soft on her feet like a ballet teacher.

"Sir," she said, "sit any place you like."

The way she said it was hard to understand, like she grew up in China or some ignorant country.

"I'll get a drink at the bar," he told her and glanced at her saggy tits. She detoured and sat with two hard hat guys, like Terry was some big hunk of nothing. He was used to that from women. They treated him rude. Something about him deflected their maternal interest.

Until they saw his roll.

He stepped over to the bar. This was a place like they wouldn't allow in the modern A.C. of today. The old days, yeah, taverns would get away with this smarmy black-and-red plastic all over everything. On the little stage here was a throne, like Cleopatra could have sat in it. Or one of them queens of ancient Rome, back when Caesar was president. He said to the barmaid:

"Hey."

At least she wore clothes. Which was good because she was old. She bent over, clank clank, fixing something under the sink. He tried again: "Hey."

She arose with a red wrench in her hand. She laid it disgusting on the bar, dripping black crud. She washed her hands in soapy dishwater. Her bazooms were too big for her body, so Terry figured that back in her youth, she'd been a medically-enhanced showgirl.

"A guy get a drink around here?"

She gawked. She never saw a guy in a Philadelphia-class suit before?

Terry said: "You have seven and seven?"

That pissed her off. Her lips turned down. "Of course we have seven and seven."

"That's what I'll have." Da dum da dum, his fingers tapped the bar.

"You got any potato chips hiding back there?"

"No food. This is a dancer bar."

Terry didn't see any dancers, but he didn't want to wise off and rile the barmaid, not before she mixed his cocktail. She backed up to the row of liquor bottles and grabbed a bottle of Seagram's 7.

Some group of guys pushed in behind him, laughing. What, they thought this was bar was a joke? The laughs would be on them, terminal, when they went home broke. Terry gave them a friendly nod. If it wasn't for suckers, smart guys like Terry would have no living at all.

Be kind to others, Terry, mom always said, *not everybody has your advantages.*

The barmaid served his drink, no napkin, no little plastic sword, no class at all.

"Twenty dollars," she demanded.

"What? The show ain't commenced."

"Twenty dollars." Her little chipmunk face got hard.

He pulled a Ben Franklin out of his inside coat pocket.

"Keep the change," he said, "Just for being Miss Mannerly."

She looked at the bill, wet on the bar.

"What do you want?" she grumped.

Terry grinned at her. "I'm in a generosity mood," he said.

"You want prostitutes, Hotel Street," she said, and wagged her finger in his face. "No customers fucking my girls."

"Lady, lady," Terry said, "you're reading my cards all wrong. I'm a businessman of uncertain esteem. You don't get my kind in here much, do you?"

The old barmaid opened the door of an office just behind the wall of cheap liquor. Terry sipped the drink. Had she put maybe two drops of Seagram's in here? These joints made a fortune, which was why they were always owned by high-marginal guys. Terry wondered who owned this one.

Then he got a glimpse of something, and it took him a moment to realize what. The barmaid held the office door open for only a pause, but Terry saw in there a big tough guy, Japanese, wearing a tight t-shirt, his arms and chest covered up to the neck in tattoos. The guy was working an old fashioned adding machine with sausage-fat fingers way too big for the keys.

He had heard of these guys only in prevaricating legend. They put the American outfits to shame, with their behavioral discipline and all. And what else did you call that? Stoical mentality. Well, this was outstanding! Here he was drinking in a Yakuza bar, a story he could spin variously to the guys back in Vegas.

The barmaid backed out of the office with a zip-bag of cash. Terry smiled at her but with a rush of enemosity, or what was that word, a classier word for hate. The Japanese were buying the Empire State Building now. And he'd heard rumors they were making offers on the Yankees. The fucking Japanese Yankees! Next, they'd move the Yanks to Tokyo. You would fly Air Tokyo ten hours to see Don Mattingly play, and they'd sell you a sushi hot dog. It would be the worst insult since Pearl Harbor.

But hey, this barmaid was just the clown princess. Proof was, she worked the bar. The high commando probably wasn't even Mr. Tattoo in the back room. Terry pictured a Yakuza chieftain, dressed in a classy suit, with gray hair, a drink and a cigar, gazing at the mountains from his Tokyo penthouse, an imported blonde in his lap.

"Hey?" he said to the barmaid, "my money's no good? Maybe you're practicing mental prejudice against my kind."

She counted fivers into the till. "What are you talking about, Mister?"

"I'm saying for your eighty buck tip, you could provide answers in an earnest fashion. I'm tracking down a little guy."

She looked him up and down, serious now. "You some kind of mainland pleesman?"

He noticed as she was counting, a rude angry-looking wound where the tip of her pinky used to be. Ah! Transgression, was that the word? This old babe had done a transgression, and paid with her pinky tip. In some ways it was elegant. You had to admire them. See, in the American outfit, this barmaid would be dead. But the Japanese, they realized the value of the second ecumenical chance. So you cut off your own fingertip when you fucked up, and made the supreme commando happy. That way the retribution was paid off, but Management didn't lose the essence of help. He hated to admit it, but the Japanese were brainier than any American gang. No wonder they were buying the goddamn Yankees.

"Eighty bucks for a yes or no," Terry said. "You seen a little guy, haircut just like mine, five foot five, could almost be my brother, but skinny? Laughs like a fucking hyena. Can't live a minute without a broad on his arm, maybe was in for the lunch shift and sneaked one of your girls home?"

She frowned. "Nobody takes my girls home."

"Save that prevarication for the cops," Terry said. "I'm in private eye practice."

"Same answer," said the barmaid.

"Have an unfortunate evening," Terry said. Leaving his $80 tip and his watered down-drink, he stalked out into the parking lot.

Prudence and her cab were both idling. Which meant the driver was living up to her name. It was prudent of her to wait, so she could increase the nature of her gratitude.

Terry slid into the back seat.

"Prudence, you didn't explain that this bar was owned by foreigners of the criminal class."

She snarled. "What did you expect?"

13

The Ted Shed

McCabe had to feel his way through the dark nightclub. Even the musicians on stage were lit dimly. The atmosphere was cigarette smoke, perfume, sour tropical sweat, sugary cocktails and loose money. The music was tourist Hawaiian, led by a lazy steel guitar.

The Estonophie brothers were sitting where they said they'd be, near the exit sign. Their table was covered by a red cloth and set with a glowing candle.

McCabe stumbled toward the table and Terry alerted like a guard dog.

Larry pulled out a chair for McCabe. Even in this indoor dusk, Larry wore huge thick sunglasses.

"Sit down," barked Terry. "Good thing you could show up. We always commended you as likeable."

Likeable? McCabe sat. Looking across the table he saw that Larry's sunglasses only partially hid a bloated purple welt under his eye.

"My brother the genius," Terry said, "comes to paradise, gets into a brawl." He gave Larry's shoulder a shove. "Can you believe it?"

McCabe nodded.

"So McCabe," said Terry, "drinks are on us."

He flagged down a waitress in pumpkin-colored blouse and a dirty apron. Upon arrival, the waitress sneezed.

"Turn your head before spreading disease germs," Terry scolded her, and then ordered: "Three volcanoes." To McCabe he said: "Wait'll you see the classic kind of drinks they serve here."

"I don't drink," McCabe said.

"You don't drink, you don't drive, you some kind of Communistic American?"

The waitress sniffled.

"Get our friend a Shirley Temple," Terry told her.

Terry sat back, his dark suit-jacket spread open on a blue-and-white Hawaiian shirt. He opened his mouth to say something, but the lights brightened and the huge room broke into applause.

Teddy Hong Kong walked out onto the spotlit stage, microphone wire trailing behind him. He stopped at a grove of potted coconut trees. Behind him, a mural depicted Diamond Head and the ocean by moonlight. Teddy wore white trousers that gleamed in the lights. His grin was almost as bright as his neon-green aloha shirt. He turned toward the audience and gave his famous thumbs up. The crowd roared. The spotlights spun. Gray haired tourists whistled and stomped like teenagers.

When the applause died, Teddy swung an arm toward the audience and crooned:

When I put
my arms around
my hula bay-bee.

The audience shrieked with delight.

"I didn't know he was so short," Terry shouted toward McCabe's ear. "Larry likes to see a short guy succeed." Terry turned toward his brother, "Don't you?"

"What?" Larry shouted.

"Stunod," Terry shouted, and made a pushing motion at Larry's head.

Larry swatted his brother's hand away. "Leave me the fack alone."

"Hula bay-ay-bee," crooned Teddy into the microphone.

"I swear to God," Terry said, "this guy used to play Vegas? He's no Elvis Newton, I'll tell you that."

"Wayne Newton," corrected Larry.

"Him neither," said Terry.

Teddy famous all over Hawaii, but his success was strictly an island phenomenon. His national TV variety show had been canceled four Hollywood weeks after it began. His showroom runs in Vegas were truncated by popular demand. But nothing could diminish the tourist crowds he drew night after lucrative night in Waikiki.

As the musicians played a long bridge, a grandma tourist in a flowery muu-muu jumped on stage and kissed a grinning Teddy. The audience roared. The musicians smiled as if they had never witnessed such an outrageous thing before.

McCabe, but probably none of the tourists, knew that this first grandma was a shill, meant to assure timid ladies that it was okay to jump out of the audience and embrace Teddy.

The waitress delivered the drinks over Larry's head, turned her head and sneezed twice.

"Aloha," Larry said. "Is that what you say when somebody sneezes?"

The drinks were served in ceramic cones meant to suggest volcanoes. A straw stuck out the top, and what looked like bright red rivers of lava oozed along the sides.

"Ten bucks a drink," Terry shouted, and shook his head. "Wish I'd thought of that."

Larry stared over his shoulder at the waitress.

"Every chick he sees," Terry shouted, and shook his head. "They're sneezing to death with the yellow flu, makes no difference to Larry."

Teddy finished his first number to wild applause. People raised their volcano drinks in approval.

"Heave 'em," Teddy shouted, and the audience drank.

No wonder he was worth millions.

"So you've got a guy who tells you to drink up after every song, at ten bucks for a watered-down drink," said Terry.

"And they call me a criminal," said Larry.

"Heave 'em!" Teddy shouted again into the microphone. The audience obeyed. McCabe, the recipient of pink liquid in an ordinary glass, sucked it through a straw. It tasted like a candy bar dissolved in 7-Up.

McCabe watched the show in amazement. He'd heard that Teddy, bored senseless by his own never-changing show, was down to four or five songs a night

now. He began to understand how the man got away with
it. As the band played an endless loop of luau music,
Teddy stepped off the stage. A line of grandmas formed.
Teddy hugged a grandma and kissed her. The official
photographer clicked his camera, and a hula girl led
grandma away. Grandma looked backward, calling to
Teddy, like she was beseeching a lost lover. Then the next
grandma stepped in. In the morning, each grandma could
claim a steel-framed picture of herself with Teddy, $69
plus tax.

"I'm thinking," Terry said. He didn't have to shout
now over the soft luau music. "This guy makes like a
hundred bucks a minute. That's six thousand bucks an
hour. Hey stunod!" he shouted at Larry. "Why didn't you
learn to play the guitar?"

Larry waved him off.

"My brother," Terry said. "No talent."

McCabe began to wish he was drinking something
knockout strong.

"So here's the deal, McCabe," Terry said. "We're
wondering, when are we going to see what do you call,
dividends on our vestments?"

"I'm working on it, guys," McCabe said. "It's not
that simple. I've got an appointment with a guy
tomorrow."

"An appointment?" Terry shouted.

"With a guy who's talked to Sam."

Terry tapped his temple. "Smart guy. Just don't get
too smart.

"You see this guy on stage?" Larry asked. "This
grandma-kissing clown? You'd never think it to look at
him, but he's one of the…"

"What my brother means to say is he forgot his manners and started talking family business in public. Right, stunod?"

"McCabe should know," Larry said, "who he's dealing with."

"He cognates everything he needs to cognate, right McCabe?"

Something told McCabe to nod, to look anywhere but into Terry's eyes, to take a defensive sip at his drink.

The rumors had been floating around Honolulu for years. Veiled references often appeared in Bobbo's *Surrounded by Water* column. Teddy Hong Kong was hooked up, depending on which rumors you believed, with the Las Vegas Mafia or the Yakuza gang known as the Yamaguchi-gumi. McCabe worked this into his own equation. First it seemed simple: Larry and Terry, on the rocks in New Jersey, had taken this Vegas job and showed up at his doorstep. But now, mix in Teddy Hong Kong. McCabe began to imagine possibilities. Teddy was always buttering up Vegas execs for another run at the Desert Skies Room. But was there more to it? Was Teddy planning on building his own casino-crooning empire right here? Was it even possible that Teddy was somehow connected to the visit of the Estonophie brothers? Either way, Teddy had dark connections all over this island, so what seemed like a simple Mainland muscle job might be much more complex.

"Cat scratched your tongue, McCabe?" Terry said. And then to his brother he said: "He is speechless from the generosity of our offer."

"Guys," McCabe said. "I'm spooked by how illegal this is."

"Illegal don't scare us," Terry said. "Does it scare us Larry?"

"Nope." Larry sucked up his drink.

"Illegal is just some kind of bad rap they give to our work. Take your thieves on Wall Street. How come that's legal? Take this guy Teddy, charging ten bucks for sugar and a squirt of rum."

McCabe couldn't answer.

"Well?" Terry demanded.

"Waitress, another round here," called Larry.

"Plus," Terry said. "Our generosity is just beginning. It's not just Uncle Sam. You, too, McCabe, would be a prized member of our exclusive club. You could find yourself a welcome guest in our domicile city. We could put you up, pocketful of chips, comp room, limo, whole thing. You and your girlfriend, the nurse. Nicest vacation in the world."

"Terry," McCabe said, "I'd appreciate it..."

"We're friends from the Boardwalk days, right? So Lazz, I can tell you things about our situation here, that, normally speaking, I would never tell a guy outside the circular trust."

McCabe looked over his shoulder at the exit sign.

"We're not asking you to..." Terry broke off to scold Larry: "Could you pay attention here, stunod?"

"I'm looking for the drinks," Larry protested.

"We're not asking," Terry said, focusing on McCabe again. "That you personally do anything non-ethical, nothing in that realm at all. Just give your politician friend a message informing him of what you would call economic opportunities."

"And they are?"

"You know how many new tourist faces would adventure to your island paradise if let's say ... imagine this joint is a casino. Full of people from California and the locals too. You think this place is a tropical paradise now, wait until gambling…"

"Gaming," said Larry.

"Do I need you to improve my fucking language? You, who dropped out of freshman year?" Terry fixed Larry with a cold stare, then turned to McCabe. "You know how to read, McCabe, so I know you'll read this situation correctly. As soon as we hear that Mr. Wing intends to spend more time with his family, we go back to the pristine desert from whence we came out of. No harm done. In fact," he folded his arms across his chest, "you could call it civic improvement."

"Who exactly," McCabe asked, "are you working for? How does Teddy Hong Kong figure?"

"We don't answer questions. Do we Larry?"

Larry shook his head.

"That's for tour guides, right Larry? Hey, Larry, am I a one man show here? Help me out."

"Shut up, talk, what should I do?"

New volcanoes were set down by the sniffling waitress, empties whisked away. Teddy, on stage, was kissing elderly twin ladies.

"My brother," Terry said. "Ever since he was a kid, he sulks. You remember what he was like, don't you Lazz? Pouty fucking kid. So what do you say? You deliver this message tomorrow and send your homies away happy. Everybody stays healthy. One thing we hate is causing trouble, right Larry?"

"No more stalling," Larry said into the drink.

"This is a job," Terry said, "that needs to be done in a time-honored fashion. Because, for one thing, I gotta get my brother out of here, already he's chasing every broad in town."

"Terry," McCabe said, "After I get your answer from Sam's guy, I drop out, right? What you are asking me to do is not in my line of work."

Larry cracked up.

Terry leaned toward McCabe. "It's in everybody's line of work."

"Right here," McCabe said, and tapped the table, "we're engaged in a criminal conspiracy. All three of us could go to prison for even talking about this."

"But first the cops would need evidence," Terry said. "And evidence …" he wagged his finger at McCabe, "can be difficult to ascertain."

Terry gave a serious look to Larry and said: "It is time for us to go for a nightcap elsewhere."

He stood up. Larry stood up. McCabe stood up.

Terry took McCabe by the arm and walked him out the exit.

They were in a dark, palmy alley, lit by tiki torch lamps, lined by a high lava wall. Teddy had taken the stage again and began crooning his famous *Waikiki Nights* tune. His muffled voice, and strong bass guitar notes, came through the Teflon skin of the big white Ted Shed.

When Larry walked out the door, Terry stood back. Larry patted McCabe down.

"Nothing," Larry said.

Terry crossed his arms, stood back underneath a flaming torch, looked McCabe up and down.

"See, Lazz, despite what the nuns prevaricated, I never did time in carceration and that's the way I intend to keep it."

"Easy," Larry said. "You promised to go easy."

"Who's this guy you got an appointment with?" Terry demanded.

"A lawyer."

"A lawyer? Are you nuts?" Turning to Larry, Terry seethed: "Am I nuts or is he nuts?"

"A crooked lawyer," McCabe said. "A dirty guy. Underworld all the way."

"A fucking lawyer," Terry said, and punched McCabe in the gut.

McCabe, gagging, slid down the wall.

Terry stood over him. "You go down so easy, McCabe. I thought you were from Jersey. I thought you were a medal-decorated veteran. Pick yourself up. There, that's better."

Larry helped McCabe get wobbly to his feet. As McCabe struggled for breath, Terry said: "You understand our business now, McCabe. It is no kidding around. Fuck the lawyer. We need that message delivered to Sam Wing, personal, and after that you never have to see us again."

"Unless you want to," Larry said.

"Shut up," Terry said.

"I meant for old times sake."

"Lazz, you are the designed messenger, it is that simple. We understand each other, us guys from Holy Infant, right? We can't afford to fool around. This is what you call a crucified operation for our forthcoming future. We only go back with the one result."

Terry put his massive forearm at McCabe's throat and pressed McCabe, sputtering, against the lava wall.

"Think of it this way," Terry said. "You're a humanitarian. You will be saving the candidate's life by talking horse sense into him, personal, not through what you call inter-mercenaries."

McCabe gagged. His hands could barely ease the pressure of Terry's forearm against his windpipe.

"It would break my heart," Terry said, "to get rough with a Holy Infant grad."

He eased his weight off McCabe's windpipe.

"So, Lazz, you were saying?"

Porky teriyaki

14

McCabe got off the bus at Ala Moana Park and headed for the farthest Ewa-side picnic table. There, in the shade of a coconut palm, tending a hibachi, stood Porky Hashimoto. Gone was the tailored suit, replaced by khaki shorts and bright green aloha shirt. The hibachi was set on the picnic tabletop and McCabe smelled the delicious evidence of teriyaki grilled pork.

"McCabe," said Porky. "Right on time. So many people in these islands conceptualize time as a loose construct but you …" he clapped McCabe on the back … "what would you like to drink? Juice? Bottled water? Coors? Primo? Or if you prefer something harder …" he picked up a blue plastic flask, "… my versatile assistant Missy makes a vicious mai-tai."

McCabe accepted an icy-cold can of pineapple juice, its paper label slipping off. That label depicted a happy blue-eyed blonde child sipping at a straw that was stuck into a pineapple. Grotton canned fruits and juices were distributed worldwide, but only Island people knew the company's secret tragedy. Charles and Andrea Grotton had been killed in an auto crash on a foggy Pali Highway. Police hid, but not very well, the reports of high blood-alcohol content. The little girl on the label had grown up to be Christina Grotton, the tormented, guilty heiress who was trying to give away the family fortune.

Porky turned the sizzling meat skewers with one hand, held a bottle of Primo Light in the other.

"McCabe, what do you see behind you? Don't bother looking, I'll tell you. The magnificent Ala Moana Shopping Center. Is it the world's largest retail mall? Indeed it is, and its revenues will soon exceed one billion dollars."

Porky slapped at his bare thigh.

"The land underneath it, McCabe, was once a swamp. Do you see the lagoon in front of you? It's artificial, created by the removal of untold tons of dead coral. The dead coral was trucked across the boulevard, dumped in the swamp, and thereupon rose the most profitable retail edifice on this rapidly whirling planet."

He removed his tiny eyeglasses and wiped their lenses with the bottom flap of his aloha shirt.

"Granted, all we can see from here is the parking structure. Joni Mitchell wrote a song about it, but she got her facts wrong. She is Canadian, so her misapprehension of Island life can be excused. This was never paradise, and the Ala Moana Center is hardly a parking lot. Now, why would you care about all this, McCabe?"

McCabe, wearing flip-flops, felt a tiny sting on his foot. Red ant. He shook it off.

"What political difficulties, you ask," Porky said, "were overcome in the building of this mall? I'm proud to say Royce Hashimoto Associates, in the days when my father was the principal partner, took the lead in overcoming the environmental hurdles. Oh the poor fishies! Oh the poor frogs!"

Porky sipped beer. "Was it easy to quiet the hypersensitive crowd? I assure you, it took great skill to outmaneuver them. What is the point of my soliloquy, you ask? Every accomplishment in human history, from the Pyramids forward, was enabled by a backroom deal."

He lifted the skewered meat off the glowing hibachi. "Suffering and progress, McCabe. They are twin phenomena. The only question is, who suffers and who progresses?"

Porky set those meaty skewers atop stainless steel bowls of cold rice. Then with his middle finger, he flicked a red ant off the picnic table.

"As with the mall's opponents," Porky said. "The bite of the fire ant is annoying, but hardly serious. No need to crush them. We just flick them off."

He sat in front of one rice bowl, and pushed the other across the table to McCabe. A tiny container held pickled ginger and cucumbers, which McCabe upended on the rice.

McCabe, hungry despite his sore gut, attacked his lunch with chopsticks. The grilled pork was tender and far more savory than any served in restaurants.

"Missy's marinade, family recipe," Porky said.

"Is she your...?"

"Maid, paralegal, cook, gal Friday and keeper of secrets. The firm would be nearly dysfunctional without her, and yet she asks so little in return."

Doormat, that's the word that occurred to McCabe. Men like Porky always seemed to find a doormat to wipe their feet on. McCabe worried that he would soon join Missy underneath the muddy sandals of Porky Hashimoto. Why had Porky invited him to this two-man picnic? He looked out across the calm green lagoon, to puka-shell hunters standing in ankle-deep water on the dead reef, to surfers far out at the breaking waves. Calm, he told himself, calm. And don't eat all your lunch. You don't want to seem desperate.

Porky held up a pink strand of pickled ginger, trapped between his chopsticks. "Palate cleanser," he said.

He chewed it thoughtfully.

"Do we enjoy an attorney client relationship McCabe? It may surprise you that, no, as of this moment we do not, and as it turns out we quite possibly never did. Of course, there's Missy's record of our meeting, which may surface some day if it proves useful, and may be destroyed if it's deemed a liability. So let us posit, McCabe, that we are merely two friends meeting for lunch on a pleasant afternoon."

McCabe drank from his sweating can of juice.

"Have I approached Councilman Wing with your offer?" Porky asked. "Who knows? You're familiar with the Heisenberg Principle, I take it. We live in a world of quantum uncertainty. But had I discussed the matter with Sam, that would be confidential. If I possessed a criminal turn of mind, which I manifestly do not, I would be frankly embarrassed to make that esteemed public servant the impoverishing offer you suggested. Speaking hypothetically, of course."

Porky smacked his lips, produced a silver toothpick from his lunch bucket, slipped it between his lips.

"McCabe, am I a financial advisor? No, I am not certified in that capricious, arbitrary and possibly bogus profession. But were I, I would advise Councilman Wing … McCabe, are you okay?"

McCabe winced, maybe because he felt like Porky was twisting a metaphorical knife in his gut, maybe because he was sore from the punch delivered by Terry Estonophie.

"It's nothing," said McCabe.

"Speaking in strictly hypothetical terms, were I Sam Wing's advisor, my counsel would be to demand an introduction fee of one million dollars."

"Introduction fee?"

"Certainly you are familiar with the concept, McCabe. In consideration of the aforementioned amount, your associates would be introduced to parties who are empowered to conduct further negotiations."

McCabe sat back and stared at Porky. Have I, McCabe wondered, fallen asleep and entered a bizarre REM state?

"Payable on demand," Porky said, "in an account we designate, on an island far, far removed from here. Could you expect a finder's fee, McCabe? I would posit that fifty thousand dollars is an entirely reasonable amount."

"I don't think," McCabe said, "my guys want to dicker."

"Nonsense," said Porky. "The shopping center behind us generates hundreds of millions, but compared to the profits from casino gambling, that will be chicken feed."

"I doubt these guys have the authority to…"

"Is it possible that you're of *them*, McCabe, and not one of *us*? Human life is conflict, McCabe. Them against us. Us against them. You're either in the cave or you're outside attacking the cave. Are you in the cave with us McCabe?"

"I …"

"You're a professional word man, McCabe. A communicator. A persuader, although in my humble opinion, you ply your trade for a pittance. Surely you can play for bigger stakes. All you need to do is convince your contacts that a billion dollars in future income is worth a paltry sum today."

He stood. He gathered the stainless steel rice bowls, packed them in an insulated bag.

"Don't look so shocked, McCabe, it's unbecoming and suggests an unwholesome naivete. This is how things are done here. It goes back to the corrupt pact between monarchs and planters. So. We carry on a grand historical tradition. Go forward, McCabe." He slapped McCabe on the shoulder. "And play your part in history."

Bang, bang, bang, the crash of hammer on steel rang from the barn behind Bobbo's house. McCabe, having hiked in from the bus stop, was covered with a slurry of dusty sweat. The banging noises had driven the rooster and his chicken flock into the jungle. As McCabe approached the barn, the hammering ceased. He paused in the shade of the barn's eaves, admiring a life-size rusty dolphin Marly Burns had hammered out of scrap automobile.

"The poor man," he heard Reiko say, and then muttering. Ah. Rei and Marly were discussing Bobbo, obviously. The good daughter was worried about the drinking and smoking habits that would surely kill her old man.

"He can't drive, he can only do office work," Rei said.

They were talking about him!

"You wouldn't say he's lazy," said Rei, "but he has no great ambitions. And whenever he gets stressed out, he falls asleep. Although ... although it's a defense mechanism. He had a rough childhood."

"Everybody had a rough childhood," Marly said.

"They moved around a lot."

"The brave embrace this world," Marly said. "Cowards want to climb back into the safety of the womb. Maybe your boyfriend is a womb climber."

Rei laughed. "A womb climber?"

"You know what I'd embrace right now?" said Marly. "Wine and ibuprofen."

As he heard their footsteps approach the doorway, McCabe slipped around the side of the barn. Beneath a shady windowsill, a red and white spider, as big as McCabe's hand, crept along its web. In the center of the web, a doomed fly helplessly beat its wings. Was that him? The fly? He thought of himself as laid-back. Did people see him as ineffectual? Was he a coward? A womb climber? A pathetic fly beating its wings in a spider's web?

He waited until he heard a screen door bang and then pretended to saunter from driveway to porch.

McCabe entered the parlor to find Bobbo snoring in a sleeping bag spread out on the piano. Atop the piano, Bobbo said, was the only place he could he get a decent night's sleep. He claimed he could feel the vibrations of the strings underneath, even when no one was playing.

How had Bobbo slept had so long, and through all the banging? The bare-wood floor was scattered with yellow balled-up sheets of paper torn from a legal pad. Bobbo had been up, maybe until dawn, writing drunken poetry. A bottle of rum sat on the piano bench, only an inch of liquor at its bottom. Two coffee cups were piled high with cigarette butts.

"Robert!" Marly shouted from the kitchen. "Your column!"

She appeared in the doorway. "Oh, it's you." She looked McCabe over as if examining a sorry specimen indeed.

"Maybe you can rouse him," Marly said. "I've been trying for a lifetime."

She turned back into the kitchen and said to Rei, "My father despises his job, but if he ever lost it, that would be the end of him."

McCabe stepped into the kitchen doorway. Bobbo's kitchen was clogged with ratty reclining chairs. Since everyone gathered in the kitchen, Bobbo reasoned, that's where the easy chairs belonged. Reiko sat, almost lost in a fluffy recliner, sipping ice tea.

As Marly gabbed with Reiko, McCabe simply admired his girlfriend. He'd been crazy for Rei ever since he'd moved in next door to her. With Rei, the wandering ghost ship SS McCabe had finally found its home port. She was attractive, honorable, sensible. But she was oddly blind to evil, perhaps because her soul contained so little of it.

Rei's mental magic had even turned the complex, chaotic world of the ER into model of simplicity. People in distress were wheeled through the big doors. The docs gave the orders, the nurses carried them out. Patients were treated, then usually sent home or upstairs to OR or ICU. Rei felt that all she had to do was follow protocol, and things would turn out as well as they possibly could.

Never before had McCabe met anyone with such a high degree of social trust. Her mind had no dark corner for dirty politics or skullduggery to lodge. Good-hearted as she was, she could offer him no help in escaping from the spider's web the Estonophies and Porky had wrapped around him.

Rei raised her glass toward McCabe. "Ice tea? We're discussing the Mainland?"

"Reiko should give the Mainland another chance," Marly said. "A few days in Los Angeles is not a fair sample. I recommended Portland and Seattle as cities with a smattering of forward-thinking, intelligent people."

Was she encouraging Reiko to leave him?

Marly stood up. She wore smudged coveralls over a black t-shirt, her outfit ending in workboots. "People cling to this miserable island so. I can never understand it."

McCabe heard Bobbo groan and turned from the doorway to the grand piano.

"Bobbo," McCabe said. He shook the sleeping bag.

Bobbo opened one bloodshot eye. "Don't tell me it's morning."

"Actually, it's afternoon."

McCabe stood back as Bobbo rolled out of the sleeping bag and climbed down from the piano. He looked like some skinny, endangered primate, naked but for wrinkled skivvies, hairless but for gray pony tail.

Rubbing his face, Bobbo stumbled across his porch and out to the edge of his jungle.

McCabe caught up with Bobbo just as he began urinating on a palm tree.

"Bobbo, I've just come back from a meeting with Porky."

"Congratulations."

"He's become Sam's agent. They're demanding a million bucks to begin negotiations."

"I'm afraid I rather overdid it last night."

"The Jersey brothers have no power to negotiate. So I'm like squeezed in a vice, Bobbo."

"Don't take up rum," Bobbo advised. "It's a noxious habit."

"And now I'm thinking Teddy Hong Kong is deep into this casino thing."

"Teddy Hong Kong, Teddy Hong Kong," Bobbo said. "I need a cigarette."

He retreated to the porch, where a bright palmy aloha shirt hung from the back of a chair. Bobbo fished around in its pocket and came out with not a cigarette, but a bent, limp joint. He lit it, inhaled, closed his eyes, sat in the big chair, the sultan of a lush, dopey realm.

"That's curious," said Bobbo. "Teddy is the spawn of the local-boy mobsters. He needs that prime spot in Waikiki, McCabe. A pair of fighting cockroaches would draw a crowd in the Ted Shed. Fifty thousand tourists a day pass it. Teddy may have friends in Las Vegas, but he's a street corner busker in Waikiki without the approval of the local gangsters."

He let out a wisp of perfumed smoke.

"Specifically, King Kimo Long. You may recall, King Kimo, McCabe, perhaps you even wrote a story about him back in the day. King Kimo of the disappearing union pension fund and the big bankrupt condo. Currently in Halawa Prison."

"Robert!" shouted Marly from the kitchen. "Either you write your column or I will."

Bobbo sputtered. "She'd do it, too."

"Okay, help me out here, Bobbo. Teddy's in league with the Vegas boys. He also has the backing of the local thugs. They want Sam out of the mayor's race so they can bring in casinos. Why doesn't Teddy just tell Sam to get lost?"

"I'm not privy to the doings of the underworld, McCabe. However, I could certainly use a cup of coffee."

"Marly!" he shouted into the kitchen. "Any java in the house?"

"If you get up after noon," Marly shouted back, "you make your own."

Bobbo buttoned the bright aloha shirt over his skinny chest and licked his cracked lips.

"With King Kimo Long in prison, I'd venture to guess that the local thuggery is somewhat confused, chaotic, nay even in turmoil. Lately I've heard pesky rumors of the Yakuza financing everything from puka shell stands to girlie bars and golf resorts. If I had to guess, McCabe, I'd say the brothers are part of a clever probe designed to discover who exactly is in charge of our darker doings these days."

"So under this scheme," McCabe said, "Bix Sanders would become mayor, and Vegas would forgive his gambling debts. Teddy would end up owning a casino showroom. And the Jersey brothers …"

"Are disposable," Bobbo said.

"Which means," said McCabe. Suddenly dizzy, he sat down on a gray Navy sea chest. "I'm disposable too."

"Harsh words," said Bobbo. "True perhaps, but harsh."

Bobbo stood and, as if he were back in boot camp, began to perform a series of jumping jacks, thumping the porch floorboards with his bare feet.

"A million bucks?" he said, already out of breath. "Sam will cave."

He quit after maybe eight jumping jacks, and stood huffing, hands on hips. "Excuse me."

In the parlor, Bobbo worked into wrinkled khaki trousers and slipped on rubber flip-flops. He ducked into the bathroom and emerged brushing his teeth. He stepped back onto the porch, spit toothpaste and saliva over this side-rail and said to McCabe: "I'm going down to file for mayor."

He stuck a Big Tent cigarette between his lips, and it bobbed unlit as he muttered: "I've finally degenerated to the point where I consider myself a politician."

"You can't run for mayor. If you get into politics, Mrs. Keeper will drop your column. She warned you."

Bobbo lit that cigarette with a Navy lighter that said: USS Kitty Hawk.

"I doubt she has the nerve. Can the population of this island exist without my salacious gossip, vicious slander and pointless self-promotion? My rusty typewriter has become the de facto headquarters of the Coconut Wireless. Social value of gossip aside, Mahalo House Department Store would cancel their ads in the absence of my daily discourse."

"Take a walk, Bobbo."

"Unhand me McCabe."

"Follow me, then."

McCabe led Bobbo down the rickety steps and into the shade of the thorny, palmy jungle.

"Why would you run for mayor, Bobbo?"

"Somebody's got to speak up for the little guy."

"Come on, you don't want to be mayor."

"Lord no, but I do want to run."

"Why?"

"You are aware, McCabe, that I operate a botanical enterprise. The enemies of that enterprise clad themselves in blue and hide behind badges. Were the master," he hiccupped, "of that botanical enterprise to run in a primary that featured only two candidates, he would get a substantial number of votes, given the perversity and ignorance of the electorate. Those votes would constitute political capital. Chief Abreu would be forced to think twice before sending his Gestapo into my verdant realm."

He ground the cigarette under his sandals.

"After all, the Chief has political ambitions of his own."

He touched McCabe's shoulder.

"With Sam out, I'd guess that at least five thousand voters are perverse enough to check the box next to my name. Yes, the candidacy of Bobbo Burns would offer me substantial political cover."

"Don't be absurd, Bobbo. If Sam drops out, we'd have casinos all over Waikiki."

Bobbo sighed. "Once upon a time there was a swampy paradise that went by the mellifluous name of Wai-ki-ki. Then a Protestant missionary named Grotton, the Devil take his soul, dug a canal. He drained the swamp, called it paradise, and invited the California steamship crowd. We enter the world crying, McCabe, and did you ever wonder why?"

"Robert!" shouted Marly from the porch. "Phone call."

She set the Mickey Mouse phone, tethered by a long cord, on the porch table.

"It's your editor," she said. "She's furious. Is your column late again?"

"I'll deliver it in person," said Bobbo.

McCabe went black. He fell through a thousand miles of darkness into a dream, in which he was drowning in a cold ocean, clinging desperately to a rock.

When he awoke to the light, Rei had a cool cloth held to his forehead and was saying, "He'll be all right. It's not dangerous except if he's driving."

The last thing he remembered before the blackout was Bobbo roaring away from the house on his red Indian motorcycle. Then McCabe, feeling dizzy, had sat on the porch step and then, darkness. He awoke with the cold realization that he'd hoped to find an ally in Bobbo, only to be betrayed. He felt shaky, like a current had passed through him, leaving a vague, electric nausea.

"Was I dreaming?" McCabe asked, "or did Bobbo go downtown to file for mayor?"

Marly returned a solemn nod.

"What did he do that for?" McCabe asked.

"Because," Marly said, "my father is profoundly self-destructive, and cannot resist anything that's bad for him. You don't know how many therapists it took to get me to accept that conclusion."

She sucked down smoke from a long twisted reefer. "Ever since I made the mistake of returning from California, he's turned me into a referee between him and his editor. He sends in his column as late as possible, inducing panic in the newsroom. It's a neurotic demonstration of self-importance, and plays to my father's obsession with defying authority."

She gave McCabe a hard-eyed look, as if he were somehow encouraging Bobbo's misbehavior.

"So," Marly said. "Passing out. Is this your form of avoidance behavior?"

"It's neurological," McCabe said. "Inherited."

"Are you sure you want to spend your life with this man?" Marly asked Rei.

Rei laughed. "He's in desperate need of a wife."

Marly shook her head. "Love does strange things to people."

"Love leads directly," said Rei. "to kaza."

Marly snarled. "Kaza? What the hell is kaza?"

The Captain's log

15

Because he was crazy in love with Pua, Larry agreed to take the bus. Parking was impossible in the Capitol District, she said, and driving The Thing in traffic made her nervous.

So they had to stand in the aisles, that's how crowded the stinky bus was. Larry hung on to a strap, and put one arm around Pua's waist. This is what a guy in love did. Protection, see, for the future mother of your children.

Wouldn't that be something? If Little Brother pumped out a couple of babies while Big Brother was still single? *Uncle Terry, meet your nephew. Yup, he's half Hawaiian and half Estonophie.*

Pua rang the buzzer and they hopped off the bus and crossed the boulevard, walking toward a humungous white building with a red tile roof. It was surrounded by crew-cut lawn and beautiful trees that sprouted lipstick-red flowers. They walked into the main entrance, thank

God it was air conditioned inside, because Larry worked up a sweat on that bus.

So this was the main Hawaiian library? Beautiful inside, like a Catholic church, minus the plaster saints. Cool. Spacious. Nice woodwork. It reminded Larry of his very first job, robbing the Poor Box at Holy Infant.

"Wow," Larry said, "it's like a thousand times bigger than the library at Rahway State."

"Is that where you went to school?" Pua asked.

"Kind of," said Larry.

"I thought you didn't go to college."

"Well, I don't like to boast."

She stuck her tongue out at him. "You're such a fibber."

"Me?" said Larry.

"I know why you lie."

"You do? Tell me then."

"Maybe when we know each other better."

Pua led them to the Reference Desk and talked to a nice lady whilst Larry looked around, hands in his pockets, remembering his pal Gambling George, the trustee at the prison library. George was in for check kiting, so you knew he was a good guy. *Hustler* and *Playboy* were forbidden at Rahway, but George had the latest issues, hidden behind the encyclopedias.

"Okay, honey," Pua said.

Honey!

That gave Larry goose-bumps and a lump in the throat. He couldn't say a thing. He followed Pua up a dark wooden stairway and past a slew of shelves until they reached a window near an empty desk.

"You sit, I'll be back," Pua said.

What was it about this girl that made Larry think of happy children? He saw himself ten years from now, dark tan from a decade in the Islands, Papa Larry, leading a happy boy and girl along the beach as they picked seashells. And little Amy, named after Mom, innocent little Amy would pick up a seashell and say: *Look at this pretty one, Daddy.*

It brought tears to his eyes. He wiped them with his knuckles. Who'd have thought! You're five thousand miles from Jersey, and finally you find a home.

Palm trees rustled in the breeze. Even the breeze had a name here: Trade Winds. The palm fronds scraped at the window, waving, like an invitation to relax underneath their shade.

Pua set a dusty book on the desk in front of Larry.

"Now who told you this?" she asked. "The clerk at the Tiki Torch?"

"Carl, you probably know him, he's Hawaiian. He wears a lava-lava."

"Silly, I don't know every Hawaiian man on Oahu. Anyway, he said Jules Dudoit was a sea captain? It looks like he was right."

"Doo-dwa?"

"Yes," Pua said. "I told you. It's a French pronunciation."

"I didn't know they had Frenchies in Hawaii."

"Well," said Pua, "you're about to learn. Dudoit is an Island name now. I went to school with a boy. Dennis Dudoit. And he was very much a Hawaiian boy. Quiet and handsome."

Larry felt the hot sting of man jealousy.

Pua flipped pages.

"Here it is, see? Captain Jules Dudoit, 1803-1866. Master of the brig Clementine. He sold his ship and bought a sheep ranch on Kauai. He sold ... are you listening? Why are you so squirmy?"

"Can't help it," said Larry. "The jimmy jumps."

"Captain Dudoit sold his sheep ranch and moved his family to Honolulu, where he became the French Consul."

"Like an ambassador, right?"

"And look at this," Pua's finger moved down the page. "He quarreled with his Chinese cook over broken pottery. He withheld the price of the pottery from the cook's pay. And the cook stabbed him to death!"

"Wow, no shit," said Larry, "let me read it." He cast his eye along the page. He wasn't really a word guy, so he focused on the drawing of a handsome man with curly hair. Must have been red hair, since Captain Dudoit was a Frenchie.

Larry looked up and through the window. The palm fronds waved. The sunny reflection he saw was not Lawrence Estonophie of New Jersey but Jules Dudoit. Sea captain! Ambassador of France!

He had to stand up he was so nervous. He felt like he did before every entry, you know, the back alley jobs. He felt this tremendous excitement that could only be relieved by going in. The best part was the feeling that you weren't supposed to be inside, you were breaking the law, defiant, you were like the The Phantom, the ghost who walks. Larry wasn't one of those nasty burglars who wrecked the place and crapped on the floor no, that was disgusting and unmanly. He was Lightning Larry, he went quick for the pills and the cash, in the cookie jar, under the mattress, in the sock drawer and then, five minutes inside max, he let himself out the window and felt calm. It was like after sex. You relaxed. You lit a cigarette. There was kind of a glow, and not just the tip of the cigarette, but an inner glow. Like it was meant to be, and here you were, a little richer, and a lot calmer, a job well done, nobody hurt, hardly any damage.

And the insurance companies covered it all.

Really, when you came down to it, he was ripping off the insurance companies, who were rip-off artists themselves. That didn't make him a terrible person, did it?

He led Pua down aisles of books, he had to get outside, he was feeling so crazy. He stopped in the lobby to catch his breath. Out there the city was mad, busy bright hot. In his mind, the brig Clementine was easing into port, hula girls trying to lure the sailors to jump ship. Captain Larry Estonophie/Jules Dudoit was steady at the helm. Belay them sails, boys, or whatever it was that Captains said.

"I knew it when I first got off the plane," said Larry. "I've seen this all before. I lived here in another lifetime and now we've proved it. Why do you think I just happened to rent a hotel on Dudoit Lane? And why did the hotel clerk tell me it was named after a sea captain? It makes sense now. I see."

"Koshu's magic words," said Pua, and from her cleavage she brought out the little gold heart with the tiny pinprick eyes. She dangled its chain, tucked it back in. "Thieves rip the gold right off your neck down here."

But Larry's mind was moving too fast to pay her much attention. Okay he wasn't a book-reading pinhead but his gut feelings were seldom wrong. Sea Captain? That was just a fancy name for a pirate. Jules Dudoit was a pirate who gave up the thieving life to settle here. Gave up the bad life for the love of a Hawaiian girl. Jules Dudoit, you suave bastard, stabbed by a Chinese cook and now come back in the body of Larry Estonophie to finish out your life.

Only in this lifetime, he was going to treat the help right.

"Downtown's this way, right?" Larry asked Pua.

"Yes, but…."

"There's bookstores, right? I need to get a book on reincarnation."

"Larry," she took his arm. "We're at the library, you can borrow one."

No, then he'd have to bring it back or Pua would get fined. Larry knew he'd never bring it back, returning things just wasn't in him. Bookstores were a better bargain. There was no need to pay for a book, really. On Terry's birthday, Larry always liberated a bunch of crossword books at the Barnes and Noble at Jersey Shore Mall.

"I'll bet we get rich," he said.

"What do you mean we?"

"You know, I'm speaking hypodermically."

"Hypo…"

"If we get rich and hire a Chinese cook, this time I'm not going to yell at him. He can break all the dishes he wants."

"Larry, let's buy a book later, at the mall. I need to stay away from downtown."

"So, like, there's an old boyfriend you don't want to meet? I'll kick his ass."

She shook her head. "It's not that. It's … a lot of people downtown lost money with Dad. They're still, you know, angry."

"Oh, so business gone bad."

Pua nodded.

"So let's go home," she said.

Well, this was working out to be the Year of the Rooster, all right. Larry was maybe a half hour from discovering the fleshy delights of Pualani Long, naked. Since he'd once been an ambassadorial Sea Captain, he deserved a taxi ride, if not a limo. Sitting next to Pua, holding her hand, the windows of the Aloha Cab open, Larry sucked down delicious breeze. As hot and crowded as this city was, it smelled of sweet flowers. Pua, Hawaiian for flower! When the cab rose up the steep slopes of the Big Wahine, the air got cooler, they left the traffic behind, a thousand feet down. The cab turned into the driveway of a white-painted ranch house nestled into a lava hillside.

Larry palmed the cabbie a $10 tip.

And he and Pua were alone in a spacy living room. It was like some burglar had come in and stolen most of the furniture. Windows ran the length of the room, and out those windows, the island looked small. Waikiki looked like a tiny white wedge, and then Diamond Head, a hole in the ground. From up here, Diamond Head looked nothing like it did on the postcards. And then the docks, and the airport, and Pearl Harbor, a mountain range behind that, and then just ocean, ocean, ocean.

Pua encircled his skinny waist with her fleshy arms.

"Like the view?"

He nodded.

"It'll be mine someday."

"Don't you have brothers?"

"Dad's cut them off. One's in Alaska. One's in the Army. There's a lot of you know complications in our family."

"Where's your dad now?"

"He's you know checked into the hospital for a while. Precaution, that's all."

"Complications?" said Larry. "Me too. Mostly my brother. He's working on a business deal. When he's done, I'm supposed to go home with him."

Her breath hot in his ear, she said, "You can tell him no, can't you?"

"You don't know Terry."

"He doesn't own you, does he?"

"He's like an … an emotional cripple."

"What?"

"He acts like a tough guy, but he goes to pieces without me." He tapped his temple with a forefinger. "Vietnam. It messed up his head."

"Larry Stone," said Pua, and spun him around. "You're preparing me to be abandoned."

Larry shook his head. "I'll figure it out," he said. "I always looked up to my brother. A couple of times back in Jersey, he saved my ass. But I made up my mind when you and me were in the library. I was meant to be here. I'm never going back to Jersey."

They kissed for a long soulful time.

Larry broke the lip lock. "And now, I want you."

Pua looked at him with the kindest gaze. "You're going to be disappointed in me," she said.

"No way," said Larry, and led her toward the bedroom.

A messy pile of prescription bottles covered the top of Pua's night-table. Larry sat on the edge of her bed thinking, man, this girl is like a drug addict. But he wasn't going to say anything. When you're roaring 90 miles an hour down Love Freeway, you don't steer for the potholes.

Pua ducked into the bathroom and gently shut the door.

Normally Larry would have pocketed at least some of those pills. But he understood that Pua really needed them. So he forced himself to look away from that tempting lineup of little brown bottles. He sat back in like a carved Hawaiian chair. He locked his hands behind his head, and scanned the room. A big rumpled double bed low to the floor. Above the bed, a painting, that crazy red Koshu heart set with the two wide-open eyes. Surfboard in the corner, a rubber leash dangling from it. Poster of some guy at the ocean, posing with a long orange surfboard.

"Comfortable?" asked Pua from the doorway. "Settling in to my room?"

She buttoned the strap over her striped overalls. At the windows, she cranked open their louvers, let in the delicious breeze.

"So, this is my girlhood place," she said. Overalls and underwear and bras were heaped near the closet, and she closed the door on that mess. Strange, this chick liked to dress in overalls, in like the hottest city in the world.

Larry thought of Karen. She had broken his heart but now he was glad she had abandoned him in Rahway. Maybe this was Kaza, fate, meant to be. He'd once thought of Karen as his true wife, and Betty and Jerri as glorified girlfriends. Karen, a chef at a Boardwalk hotel, was the only one of his wives who brought home a paycheck, and the only one who could fry a decent burger. Plus she was a wild animal in bed.

But the minute they got out of bed, they started arguing, him and Karen.

Pua sat on the bed with a sigh. "Dad never likes my boyfriends."

"How many boyfriends do you have?" Uninvited, Larry joined her on the bed, ran his arm around her waist.

"You know something?" said Pua, looking at her hands in her lap. "There are things I can't tell you." She stretched out on the bed, lying on her side, facing not the windows but the wall.

Pua stared at her poster of that surfer.

Larry's hand started playing with her front snap.

"Who's Surfer Joe? You know him?"

"That's Koshu."

"That surfer is your holy man?"

"Koshu Kai, that was his name before he had his visions. He's not even from Hawaii. He was a San Diego Hawaiian. Oh, from a very strict family. Mormons. Haole mom and Hawaiian dad. I think his dad was in the Coast Guard. He came here to surf, but guess what, there's no money in it. He got a degree in sociology and then went to work for Hawaii Guardians. It's a Grotton charity for children."

"And then?"

"He had his visions. Christina gave him money. He founded the Kaza School, it's for wounded children."

"Wounded? Like war orphans?"

"Oh you know, wounded in the heart. Koshu was meditating one day when he burst out with: *'I See.'* Because he suddenly realized how much of the world's trouble comes from wounded children. Wounded on the inside."

"You were in love with this Koshu."

Pua shook her head. "Unh uh. He was a *mahu*."

"A what?"

"Gay."

"How did he die?"

"You've been to the temple. He died there. Swept off by a big wave. As the wave took him under, he shouted: *I see*. And that's the last we ever saw of Koshu. His body was never found."

Pua said, "Oh," and rolled over, began hiding her pill bottles in the sock drawer. Larry wanted to say, Honey, I've already seen them. Pills, they were even better than money when you did an entry, and Larry would never miss a bottle of pills.

"So this Koshu guy, he just… turned his life around, like from surf bum to kind of a god?"

"After his revelation."

"Revelation?"

"Kind of like when a cute guy comes here from the Mainland, and finds out he was a sea captain in another life."

Cute guy? Did she mean him?

"How about you?" she said. "Is there some pretty blondie waiting for you on the Mainland?"

"Nope." He nuzzled her ear.

"A wife?"

"No wife."

"Ever been married?"

"Me?" he said.

"No keikis?"

"What's that?"

"Children. No little Larrys running around the mainland?"

"Is this like twenty questions?"

He unsnapped her overalls and pulled them off. He ran a hand gentle over her gorgeous legs. He unbuttoned her white blouse, she turned over so he could unhook her bra and then there she was, his beautiful chubby bunny lying naked.

"Maybe I'm just a curious girl," she said. She rolled over, took control of his hand, flattened it against her stomach. "But I want to know if you have children."

"No kids that I know of," he said.

"Larry, here's..." she gulped... she stared at the ceiling, at the surfing poster, turned her head to look out the windows.

"I can't give myself."

"You're what? Not a virgin?"

"I didn't say that."

"Oh, great," Larry said and took his hand away.

"Don't get me wrong," she said. "I like you."

Larry pouted.

"I can't do everything you want," Pua said.

"What the hell?"

"It's like sex, you know," and then she broke off. She let out an animal grunt, "Unnnh," and stared at the ceiling like it was all hopeless. "You have to keep your clothes on," she said.

"Just like last time," he said.

"What?"

"Like in our past lives."

"Oh, please."

Larry rolled over on one elbow. He looked directly into her eyes like he was searching for her soul. Man, did she have beautiful big brown eyes. He could see himself in them.

"The Princess and the Pirate," he said. "We couldn't make it back then either. It's like fate or the other thing … "

"Kaza. Fate becomes kaza when you welcome it, good or bad."

"Okay, kaza."

"You can kiss me, though," Pua said. "I'd like that."

Larry sucked down a big breath and began, reluctantly, to kiss her lips. It was like his duty as a man. But he asked himself: Why put in a day's work if there's no paycheck at quitting time? He decided to test her, in case she was goofing him.

He moved his hand down her belly.

"Don't do that," she said, and pushed his hand away.

He had never been with a girl so big and strong. He could smell her woman scent, it went straight to his brain and made him tingle. He could feel her trembling, why he didn't know. He broke away from her, got on his knees near the foot of the bed and began caressing her bare feet.

"What are you doing. Wait!" she said.

Okay, Larry was not a high school graduate, but his Little Fox made up for it. Mom had first told him about his Little Fox. *Always listen to your Little Fox, Larry.* And right now his Little Fox was telling him something.

He backed away and sat in Pua's Hawaiian chair. He looked at the windows. They were not like windows back home, they were louvers, you couldn't open them up and jump out into the yard. It must have been tough on entry guys, these houses with skinny windows. He looked at Pua. This girl had never said much about her mother, except she had died long ago.

Larry's heart broke to see her there, a child brought up without a mother's love, her father always in some mysterious trouble. She wasn't going give him her body, but he didn't feel all angered up about it. He realized what Pua's problem was. His Little Fox helped him understand. Her fear of love, her sex freeze up, the cut marks on her wrists, the bottles of pills.

"I know," Larry said. "It's all right."

"It's not all right," she said. She drew a blue sheet over her body, covered everything but her head, tears streaming down her face.

He knelt at the bed, kissed a tear that ran down her cheek.

"Okay, it's not all right," he said. "There, does a tender kiss make you feel better?"

Beginning to blubber, she nodded.

Dad the Pervert, eh? Larry had known bastards like that in Rahway.

"Princess," he said. "My Hawaiian princess. I'm going to show you what love is. I'm going to kill your father."

"Don't, no, don't do anything mean, I love my Dad."

"He did bad things to you, didn't he?"

"I love him anyway. It's not his fault. Mom wasn't around. Koshu says we should love those that hurt us. We should try to see their pain, understand their pain. You see? Koshu's big heart."

She pointed over her head to the painting of the two-eyed heart.

She put a hand inside Larry's shirt, lay it on his chest at the Friendly Devil. "You have a big heart too, Larry Stone. Feel how strong it's thumping."

Plan B

16

"My brother the Chinese," grumped Terry.

They sat on a low concrete wall bordering a shallow pool. In that pool swam big fat goldfish. Larry held a paper plate in front of his mouth, and used chopsticks to scoop up Chinese noodles.

"Now you wear aloha shirts?" Terry said. "And look at your tan. Chopsticks! Next thing you know, you'll be talking Polynesian."

Larry swallowed noodles. "Don't laugh. I might come back here some day. For a long term visit, you know."

"McCabe is late," Terry said.

"You scare him shitless, that's why. He's meeting us in daylight so you can't beat him up."

"That was a beating? No. Words, Larry, someday you'll show discernment about corrective words. Reminder. A reminder is all McCabe got."

"This crispy duck," said Larry, "is fantastic."

"McCabe late again, that's insulting our professional livelihood. Late is what you call uncourteous."

The brothers sat in a shaded corner but still it was sweating hot. Terry unbuttoned his gray suit-coat, tugged at his purple tie but did not loosen it. People here dressed what you called slovenly. Colorful, but slovenly, walking in sweaty sunshine, carrying shopping bags.

"You sure we're in the right place?" Terry's anger glowed hot in his face.

"Fish pond. Second level. Ala Moana Shopping Center."

"Because if we're in the wrong place, Larry…"

Larry dangled a noodle strand in the pond, but the fat red fish did not take the bait.

"There's only one fish pond in this mall," said Larry. "Koi. The fish are called koi. You know what I found out? They cost like a hundred bucks a piece. Maybe we should get into fish smuggling when this is over."

"Here comes the pansy now," said Terry.

McCabe, at the top of the escalator, waved at the brothers.

"What's he think," muttered Terry, "this is a Boy Scout picnic? Ditch the lunch, Larry, in all seriousness."

Terry stood, hands in his pockets, and watched McCabe approach. He wore gold-and-white aloha shirt and white trousers. If he'd been carrying menus, he'd look exactly like a waiter. Which was why Hawaii was such a sad excuse for sartorial, Terry figured. Everybody dressed like they were going to tell you about the early-bird special.

"Sorry," said McCabe and held out the fake hand of friendship. "I missed the bus."

Terry's lips formed the word *pathetic* but since this was a business meeting, he did not pronounce it. He let McCabe's hand hang out there like, what would you call it, a dangling participle.

"What you got for us?" Terry asked.

McCabe stuttered.

"And let me say," Terry added, "the answer should be yes, without what you call disqualifications."

"Well, I've been talking to Uncle Sam's man," McCabe whispered, and then looked around. "Can I sit down? I feel dizzy."

He sat on the pond ledge, trailed one hand in the water. Behind him the glaring sun made a slow-cook oven of a gazillion tons of coral, lava and concrete known as Ala Moana Shopping Center. McCabe, it was like he was looking right out of the sun when he said: "He wants a million bucks."

Terry sputtered.

Larry slapped his own face. "Did I just hear that? A million bucks."

"Unfortunately," McCabe said, "that million would only buy an introduction. Further negotiations would be necessary."

"Further negotiations?" Terry snorted. "McCabe, this ain't Let's Make a Deal. This ain't what you call a nautical negotiating ploy. This is a gregarious offer. It's the only offer your friend is going to get. The next time we speak, the language will not be mercenary."

Terry, hoping the keep the sun out of his eyes, sat on the pond wall next to McCabe.

"The deal," Terry said, struggling to keep his voice quiet, "is a fantastical win at roulette, like we verified to you. You get it? You think we can go back to Management and say, oh guess what, remember that figure you gave us, well multiply it by ..." he paused to work the math ... "six and you got it. Even double would be a fatalistic insult."

McCabe laughed, but Larry understood this was nerves in disguise.

"McCabe, you want us to call and activate Plan C? You wouldn't wish that on your most triumphant enemy, believe me."

"I thought you had a plan B?"

"You'll find out about plan B and so will Uncle Sam unless you bring me back a verifiable yes, on the original terms, by midnight tomorrow." Terry stood up. "I didn't know you were such a fuckup McCabe. I thought you were the valley dictorian of Holy Infant."

"Terry," McCabe said, "I don't want to be involved." Sweat poured down his face like he had run panting all the way from Waikiki. "I want to put you directly in touch with this guy, he's not like a godfather or anything, he's just a lawyer..."

"A lawyer?" fumed Terry. "It's a no-paperwork deal, what do we need a lawyer for?"

"Just meet with him, and leave me out of it. I'm sure you can negotiate a compromise."

"Negotiate? Who do you think I am, Harry Kissinger? Compromise is when I refrain from kicking your ass, okay?"

Terry looked at his brother for support, but Larry was watching the wahines stroll by. "Stunod, attention here."

Larry told McCabe: "You gotta listen when my brother speaks the truth."

"Go back and consult your lawyer," said Terry. "And the next time I see you, the one-word answer of *done deal* should be on your lips."

The brothers abandoned McCabe at the koi pond and stomped down the stairs to a shaded parking deck. "Fuck it," said Terry as he slammed the door of the Crown Victoria. "Plan B."

Larry fidgeted beside him as Terry drove the sweltering car away from Ala Moana Shopping Center. Anger was getting ahold of Terry. His temper would be his demise, was how Sister Helen put it. She said she saw great things in Terry, especially in his studious nature, but he had to put aside his anger, offer it up to Jesus.

No fucking way.

Maybe he would go soft when he was an old man, perusing his memoirs. But right now he was battling life versus death for his career. He dropped Larry off at the rental car agency, which like so many places in Waikiki, was disguised as a grass shack. He waited in the Crown Vic, impatient, air conditioner roaring, down the block. In twenty minutes Larry pulled up behind him in a blue Camaro and honked.

Stunod, he mentally scolded his brother. I said white car, not flashy. And no honking.

Landmines! Terry had, maybe 40 times, driven the scout jeep in a convoy down Vietnam's Highway One. Scout jeep! That's the one that gets blown up, a sacrifice to save the cigarettes, booze and ammo in the trucks. Only the brave drove scout jeep.

He could remember it perfect. Himself at the wheel, Cameron beside him riding shotgun, Indiana Stubby standing up behind the M-60. The VC had all kinds of tricks, invisible wires strung across the road, landmines, lumber barricades, roadside ambushes ... but not once had the enemy stopped Terry from leading the convoy through.

Okay, one dunk in the Mekong, that was a mess. Weird how life turns out, but it was a couple of pajama-wearing VC, paddling a leaky sampan, who saved him from drowning.

No matter how you looked at it, life could be ironical in stature.

Terry, gas station map spread out on the passenger seat, drove to the campus of the University of Hawaii. Larry in the Camaro followed. You'd think something educational went on in these colleges, the way everybody yammered about them. But all Terry could see was a bunch of pinheads running in and out of concrete buildings. College, Terry figured, was a battle of old versus young. It was like the professors had captured the students and were holding them hostage. Pay the ransom, said the professors, or we'll never let you go. Yup, it was pretty much like a kidnapping, that's what college was.

A massive building was going up, in raw cinder blocks, at the edge of campus. It was surrounded by chain link fence, to foil construction thieves. When casinos came in to AC, Terry and Larry had worked the construction scam, but it was a payoff in peanuts. It got worse when the builders wised up and stopped using copper plumbing. So Terry and Larry left construction site rip-offs to the skids and graduated to the airport rent-a-car scam.

That was beautific in its simplitude. The facilities boss at the AC airport was a Holy Infant grad who'd accelerated into community college and protruded with a management degree. In return for remunerative consideration, he granted Terry the towing franchise for all the airport's rental car agencies. Whenever Terry needed money, he would send his one employee, Larry, into the dark parking lot to pull distributor wires on a couple of rental cars. Car won't start? Black Horse Auto Rescue was your only call, at $125 minimum service charge.

Plus parts and labor. And all's Larry needed to do was plug in the distributor wire.

Of course the brothers got greedy, because that is built into the inevitable nature of us humanitarians. Some Philadelphia accountant had figured the scam out, Terry got threatened with jail, and the contract was canceled. But it was a good three-year ride, and nobody could prove nothing except that a lot of cars had trouble starting at Atlantic City airport.

Must have been the salty air.

Behind this campus construction site was the faculty parking lot, with an automatic gate to keep the students out. *Students, stunods,* amazing how close those words were in pronunciation. Anyways, it was just before four o'clock, the perfect time. Terry waited, eyeballing Larry in the blue Camaro behind him, then watching the doorway of the big classroom building at the edge of the parking lot. They weren't waiting five minutes before Claire Wing walked out, and this timing suggested to

Terry that God and maybe Sister Helen were smiling upon Plan B.

Claire Wing was Uncle Sam's only daughter. Terry had eyeballed her a couple of times now. He'd been delighted to discover that college class schedules were the most dependable things in the world. You could set your Rolex by them.

Claire was about five feet tall, her shiny black hair cut so short it barely covered her ears. She wore a white blouse, pink shorts, and walked in flip flops. She carried a beat-up backpack lumpy with books, a quilted bunny sewn to the flap. Her father, city big-shot, had arranged for her to park in the professor lot.

She drove her green Honda Civic to the gate, inserted a card, and windshield glaring in the sun, turned toward the boulevard.

The brothers had practiced the two-car follow, but Terry cursed Larry for renting a bright blue car. He knew why the kid had done it. Larry loved to disobey Mom, the Nuns, and big brother. The kid, you told him jump and he'd duck, you said buy me a pack of cigarettes and he'd come back with gum. Larry was anti, what was that big professor word, dish establishment terry-ism.

Terry tailed Claire's Honda Civic onto the freeway and then down the off-ramp a mile later. Larry zoomed by to take the next phase. Uphill they headed on the Pali Highway, which rose steep up the green mountains, headed for the clouds.

Plan B was simple. Once they reached the other side of the mountains, down a very steep decline, there would be a turnoff to the Wing neighborhood. Terry car would force Miss Wing's car off the road, alongside a park, no witnesses. He would roll down the window, point his .45 at Claire Wing's eyes, and drive away. If Terry had to bang up the Crown Victoria to get Miss Wing to pull over, no matter. They would abandon that car, escape in Larry's Camaro, and a half hour later they'd be in Waikiki enjoying a steak dinner.

Unless they hit some kind of landmine.

Miss Wing in that Honda Civic was suddenly driving fast, crazy fast, Larry tailgating. Larry had spooked her. Shit!

Terry stomped on the gas to keep up. They couldn't force that Honda off the road here, there was no shoulder, only guardrail, and then a steep drop. Anybody spinning off the road would be dead 2000 feet down in smoldering wreckage.

Dead was not in Plan B.

Miss Wing dead would be a disaster in Plan B.

Volcano! They were driving up a volcano and Terry felt like he was going to blow. He imagined throwing his brother off these cliffs. He liked it so much here, maybe he should die here. Larry, this is your last fuckup, I swear to God.

Miss Wing's Honda veered off at a sign that said NUUANU PALI STATE WAYSIDE.

Larry's blue Camaro drove onto that steep side road too, but he pulled over and Miss Wing's Honda kept going. Terry parked the Crown Victoria behind the Camaro and lurched out of the car.

Larry rolled down tinted windows and said: "She almost got loose."

"She almost got loose," Terry repeated between his teeth.

"I had to speed up," Larry said.

"Wait here, stunod. If you're not here when I get back, I'll hunt you down and blow your prevaricating brains out."

Larry flipped him the finger and up rolled the tinted window.

Terry saw two parking lots: one clogged with tour buses, the other for cars only. About a hundred tourists, wearing their cameras and leis and straw hats, crowded around the buses in the lower lot. But the car parking lot was nearly empty. A few stray tourists were lined up behind a lava-stone wall, looking out over blue sky and windy sea. Among them stood Miss Wing, minus the backpack, her hair standing up in the stiff wind, talking into the outdoor payphone.

Terry hopped into the Crown Victoria and sped toward Miss Wing.

Just as the Crown Vic approached she hung up the phone and hustled for her car. She did not seem to recognize danger in a Crown Victoria. She was staring downhill at that Blue Camaro. She slipped into the Honda Civic and Terry saw her reaching around to lock the doors.

Terry figured she'd phoned the cops, or maybe her Dad. She probably thought she was safe here, with tourists around, and she could wait locked in the car for her rescuers to show up. But it was a long drive up the mountain road, from either Kailua or Honolulu, with no towns in these impossibly steep cliffs. Sheer, that was the word. Not even a mountain goat could live up here. No towns meant no cops. Help was fifteen, maybe twenty minutes away. Lady Fortune had finally whispered sweet nothings into Terry's ear. He had a vision, of himself in the scout jeep, leading his convoy safe through the gates of Can Tho Air Base, hero patriot, convoy master of another good run, enjoying beer and steak with the Delta Warriors.

Terry circled the parking lot in the Crown Victoria. Claire was sitting low behind the wheel of her Honda. Terry threw the big car into reverse and plowed into the driver's side of the Honda.

Crunch, screech.

It was like a slow motion hit, meant for destruction and fear only. The Crown Vic's theft alarm blaring in his ears, Terry put the car in low gear and lurched forward. Then he threw it in reverse and again slammed the Honda. The little car rocked, and its windshield cracked in a spider web pattern. There could be no mistaking this now for an accident.

With the Crown Vic still in reverse, Terry stomped the accelerator and the Crown Vic pushed the Honda into the lava wall. He smelled hot engine and burnt rubber. He felt a tremendous surge of elation, like he was drunk in a strip club and having a swell time. He heard shouting as a couple of dumb tourists began running toward his car.

He drove away calm, metal pieces falling ding ding off the Crown Victoria. He could see in the rearview the Honda was smashed all along its driver's side. When he reached the bus parking lot, he braked to a stop, stepped out, put the car in neutral and let it go. The Crown Vic bumped up against a rock, turned, then rolled down the sloping road gathering speed. Bump, it flipped over a guardrail and crashed down the steep cliffs.

He couldn't see the Crown Vic hit bottom but he heard it tumble and roll. By then Terry was in passenger seat of the Camaro, and Larry was screeching into a U-turn. Terry took a last look behind to see dumb tourists helping a stunned, wobbly Miss Wing out of her Honda.

Now here was the danger part and both brothers were nerve-wracked as Larry drove them downhill. Five minutes at most, Terry calculated, and the Honolulu cops would be looking for a blue Camaro coming down the Pali Highway.

"What name did you use up?" Terry asked as Larry sped along.

"No name," said Larry.

"What license did you give 'em at the rental car agency?"

"No license."

"No license, then how did you … asshole, you stole this car?"

"Not really. It was sitting on the lot with the keys in it."

"We're driving a stolen car?"

"I'll bet they haven't even noticed it's gone yet."

"Can't you do nothing honest even once in your life?" Terry said. "Rent, I said, rent. Management gave us all them IDs for a reason."

"Yeah, and you can sell them IDs if you don't use 'em."

Terry threw his head back and looked up as if he were imploring God. "My brother," he muttered. "World's dumbest criminal."

Larry was streaking downhill, passing cars like a maniac, and soon Terry saw, to his relief, a golf course below them. He could see the whole city and the layout like a big green map. At the golf course civilization began again, a suburb and curvy streets. He directed Larry and once off the highway they drove normal, zig here, zag

there, into a strip mall, hide the Camaro around back,
behind a trash dumpster.

Larry waited for the bus at a shady bench in front
of a jewelry store. Terry ate dinner at a counter in a
Filipino diner, ordering the daily special, cut up pork
chops mixed with peas and rice. It didn't taste too bad.
Kind of heavy on the variety spices, though. Five, six
minutes passed and not a cop car, not speeding up the
Pali Highway, not cruising for suspects at the strip mall.
When the bus arrived, Terry watched Larry board and
breathed easy. He finished his pork and peas and walked
out of the diner, called for a cab from a shady pay phone.

When the cab arrived, Terry first checked out the
driver to make sure it wasn't Prudence, and then hopped
in. It was a skinny pale white guy, scant blond hairs on his
head, like nineteen years old, a military dropout loser,
maybe. Terry loosened his tie. He couldn't get fast
enough back to the hotel room, thinking of a shower, a
room service martini in air conditioned comfort.

"Iolani Palace," Terry commanded the driver.

A couple of tourist stops would throw off any cop
tail, Terry figured. Meantime Larry would be on a bus
headed auspiciously for Dudoit Lane. Although you could
never predict Larry, he might accomplish something
stupid on the way home.

After ten minutes of air-conditioned, quiet ride, the
wordless cabbie accepted fare and tip and Terry got out at
Iolani Palace. He climbed the stone steps to where, lo and
behold, they had a museum-quality gift store. Did he care
enough to spend $8 on a Hall of Island History entry?
No. They were just about closing for the day anyways.
They obviously had kings and queens here once upon a
time, and it had done them no good. Like the kings of

England, the Hawaiian royalty had bowed to the Armed Might of the United States of America, one if by land, two if by sea.

What the fuck did Terry care about the history of loser kings?

However, he did care enough about Larry to drop a quarter into the gift shop pay phone.

"Stunod!" Terry said, surprised that his brother answered on first ring. Gulping breaths, maybe, but he answered.

"Now what?" Larry said.

"Turn on the TV and watch all night," Terry advised. "Call down to the Chinese joint for dinner, have it brought over. Lay low, keep quiet, no girls, no taverns, and remember, Mom always told us never talk to strangers unless you know who they are."

"Then what? This job is turning me into like a horny monk."

"Soon we go our separatist ways. And that will become a permanent feature of our life existence. With you along, the risk is nothing like the award. You and me, this is the last partner job."

"I don't know why you had to wreck a beautiful car," said Larry.

"Shut up when you're talking on the phone," Terry said. "Don't worry, it's all part of Plan B."

Honolulu Record
Tuesday, March 24, 1981
Page 3A

Surrounded by Water
By Bobbo Burns

The tourists are finally getting out of hand.

Either that, or Island politics took a nasty turn up at the Pali Lookout t'other day. Daughter of Sam is now under police guard. The Coconut Wireless is telegraphing paranoid rumors into the tiled hallways of Honolulu Hale. **Miss Wing** is frightened and has minor bruising, but is otherwise unharmed. Her father is deploring the assault, even as the Gods of Irony are providing a sympathy bump in the polls. His opponent **Bix Sanders** stopped just short of calling on his TV alter ego, Mick Danger, to solve the crime. **Governor Lee**, fond of blaming "mainland influences" for every malaise, may be correct for the first time since his descent to office. My sources are whispering about two thugs with Jersey accents. Who are my sources? The usual Waikiki deadbeats. They're the only ones on this island who can afford to tell the truth ...

Larry's Dream

17

Larry woke up and started dreaming.

He was lying in a big sloshy waterbed, alone. Above him hung a huge sheet of canvas, strung from bamboo poles. The bedroom glowed with bright sunny louvered windows.

Through those windows drifted the cheerful chirping of about a hundred birds.

Oh right, Larry reminded himself, I'm in paradise.

He rolled out of bed and stumbled to the windows. So this was life on the mountaintop. A tropical rain forest, with the Pacific Ocean just a blue stripe in the distance. He picked up binoculars and scanned the forest for birds. He heard the soft cooing of doves, but could not see them. On the lawn, mynah birds hopped and whistled, pecking for breakfast. On a tree branch, a beautiful green parrot landed, shuddered, and took off.

"Bird sanctuary," Larry muttered, looking through the binoculars. "What a fabulous scam."

It came to him then, the dream he'd had last night. The dream was a confusing jumble, but in the background was Mom's ghostly face. In the dream Mom was trying on clothes. She was being helped by a seamstress who was freaked out, a nervous wreck, flitting around the dressing room.

But Mom was calm. *You can't be alive, Larry, if there are no dead*, Mom's ghost said.

In the dream, Larry could hear her voice just as plain and strong as if she were in the room.

No death, no life, Mom said. *So I hope every day you thank the dead, Larry, including your father. I know you two didn't always get along. Be grateful to him, and to all the dead. We all can't be alive at once, you know.*

Wow! What kind of crazy dream was that? He couldn't make nothing of it right then, maybe some day he'd read up on dreams in the Library. The dream made him wonder about reincarnation, and whether he really had been a Sea Captain in another life. If so, did he like, have the same mother in that sea-faring life? Did Mom too have another life, in France, married to a man named Dudoit. Did she give birth to a baby named Jules who went to sea at an early age? How did this reincarnation thing work, anyway?

Either way, he felt sad that Mom's ghostly visit was so short. She'd had a hard life, a rotten husband, and selfish sons. Someday, Mom, he promised her, you'll have beautiful Hawaiian grandchildren. I'll bring them back to Jersey and show them the casino parking lot that used to be our home.

The mynahs pecking for breakfast on the lawn reminded Larry he was hungry, so after a trip to the bathroom, and a pause to admire its classy all-white tiles, potted bamboo plants, and piles of fluffy towels, he barefooted into the kitchen.

The table was set with two bowls, a pitcher of milk, and a box of Wheaties. There was some baseball player on the cover of the Wheaties box, but Larry had given up on the game, what with the players threatening a Communistic strike. Why did rich guys need a union anyway? His eyes fixed on Pua, out on in the flowery yard. She mounted the porch steps carrying a bowl of fruit.

"Good morning, handsome," she said.

He stepped aside.

"I see you slept pretty well," Pua said.

"Cool air up here," Larry said.

She set the bowl on the table. It contained two bananas and two papayas. Pua poured Wheaties, sliced bananas on top, then split the papayas. With a big spoon she flicked out their round black seeds.

"Don't you talk in the morning?" Pua asked. She popped open two cans of Grotton pineapple juice. "Maybe your tongue's stuck to the roof of your mouth?"

Larry didn't want to say it, because he was afraid to sound like a rube, or as they put it here, like a dumb haole. But holy mackerel, when these people wanted fruit for breakfast, they just picked it off a tree. In their backyard!

He pulled back a chair.

Dangling from the kitchen ceiling, held by fishing line, were bright-painted wooden birds, twisting in the breeze, like they were flying. The breeze itself smelled delicious, flowers and fruit and grass and rain.

He picked up a gleaming silver spoon and examined it in the sunlight. He could tell real silverware. Every guy who made his living doing entries could tell silver, even in the dark, just by the feel.

"So it's like a world-class scam," Larry said. "This bird sanctuary."

"It's not a scam, it's enlightened," said Pua.

"The Grottons own this big chunk of mountainside," said Larry, "which they got from the King for like a dollar. And they donate all but one acre to the Bird Lovers Society. Then they build their house on that one acre in the middle of the forest. No taxes, no neighbors, no trespassing." He slapped his head. "It's the genius scam of a lifetime."

"Shh," Pua said. "Chris is coming over."

"For breakfast?" asked Larry.

"She doesn't eat breakfast," said Pua. "Half the world wakes up hungry, she says, so why shouldn't she experience that too."

"She's crazy, right?"

"She's a wonderful person," said Pua. "She can't help it if she was born to a dirty fortune."

Pua pushed a big bowl of limes across the table.

"You grow limes here too?"

"Of course."

Larry had never tried papaya before and no wonder, his first spoonful tasted like old socks.

"Bleh," Larry said.

"Silly," Pua said. "Don't you know anything?"

She squeezed a lime over the papaya.

"Try it now."

All of a sudden, it was delicious. Like magic. Okay, it didn't really beat a Taylor Ham breakfast at the Shore Thing Diner, but he could get used to this cereal and backyard fruit routine.

The absolute beauty of this morning. He couldn't stop looking. An entire city at their feet, they were higher than the planes circling the airport. He stared at the freighters waiting at anchor out there, beyond the Aloha Tower. Every building in the city was a speck.

Up on the wooden deck strode a peacock. The bird shook his feathers and let out his jungle cry. Larry walked to the window to watch him, those feathers glowing like jewels in the sun.

"They crow in the morning just like roosters," Pua said. "Isn't it a beautiful sound?"

"I thought it was a monkey call when I first heard it."

"Silly, we don't have monkeys in Hawaii."

"Well, you used to in ancient times right?"

"No."

"Why not? It's hot enough for monkeys, you got jungle, you got bananas, where's the monkeys?"

He stood back and admired his surroundings. Nine in the morning and warm enough to go for a swim. Pretty little wooden birds flying over the kitchen table, real birds peeping in the forest, peacock shaking his feathers on the desk. Tropical fruits growing in the backyard.

How could he get a piece of this scam?

The sight of the distant airport brought to Larry's mind the rent-a-car business, but some local guy probably had that locked up. Nobody was hiring ex-cons, especially ones who didn't even have a Hawaii driver's license. So entrepreneur and job hunting, they were out.

Pua, reading the Honolulu Record, shouted: "Oh my God! Claire Wing."

"Who?"

"I know her," Pua tapped the newspaper. "We know her dad, too."

"You know everybody," Larry said.

"She was almost killed," Pua said. "At the Pali Lookout. Two maniacs followed her and rammed her car. Look."

On the bottom of Page One was a photo of Claire's dented Honda, and another picture of uniformed cops climbing down a rocky hillside to inspect a wrecked Crown Victoria.

"Maniacs?" muttered Larry. "What'd they do?" He grabbed the newspaper. "Thank god she wasn't hurt badly. She's your friend?"

"Not friend, I just know her. Actually, she's kind of stuck up. Her dad and my dad had a couple of, you know, deals together. Real estate."

Footsteps sounded on the wooden stairs and Christina appeared at the screen door. She wore khaki shorts out of which extended long pale legs. She wore leather sandals, pink blouse, short hair, and everything was set off a little wacky by those bulging blue eyes.

"Did you see this about Claire Wing?" Pua asked.

"Heard it on the radio," said Chris. She didn't seem shook up about it. She looked happy. "My dad would approve."

"What?" Larry said.

"Of your breakfast. He was a vegetarian. He hated when people cooked meat in the guesthouse."

"Why would anyone smash Claire's car?" Pua asked.

Christina shrugged. "Evil world."

Larry said: "Maybe it was an accident."

Pua read from the news story: "Witnesses said the driver of the Ford appeared to purposely target the Wing vehicle, and tried to accelerate even after the collision."

Larry jumped up. "We're going to the hot tub, right?"

"That was the plan," said Chris. "Unless you've got a Plan B?"

"A what?" said Larry.

"An alternative. Maybe you two want to take a walk through the forest. I've got a map back at the big house."

"Hot tub," said Larry. He looked into Pua's deep beautiful eyes, and her eyes, too, said hot tub.

The guesthouse, you would think, for all the Grotton family's money, would be plated in gold. Although luxurious inside, it was clad in dark cedar shake, a little moldy from all the night rains. It had rained all night, loud on the tin roof. The noisy deluge had woken him up in the middle of his dream about Mom and Death.

That's why he was late arising. But it rained every night in the mountains, he was learning, and the clouds sooner or later were driven off by the tropical sun.

Larry tripped into the bathroom, grabbed a big white towel. He didn't really have a bathing suit, so he slipped into blue-jean cutoffs. Bare chested, a little embarrassed about his Friendly Devil tattoo, he draped the towel around it.

By the time he reached the deck, Pua was soaking in the hot tub.

"No suits in the tub," Christina declared. She sat in a deck chair, hiding her face behind The Honolulu Record.

Larry turned his back, embarrassed, and dropped his shorts. He wasn't one of those porn stars, with the big honker. He backed down the ladder and eased into the warm water. Pua stood on the far end of the tub, like a mirage in steaming water. The tub was as big as a small swimming pool, the water chest deep and body temperature. Larry was, like, hypnotized by the sensation of the warm water, the chirping birds, the sweet breeze, the mountaintop view.

Christina kept reading the newspaper, but Larry figured she was only fake interested in the news. Chaperone, that's what she was.

"Christina!" Pua called. "Read my horoscope."

"What are you again?"

"Horse."

Pua whispered in Larry's ear: "She doesn't believe in the Zodiac."

Christina read: "Horses crave love and intimacy, which is a double edge sword, since it often leads to them feeling trapped. Your wind today, mauka."

"What's this wind stuff?" Larry asked.

"The four winds of Oahu," Pua said. "Makai, the sea, new adventure. Mauka, warmth from the mountain gods. Diamond Head, your lucky day. Ewa, caution, maybe you'd better stay home."

"What's my wind?" asked Larry. "I'm a Rooster."

Christina read: "It may seem that you're moving at a snail's pace, but actually you've made very good progress at work. Direction of your wind: Diamond Head."

"Lucky boy," said Pua and kissed him. "Come on, get on my back. Rooster rides the Horse."

She was a strong woman. She gave him a ride through the water, and then they switched, she clung to his back for a ride across the tub.

She hopped off, swung around and kissed him.

"E como mai," she said. "That means welcome, come in."

He kissed her, let his hand drift down and touched her between the legs. He expected her to flinch but she kissed him like she was trying to devour him. He looked over her bare wet shoulder, and Christina had risen from her chair.

"Should I leave you two alone?"

Pua nodded.

Somehow, here in this steaming tub, Pua had overcome her fears and let Larry in. Guided him in. Her lips clinging to his. Her eyes closed. Her hair floating a dark halo in the water. Hip against hip, her breasts pressed into the Friendly Devil on his chest, lips locked. Larry closed his eyes and became Captain Jules Dudoit, locked into a love embrace with his beautiful Hawaiian princess. He'd waited a hundred years to love her again.

Maybe it was the warm water or the sweet breeze or the songs of the birds, but Pua relaxed and opened up to him, and they made love, gentle, easy in the water. Clinging clinging clinging, Larry closed his eyes so overwhelmed by the good feelings that he had to bite his lips in order not to cry. Stunod, he scolded himself, you don't cry when facking your girl.

He was so excited he didn't last very long but it didn't seem to matter. He shuddered with a thrill but for a while Pua wouldn't let him go. She pushed him against the wooden wall of the hot tub and just about smothered him. Only manly pride kept him from crying out in pain.

She put her head over his shoulder and breathed into his ear.

"Do you really like me? Just as I am?"

He nodded.

"That's all I want," she said.

He realized now he'd been set up. A night with Pua at the guest house, a morning in the hot tub, under supervision until Pua felt safe. Pua did not quite trust him yet, which was okay, she'd been hurt as a little girl and trust would be quite a while coming. Hurt as a little kid? That Larry understood. What if your old man came home from the Knights in a foul mood and whipped you with a belt? Not once, not twice, but whenever he felt like it?

He cradled Pua like she was a baby. Big gal though she was, it was easy to hold her afloat in the hot tub. It made Larry feel he-man strong.

Larry heard the door slam in the big house and saw Christina pause on the porch steps. Larry felt sorry for her, a tall blonde lonely rich girl walking through her own private rain forest, but no man for her, no husband, no children, no lover, no friend.

"She wants us to be together, doesn't she?" said Larry.

"No," said Pua. "I asked her to set this up. I begged her to put us up in the guest house. I'm the one. I wanted us to be together."

Christina, binoculars around her neck, bird book sticking out of her back pocket, walked toward the forest.

"Man," said Larry, "how lucky can you get? Born to a pineapple fortune."

"Larry, you wouldn't want to be Christina, believe me. She was a mess until Koshu helped her accept her kaza."

"It's horrible to be rich?"

"She once confessed to me that she didn't own a fortune, the fortune owned her. Pua, she said, you are free to be anything you want, but I can only be the administrator of an ill-gotten fortune. She's destined to be lonely because men are more interested in her money than in her."

"She should give her money away then."

"She's trying, but there's a Board of Directors, and investors and lawyers, and bankers…"

Larry climbed the ladder out of the hot tub and turned to put a hand out for Pua. They dried each other off with big white towels, playing like nature's children on a wooden deck in the intense sunshine. Larry sat in the cushioned lounger and covered his man parts out of, like, modesty.

Pua lay in the lounger beside him, naked, and they held hands. Then she dropped his hand and shifted to her side, shaded her eyes.

"That's not a sailor's tattoo," she said.

Larry crossed his arms to help cover up the Friendly Devil. The Devil was red, shaped like a teardrop, and smiling. Although The Devil carried a blue pitchfork, it was just for self defense, he wasn't going to stab you with it.

"Christina said you'd been in the Navy. Did you tell her that?"

"I can't ah remember," said Larry.

"Were you in the Navy or weren't you?"

"Briefly," Larry said.

"Larry Stone," she said. "I believe you're telling tales again. I know why people lie, Larry. It's because the truth is too lonely. So tell me the truth now. You can lie all you want to other people, but not to me. Where did you get that tattoo?"

"Boardwalk," he said. "Atlantic City."

"How old were you when you got it?"

"Eighteenth birthday."

"Did it hurt?"

"I don't know, I was drunk."

"Were you ever in the Navy?"

"No."

Pua pursed her lips.

Larry said: "My brother was in the Army, though."

"I told you some lies, too," Pua said. "So it's okay. I understand."

She looked seriously at Larry. She took his hand and kissed it. "No more lies between us."

Larry kissed her hand.

"Now," Pua said. "Tell me why you came to Hawaii?"

"Because my brother's got a business deal here, but I can't say anything about it. It's secret."

"And that's the truth?"

"I swear to God," Larry said.

Pua lay back and sighed.

"I feel better now. Christina had her suspicions."

Although Christina was off in the forest, Pua whispered when she said: "Christina thought you were running from the law."

Man o' War

18

Bobbo played bishop takes the knight, muttered "check" and lit a Big Tent cigarette in rum-shaky hands. They were playing in the shade of a giant banyan tree and as McCabe pondered his counter-move, a rumbling GTO drove in, raising a dust cloud.

"Friend of yours?" inquired Bobbo.

"Cop," said McCabe. "Don't worry, he's not a narc."

As David Shimada stepped out of his hot-rod, Bobbo shouted: "If you don't have a warrant, get back in the car."

Shimada held up both hands. "Off duty," he said.

Bobbo upended the board and scattered the chess pieces on the picnic table. They looked like medieval soldiers who'd died defending a towering bottle of rum.

"I'm calling my attorney," Bobbo said. He mounted the porch and picked up the Mickey Mouse phone. "And my attorney is Porky Hashimoto."

Bobbo's rooster eyeballed Shimada sideways, kicked dust at him, retreated in a huff of feathers.

"Come on Bobbo," McCabe pleaded. "David and I were Army buddies."

Shimada was dressed in a blue-and-white aloha shirt that depicted whaling ships. Khaki shorts ended in shreds at his knees and he shuffled toward the banyan tree in cheap rubber sandals.

McCabe walked into the sunshine and said: "What's up?"

"I'm not welcome here," Shimada said. "Let's ride."

As Bobbo flipped them the finger, Shimada executed a U-turn in the driveway. Air conditioning on blast, he drove McCabe toward the highway. The police radio at McCabe's knee squawked and hissed. Shimada donned chrome sunglasses and said: "How you getting into work?"

"Rei drops me off at the newsroom at three, pulls her shift, picks me up at midnight. That's how we met, you know. Rei and I. We were both hanging around the apartments all day."

"So the Jersey brothers know where they can find either of you."

"Sure, at the newspaper or the hospital. But out here I can sleep at night. I can't sleep in that apartment knowing they can knock at any moment."

"Bobbo's hosting you two indefinitely?"

"Who knows when he'll kick us out in a drunken rage. He's threatening to file for mayor. He sees politics as a way of keeping the narco squad out of his marijuana patch. He doesn't realize his candidacy would complicate things. It's all about what's in it for Bobbo. He's selfish, that's what it is."

"Selfish is like gravity. Law of the universe."

David made a hard, squealing turn onto the main highway. The tachometer flickered like it was measuring McCabe's blood pressure.

"Friend I want you to meet," Shimada said.

"Am I under arrest?"

"Don't joke."

"What if I don't care to meet your friend?"

"Then you're under arrest."

McCabe choked down a wave of nausea and blacked out.

He awoke sweating and coughing. Shimada opened the GTO's door and stepped aside.

"Who lives here?" McCabe asked.

Whoever it was, they hadn't cashed a paycheck in years. The GTO was in the driveway of a pumpkin-colored tract home. It was one of those cheap houses that begins to tilt toward demolition the moment the construction workers leave. A glance around told McCabe they were in Waimanalo, that narrow settlement squeezed between sheer green cliffs and the deep blue Pacific.

"You want to give me a clue?" McCabe said.

"Chief wants to meet you."

"Chief Abreu?" McCabe said. The pumpkin-colored house was only one step up from a mobile home, with a moldy roof, salty windows, the biggest one cracked. Its weedy yard was littered with rusty car parts, dinged-up surfboards and windblown plastic bags. A white cat hissed from beneath a rusty hunk of corrugated tin.

"He lives in this dump?" McCabe whispered.

"Friend of a friend of a cousin," Shimada said. He put a hand on McCabe's shoulder as he escorted him in.

Despite the ferocious sunshine, the living room was dark. Its centerpiece was a velvet painting of a white-robed Jesus. Children's crayon drawings were taped to concrete block walls. The seat of a junked auto stood for a couch. A fishing pole and seaweed-encrusted net slumped in one corner.

"Around back," David said.

They walked through a ruined kitchen to a yard of blasted grass. There, under a rusty tin roof, sipping a white cup of coffee, sat Chief Abraham Abreu.

Had the Hawaii Visitors Bureau chosen a poster grandpa, Chief Abreu might be it. His surname was Portuguese but he looked unmistakably Hawaiian. He was six-foot-plus, ruggedly handsome, with easy going features and salt-and-pepper hair. He wore a flowery red aloha shirt. He seemed to be staring into his coffee, almost meditating on it, as McCabe sat at the table across from him.

Shimada brought over coffee in a pot, and a greasy pink box of sugar-dusted malasadas.

"So you and David are friends," said the Chief. "All the way back to Tropic Lightning."

McCabe nodded.

"Monday, December 8th, 1941," the Chief said. "My personal day of infamy." He flashed McCabe an easy smile. "I didn't wait to be drafted. The friends I made in Tropic Lightning became friends for life."

David poured coffee for McCabe.

The Chief put a hand over his cup.

McCabe stifled the urge to eat a malasada. He also stifled a laugh because malasadas were essentially elongated donuts and the man across the table was the essence of Hawaii cop.

"And now you work for The Record?" the Chief asked.

McCabe nodded.

"Mrs. Keeper," the Chief said. "Good friend of mine. The Record is in steady hands, agree?"

McCabe did not agree but he nodded.

"So your friends from New Jersey ..."

"They're not my friends."

"Schoolmates then? They asked you to transmit an offer to Sam Wing. Who did they say was behind this offer?"

McCabe glared at Shimada, those eyes hidden behind sunglasses. So Shimada had narked him to the Chief. Thanks a lot, David, you selfish bastard.

McCabe answered the Chief: "They didn't say."

The Chief reached into a briefcase at his feet, brought out two mug shots and set them on the table.

"Lawrence Estonophie. Terrance Estonophie. Correct?"

McCabe nodded.

"One's a felon, multiple counts of burglary," the Chief said, "the other, arrests for assault but no convictions."

"I don't know their police record," McCabe said.

"Then there's the episode of Miss Wing, terroristic threatening and assault by vehicle. Did you know anything about that before it occurred?"

"I only knew they had a so-called Plan B, which they would put into action if Sam didn't respond."

"Plan B?"

"And there's a Plan C, but they never said what that is, either."

"And did you deliver their message to Candidate Wing?"

"I did. Through an intermediary I can't name."

"You don't have to," said the Chief. He drew a cigar out of his shirt pocket, admired it, as if it were a fine, fine thing, a work of art, a blessing to all humanity. Chief Abreu's laid-back demeanor seemed natural enough, but McCabe figured that any man who ascended to the top of a 1,000-member police force had a ruthless core. That cigar hinted at an ego that was self-satisfied, maybe even arrogant.

McCabe glanced at Shimada and realized that David had held nothing back from the Chief. Since it was David who'd suggested McCabe see Porky Hashimoto, the Chief knew about that too. McCabe felt the hot sting of betrayal. Now David was looking off toward the Pali cliffs, as if he wasn't part of this conversation.

"Do you feel," said the Chief, and lit the cigar, "that the Estonophie brothers are a physical threat to your person?"

"Yes I do."

The Chief blew smoke.

"Would you be surprised if it turned out that these brothers are emissaries of Nevada mobsters?"

"No."

The Chief rose. He put out one hand to lean on a concrete-block column. He stared toward the ocean.

"Mister McCabe," he said, "we're on Hawaiian Homes Land. You're familiar with that designation? It's a trust that, by some miracle, has preserved slivers of these islands for the native people. Tiny slivers. These slivers were the left-overs, after the sugar and pineapple planters carved up these islands."

He walked around the table puffing the cigar.

"When we local fellows came home from the war, we started a political revolution. For the first time since the monarchy, it was local boys took charge. We used the power of the unions and machine politics to wrest control of the state and county governments. Thirty years now we've been captains of our own destiny."

He pointed the burning cigar at McCabe.

"Once again, foreigners threaten to take over. Nevada haoles. If they put casinos in Waikiki, the money pouring into those slot machines will make these Nevada haoles kings of our island."

He waved the cigar.

"Mister McCabe, your friend David's grandfather lived in a barracks and cut sugar cane under threat of the whip. The whip! Like he was a mule."

The smoke from his cigar drifted in the Trade Winds.

"Nobody is going to bring the whip back to these islands," the chief said. "They may be tough in Las Vegas, but we have our own tough guys here."

He shot Shimada a look that made him stand up.

"David," the Chief said, "do we currently have a Public Relations Officer at the HPD?"

Shimada shook his head.

"But we had Joe Cockett until last January, correct? So that means there's authorization on the books?"

"Right," said Shimada.

"Mister McCabe, I understand your duties at the Record include rewriting horoscopes to fit the local tastes, and deciding which letters to trim from the Ann Landers column."

"Well, there's a little more to it…"

The Chief touched McCabe's shoulder.

"Go with David," he said.

Shimada was already standing at the smudged sliding glass door that led to the kitchen. As McCabe followed him through the house, Shimada said: "I can't help you, blala, unless you help yourself."

They let themselves into the Goat, which had more or less become a solar oven.

"What does that mean?" McCabe asked.

"The nail that sticks up gets hammered down."

"Quit speaking in riddles."

David started the car. "First we get out of here," he said. "Druggie neighborhood. Gives me the creeps."

David drove to Waimanalo Beach and parked in the shade. Without saying a word, he led McCabe past a row of stubby, wind-blown Norfolk pines, then down a narrow sloping beach where waves washed in exhausted after a five-thousand mile journey. The ocean was every shade of blue-green imaginable. The Trade Winds whistled in McCabe's ears, and brought the taste of salt to his tongue.

Shimada stooped, picked up a stick, dug at something in the sand and held it up to the sunlight. It was like a long string of jelly attached to a tiny purple bag.

"Portuguese Man o' War," he said. "You ever get stung by one of these?"

McCabe shook his head.

Using the stick like a poker, Shimada buried the jelly creature in sand.

"I was. Once. I never told you? It feels like you've grabbed a live electric wire. I ended up in the ER, could hardly breathe, my throat closed down to the width of a straw. You wonder why you never see me in the ocean? That's why. Not the way I want to die, blala, gasping for breath."

He kicked sand over the creature's burial mound. "Those windblown little monsters kill more people than sharks." He lifted his sunglasses and focused on McCabe.

"If Sam drops out," David said, "that would be okay with the Chief."

The blue-green waves rolled in, rolled in, relentless. Any one of them might deposit the Jellyfish of Death at McCabe's feet.

Feeling faint, McCabe plopped down in damp sand. "Sam. Drop out?" was all he could say.

"Leaving Bix Sanders versus the Chief as a strong write-in."

"Write-in?"

"Even if the Chief loses, it's only a special election. Twenty-two months later, regular election, he's on the ballot as the main challenge."

"The Chief wants to be mayor?'

"Like a dog wants to bark."

"David, why did you rat me out to the goddamn Chief?"

"After your boys tried to knock Claire Wing off the Pali, I figured you were in serious trouble. So I lobbied for your carry permit."

He took a folded piece of paper out of his shirt pocket and handed it to McCabe, who stared at it without comprehension.

"I had to square up with the Chief," David said, "you know how stingy he is with the permits."

"I'm doomed," McCabe said. "So HPD is on the side of the Estonophie brothers?"

Shimada sat down beside him. "If Sam takes the bait, the Chief has the option to move in, you see? *Samuel Wing, you're under arrest for felony bribery.* Boom, political battlefield is clear. With Sam under indictment, it's noble local boy Chief Abreu vs. Bix, the drunken Hollywood haole."

"And my role would be …"

"Put Porky in direct touch with the brothers, and then step out of the way. That simple."

"So you say."

"We'll be watching."

"Oh, yeah, the ever vigilant HPD."

"When Porky and the Jersey brothers meet, we have a safe house for you."

"How about Reiko?"

"Her too."

"We can't just quit our jobs."

"We can arrange police escorts. But soon the Jersey brothers will be busy fending off bunkmates in Halawa."

He slapped McCabe on the back.

"You were already in this mess, Lazarus. This is what we can do. This works for everybody."

"Especially your boss."

"Let me tell you something I'm not supposed to tell you. After your Jersey boys meet Porky, their Nevada masters will be singing a new tune, in Hawaiian slack key. That's all I can say."

"That's not enough."

"McCabe, it's my job to know what's happening in this town. There are 17 resort hotels on Oahu owned by Japanese interests. The Japanese have bought up every public golf course except the Ala Wai. The hostess bars with Korean girls? The Yakuza doesn't even try to hide the ownership. In Japan, gangsters and corporations are hand in glove. You know that in Japan, golfers wait months for a tee time? Our tattooed friends are using Honolulu as a playground. Bring over the execs, put 'em up in beachfront hotels, golf all day, girls all night. There's nothing we can do but watch, since their every move is legal, and protected by a well-known law firm. None of this could you glean from the happy pages of the Honolulu Record, but the Yamaguchi-Gumi, the Yakuza clan that runs Osaka, has got a dog in the Honolulu mayor's race."

"A dog named Wing?"

"Did I say that?"

McCabe took a moment to do the calculation. If Sam Wing was backed by the Yakuza, and he quit the race, was the Chief hoping to take his place as favorite son of the Japanese mob? Trying to figure it all out made him dizzy.

"David, how about the Chief uses his magical powers to get Reiko a leave of absence? We stash her for the duration."

"I'll ask," David said. "Lazarus, I know you want to stay in the Islands. I understand. You did nothing but move house as a kid. But Hawaii's a tough place to make a living. A lot of waiters and bellboys. The Chief is offering you, once the smoke clears, a civil service position with the HPD. Nobody can squawk, you're well qualified. All you would do is take reporters' phone calls. Good pay, easy work, lifetime job, full medical, strong pension."

"You can't just arrest the brothers?"

"For what?"

"Claire Wing!"

"The Crown Vic traces back to a fake driver's license. The Camaro was stolen from a car rental lot. The witnesses were tourists, half of them already back on the Mainland. Claire never got a good look at either driver and all she remembers is the crash."

"You're right, it's no use anyway. The Chief wants what he wants."

"This is the safest way to get the Estonphies off your neck."

"David, if the Chief wins mayor, you get a big promotion and maybe some of your financial problems are solved."

"Only eased," said David. "I've got a decade of child support, and then college tuition."

He tapped McCabe on the shoulder. "We could be surfing the same wave, blala. Be selfish. Be one of us, not one of them. Don't be the nail that sticks up. Like the Chief said, we're in a struggle for the soul of this island, and we cannot lose to Nevada mobsters."

"So we win with Japan's mobsters?"

"It's the least bad scenario. Gentlemen's agreement, they promise to commit no serious crimes here. It's in their best interest to stay clean here. In the islands, they're big spenders, and that's all."

"Porky Hashimoto claims to be speaking for Sam. They want a million bucks on the table."

Shimada shrugged. "In Vegas? That's chicken feed, bla."

"I'm pretty sure the brothers don't have the power to raise the ante. Would the Yakuza consider a partnership with Vegas? Is that what's going on?"

David shrugged. "Put Porky and the Jersey guys together, see what happens."

"David, what if their Plan C calls for an assassination? If the brothers go away mad, maybe the mob sharpshooters come in."

David shook his head. "Not going to get that far," he said. "Believe me. The brothers and their Vegas masters are about to run out of luck."

Avoid pilikia

19

The finger of time, as told by the newsroom clocks, moved relentless around the globe, stranding McCabe in a world of procrastination. The New York, Chicago, Denver and San Francisco hour hands had applied early pressure. Now even the Honolulu clock was ticking toward deadline. Had he done anything tonight but read the news wire, nap, eat malasadas, drink coffee and worry?

The Tropic Lightning Division had been dominated by returned Vietnam vets, men whose hard-eyed stare and no-bullshit attitude intimidated McCabe. He wasn't one of them, and they knew it. No other soldier in the Division had such weak weapons skills. A week of target practice during Basic, and a half hour on the range at Fort Shafter, summed up McCabe's rifle experience. So even with a gun permit, McCabe was no gunslinger. Twice this evening nightmares had awoken him from desk naps. Each time he'd been dream-stalked by that psycho Nam vet, Terry Estonophie. Each time, McCabe reached into his waistband for a gun that wasn't there.

In the morning, McCabe promised himself, he would shop for a pistol.

Or maybe he'd put it off.

Eleven-twenty, time to shape up the horoscopes. Over at the horse-shoe shaped copy desk, editors were reading the City Final proofs. McCabe ambled over and nabbed the back pages.

The comics were in order. The crossword and Jumble showed the correct dates. Ann Landers had been rearranged, and now began with a letter from a pregnant teenager. This would placate Editor Norma Keeper, who believed a newspaper should function as moral scold. Promiscuity, Mrs. Keeper claimed, was undermining island society. Her daughter had three babies by three different men, which may have explained her anxieties.

McCabe checked the obits against the lists sent from the funeral homes.
Today's dead were accounted for. Some perverse impulse made him pull Sam Wing's pre-obit out of the files. It was two sheets of typewriter paper, headlined:

SAMUEL KONG WING, DEC. 11 1925 –

City Councilman Sam Wing, known for his flamboyant dress and aggressive street campaigns, died _____ He was _____

It needed updating, to acknowledge Sam's promotion to Council Chairman. McCabe left Sam's obit atop the file cabinet, intending to work on it after deadline. He turned his attention to the horoscopes.

YEAR OF THE SNAKE
It's important never to betray a Snake's trust, for the Snake is vengeful and will get even some day!

That line he'd copied out of an astrology book, correcting *too* to *to* and *someday* to *some day*. He left in the exclamation point because Mrs. Keeper loved! exclamation! points!

Uncle Sam Wing was partly responsible for the switch to the Chinese Zodiac. Sam obsessively read his own horoscope and those of his political opponents. He'd informed Mrs. Keeper that it was culturally insensitive to run "haole horoscopes" when most Island people followed the Chinese Zodiac. Sam was on the Mai-Tai Circuit, the movers and shakers who met at sundown Thursdays at the Mynah Bird. That club also included Mrs. Keeper and Chief Abreu.

Before Sam's intervention, McCabe's horoscope job had been easier. He'd just rip the "haole horoscope" off the wire, walk it back to the typesetters, and be done. He knew as much about Chinese Astrology as he did about nuclear physics. But now his job was to make the horoscopes appear local, inserting island color and Hawaiian or pidgin words.

If you encounter a Snake on Da Bus today, or at the beach or your workplace, walk a wide circle around da kine. He may be in the mood to

strike. Be akamai! Avoid pilikia! Direction of
your wind: Ewa.

Be smart! Avoid trouble! Who could argue with
that? The warning matched McCabe's mood, the spellings
were correct, there were two exclamation points, and the
item fit in its typographical slot. McCabe signed the
proofs and walked them to the copy desk. He picked up a
bulldog edition of The Record, warm from its journey
through the press, and plodded down the back stairway.

It seemed sinister in that dark stairway, this close
to midnight. McCabe held the handrail, the steps slick
with ink from the printers' shoes. He burst out the steel
doors into a half-dark parking lot, one bank of lights
flickering dim. Across the lot, the Columbia Inn, on a
normal night, would tempt him with the camaraderie of
his fellow editors, political gossip, and a warm bowl of
saimin.

But tonight he hustled to a red-and-white Mahalo
Cab and hopped in.

"Queen's Medical Center, please."

Bartenders and cabbies were often pleased to get
the Record's bulldog edition before it hit the streets. So
McCabe dropped the newspaper into the passenger seat.
"Hot off the press," he boasted.

The cabbie turned around. She was a scowling,
hefty woman with long dark hair.

"Five blocks?" she said. "Too lazy to walk?"

When McCabe recovered his wits, he said: "I've
got to be there now, please."

"I've been waiting half the night for this fare, and
you want to go five measly blocks?"

"I'll pay you for ten blocks," McCabe said.

She grunted and jammed the cab into gear.
McCabe glanced at her license. Prudence Yamanaki. He
vowed to report her to the Taxi Commission.

If he survived the night.

As she drove, McCabe worried. They passed
Honolulu Hale, the Spanish-style city hall, and he
imagined Mayor Bix, Mayor Sam, Mayor Abe, even a
drunken Mayor Bobbo on its broad tile steps. Along dark
Punchbowl Street the shadows seemed evil, and the
looming Big Wahine, in McCabe's imagination, morphed
from a suburban mountainside to a volcano glowing with
dangerous lava.

The cabbie cursed at a hot-rod that roared past a
red traffic light. The smell of her cigarettes, greasy lunch
and body odor mixed with the sweet aroma of night
blooming cereus. McCabe shuddered, this awful ride
taking five blocks of eternity. Panic hit him like a
lightning bolt, and he leaned forward to tell the cabbie:
Take me to the airport.

But Rei!

"What are you?" Prudence Yamanaki demanded.
"A reporter or something?"

"I used to be," McCabe said. "Now I write the
horoscopes."

"Somebody actually writes those stupid things?"

"Well, they're just for fun, you know."

"I'm a Dragon," she said, and blew a stream of
cigarette smoke into the windshield. "You think it's *fun*
being a Dragon?"

As the cab approached the hospital, Prudence said:
"I know you'll tip big, but don't think you're buying my
soul. Dragons can't be bought."

She wheeled into the circle reserved for ambulances. Rei, in light blue scrubs, stood beneath the glowing word: EMERGENCY.

The sight of her plunged McCabe into a pool of relief. He'd been fighting off a nightmare: Rei bound and gagged in the trunk of Terry's car.

He handed the cabbie $10 with shaking hands. As he took Rei's arm he scanned the parking lot, hoping to see David's GTO. But the only police presence he saw was the ancient guard in his bright lit booth, reading a comic book.

He hustled Rei toward her yellow Beetle.

Terry stepped from behind a banyan tree. Backlit by the hospital's white glow, he seemed an enormous shadow. "McCabe," he said. "And the delightful Mrs. McCabe of the future."

Now McCabe wished he'd manned up and bought a gun.

"Leave her out of this, Terry."

"Such is my honorable intent," said Terry. "Let's all walk in to where the lights are bright and we can see transparently."

They walked to the emergency room and at a bank of payphones, Terry said: "Do you know anybody can ignore a midnight phone call?"

An ambulance crew unloaded a bloody, moaning crash victim.

Terry said: "In accordance with my speculating nature, I am now prospecting that a million dollar fee is a mute point. Do you get my drift? I demand a meeting of urgent proportions with your intermediary. Not proportions, what am I trying to say? Parameters. Urgent parameters. No fee necessary, as we have pre-demonstrated our serious intent."

"By terrorizing a college girl?" McCabe said.

"Call," demanded Terry.

"Have you got a quarter?" asked McCabe.

"McCabe, I'm surprised, an Army guy like you. You never carry change in a combat situation."

Rei found a quarter in her purse. From his wallet McCabe retrieved a card that said ROYCE HASHIMOTO ASSOCIATES and dialed not the printed number on front, but the one scrawled on back.

"Porky?" he said, surprised at the quick answer.

"Have I been waiting for your call, McCabe?" said Porky's voice. "Indeed I have. What took you so long?"

"Look, I've got the big man here and he'd like a meeting as soon as possible, but he doesn't have the … he doesn't have the money."

"Is now too soon?" Porky said.

"Now?"

"Punchbowl Cemetery, ASAP," Porky said, and hung up.

Dazed, McCabe draped his arm around Rei's shoulder and said, "Let's ride, honey, you're going home."

McCabe walked Rei through the shadowy parking lot, Terry following. Larry was leaning on Rei's Beetle, smoking a cigarette. He stepped aside as if he were a chauffeur, and bowed.

McCabe let Rei get behind the wheel and then kissed her.

"I'll be home in two hours."

She shook her head. "We're coming with you."

"Rei, don't be stupid."

"We'll follow you if we have to. We're not going to let them push you off a cliff."

"Who's we?" asked Terry.

"She's talking about herself, just her alone."

"We?"

"It's a small town island thing, Terry, I can't explain it."

"She too can accompany a ride of enlightenment," said Terry. "I don't see the harm in it, do you Lawrence?"

"Fack no," Larry said.

"Two heads are better than one," said Terry, "especially if you've got a guillotine."

He clapped McCabe on the back. "I see you two as having dueling fates. But this is not a hurtful premise, am I making myself clear? Miss Nakayama, you are made of a courageous nature."

"Nakamoto," said Rei.

Larry opened the back door of a black Dodge van. This was exactly the vehicle a killer-kidnapper would use. McCabe, desperate, cast one more glance at the parking lot hoping to see Shimada's car.

And he did.

Off in the shadows of the Emergency Room were parked three ambulances, the taxi that had delivered him, and one hot-rod GTO.

The sight of that GTO gave him courage. He and Rei stepped into the van. It was lit in soft blues, like a cocktail lounge. Two recliners took up most of the space. McCabe sat in one and pulled Rei into his lap.

He was shaking, she was not, except for a lip tremble barely noticeable in the dome light.

Terry said: "Once our contract is successfully executed, which I anticipate will be recumbent soon, we'll

retreat to some prestige establishment for a celebration.
Drinks on my account."

Terry drove. Larry sat in the passenger seat,
chewing gum, legs jumping.

McCabe directed Terry to Punchbowl National
Cemetery, uphill all the way. It was dreadful dark. Only
because McCabe had been here during daylight did he
know they were driving into a volcanic cinder cone, a
natural amphitheater, filled with the graves of Pacific war
dead. When Terry parked, the view through the
windshield was downtown skyscrapers, the dock lights at
Sand Island, the glowing Aloha Tower, then three
thousand miles of black ocean.

Terry checked his Rolex. "They got ten minutes."
He switched the dome light on and picked up a
crossword book. "In our business," he said, "there is a
pre-eminent amount of waiting."

He filled in a crossword clue.

"McCabe," said Larry, "how long have you lived
here?"

"Eight, ten years, depending."

"Depending on what?"

"On whether you count my Army time as living
here."

"So it never snows, right?" Larry asked. "How
about sleet? They got sleet? What's the coldest it's ever
been, McCabe? And what are the rents like, reasonable?
Are the landlords a bunch of thieves?"

"Forget about it," Terry grunted. "You can't live
here, Larry."

"Why not?"

"Two words. Pro Bation."

"You can travel out of state if you clear it with your P.O."

"This ain't a state."

"It is so. Ain't it McCabe?"

"Since 1959," McCabe said.

"But it ain't a regular state," Terry said, "it's one of them what you call territorial states, right? I mean it ain't attached to nothing, how can it be a state? It's like Puerto Rico, a non-regulation state. All the regulation states are next to one another."

"But the Pacific," Larry said, and held up one learned finger, "is American territorial waters."

"What's the word I'm looking for?" Terry said. "It's an irregular state. Like Alaska."

"Fiftieth state," said Larry. "Look it up in your dictionary."

"Stunod," Terry said. "Take a walk, surveillance."

"What am I surveilling?"

"Should you see someone parked on this dark road behind us, that would be inappropriate for this appointed hour."

Larry, muttering curses, stepped out of the van.

Reiko said: "It stimulates the brain."

"What?" Terry asked.

"Crossword puzzles," she said.

"Sitting duck," said Terry. "That's your clue."

"Dupe?" suggested McCabe.

"Chump?" said Rei. "Patsy?"

"No, no, no," said Terry. "Eight letters."

"Fall guy," McCabe tried.

"Eight!" Terry barked. "Blank blank S H.

"Pushover," Rei said.

"It fits!" said Terry, working his pencil. "Thank you, nursey. I needed that R at the end."

McCabe kept his arms wrapped around Rei's waist and began to feel better. Somewhere in the dark, he was pretty sure, waited David Shimada and the HPD swat team. Perhaps McCabe had watched too many episodes of *Danger, Hawaii,* for he wanted to believe its unlikely premise: that the police had no other agenda but to nobly protect all citizens. The show would always end with Mick Danger slapping the bad guys in jail and winking at a pretty girl. But that TV fantasy was punctured by McCabe's recent talk with Chief Abreu. The Chief was no noble TV cop, but a scheming politician.

McCabe mentally rehearsed shoving Rei to the floor, lying on top of her, as the cops and the Estonophies shot it out. He had learned at least one thing in Basic Training: when the bullets fly, lie down.

McCabe's mind wandered back to Pleasantville, a city that held distinctly unpleasant memories. Had Terry really gut-shot his father and left him to die in an alley? Was it Larry who had burgled their home when the McCabe family was at Disney World? What nasty tricks had Larry learned during two years at Rahway?

As McCabe was refereeing a wrestling match between fear and denial, the passenger door opened and Larry hopped in.

"What's the report?" Terry said.

"Nothing," said Larry. "There's one car back around the curve. Two people making out."

"You're certain of this?"

"Yep."

"It's a big make-out spot," Rei said.

"Especially late," McCabe added. "You know, bar pickups, you come up here, romantic city lights…"

"Shut up," snapped Terry. "Larry. Hey. Young couple, old couple, what?"

"I didn't shine a flashlight on 'em," Larry said.

"New car, old car?"

"Old. GTO hot rod. A teenager car."

"What's a five letter word for breakfast staple?"

"Staple?"

"Like what do you eat for breakfast?" Terry asked.

"I'm hungry," Larry said.

"Bacon," said McCabe.

"See?" said Terry. "McCabe went to college."

Rei kept quiet and calm. This always astonished McCabe, the woman seemed to have no nerves. Whatever happens was meant to be, she liked to say. We're little paper boats on a big stormy sea.

Terry flicked the radio on. Some DJ was blathering about: Let's tear down the Berlin Wall, so he switched to a station that loudly announced its call letters as KPOI. A ragged-voiced woman began singing *She's Got Bette Davis Eyes*.

Larry snapped his fingers.

"That's it!" he shouted. "The chick, the Pineapple Heiress, that's what she's got, Bette Davis eyes."

"So fuck, you gotta talk about that now?"

"It's been going through my mind, them bulging eyes. You'd think with all her money, she'd get an eye operation."

"She's being treated," said Rei.

"For what?" asked Larry.

"Can't say," Rei answered. "Shouldn't have said anything. Patient confidentiality, you know."

"Confidential?" Terry asked. "Speaking of that, let's all shut up. Let's listen to the radio, look at the nice lights below us, without all this blathering inhumane talk."

"Hey I'm nervous too," said Larry.

Terry snapped off the radio. "I ain't nervous," he shouted.

Long minutes of nervous silence passed.

Then Rei blurted: "Oh, dear."

Headlights swept around the curving drive. A Cadillac sedan pulled up behind the van.

"Our appointment rounds," said Terry. "Let's go."

McCabe and Rei followed the brothers out of the van as a stranger stepped from the Cadillac. In silence he opened the rear door and Terry, Larry, Rei and McCabe squeezed into the passenger space.

Porky Hashimoto was driving. He was dressed in tan slacks and yellow aloha shirt.

"Are we in the mood for a late supper?" Porky said, glancing into the rearview mirror.

Late supper, wondered McCabe, or last supper? Whoever the stranger in the front seat was, he was no thug. He wore a tailored suit. He was late middle age, barely five feet tall and a hundred-some pounds. He had gray hair, slicked back perfectly, and a sharp, handsome face. McCabe had seen this fellow somewhere.

Nobody spoke as they drove downhill toward the city lights. If they passed Shimada's GTO on the curvy ride down, McCabe missed it.

The Cadillac navigated the dark streets, and for a moment McCabe thought they were headed to the police station. But they kept going another block and pulled into reserved parking behind the Cherry Girl Lounge.

"The young lady waits in the car," said the little man.

"You'll be okay out here?" McCabe asked Rei.

"We're okay with waiting, Lazarus," she said.

The men got out of the Cadillac. Porky, under a spotlight, used a key to open the strip club's steel door and stood aside. The well-dressed little man followed them all in.

The raucous sounds of a strip show faded when Porky shut the group into a plush room. Set on a long table was a huge dead fish, its top a dull blue, it bottom yellow and silver. It had yellow fins. This fish was almost as big as Larry. Its mouth gaped open. Its eye bulged, blind to everything but death. Terry realized it was half a fish, slit lengthwise and set on chipped ice. At its head and tail were small buckets of mustard and soy sauce, beside a platter of sliced cabbage.

Porky said: "Business before pleasure?" and the little man sat on one side of the table. McCabe sat opposite, alongside the brothers. Larry grabbed a Suntori beer from a bucket jammed with ice and bottles.

Porky picked up a long thin knife, sharpened it on a round stone. "Gentlemen," he said, and looked at Terry and Larry. "I hope you appreciate that we've waived our introduction fee."

"Whom am I dealing with?" asked the sharply-dressed little man.

"Me," Terry said, and pointed to his chest.

"And whom do you speak for?" asked the little man.

"We came here to make an offer of generosity to a politician whose skills we admire," Terry said. "We calculated that it would be a great waste of talent should

Sam Wing settle for the mayorhood of your fair city. We would appreciate an opportunity to speak with this man on a facial basis."

Porky cut into the side of the fish, lifted out a bloody raw steak, presented it on butcher paper to the little man, who nodded.

Then the little man refocused on Terry. "Who is *we?*"

Terry shrugged. "We are not at libertines to disclose such information."

Now McCabe realized who the little man was. He had seen him around the Capitol during his reporter days. This was Spike Murakami, a land developer who had tons of influence but hardly an ounce of public profile. And why was he dressed in a handsome suit, while Porky wore an aloha shirt? McCabe realized this was to demonstrate that Spike was in charge, and Porky merely his assistant.

"Your offer represents," Spike Murakami said, "and I've already discussed this with Attorney Hashimoto, a failure of imagination. Whoever sent you here has failed to imagine Island life in all its complexity. Hawaii is not some hula-girl paradise. This is our home. We have our own ways here. If someone from Nevada wishes to pitch a tent in our backyard, the proper approach is to first negotiate with Royce Hashimoto Associates."

Porky, cutting tuna steak into long slices, nodded.

"Before you develop a property," said Spike, "you must first deal with the man who owns it. Am I making sense?"

Spike Murakami stood up. "Everyone who develops a significant property here requires the services of Royce Hashimoto Associates. Local or mainland, it makes no difference. Royce Hashimoto Associates is the bottleneck through which all major development on Oahu must pass."

He leaned over the table and stared down Terry. "Clear?"

Terry nodded.

"I'd prefer," said Spike, "to speak directly with a decision-level executive. But in your case those executives are three thousand miles away, so here is my message for them."

Spike glared at Larry. "No smoking," he said.

Larry closed his pack of Big Tents.

"The kind of development your backers are proposing," Spike said, "has been fought locally for years. Bix Sanders and the entertainer who calls himself Teddy Hong Kong have been plotting, ever since they met in some cheap cocktail lounge, to bring casino gambling to Waikiki. We have opposed them. There are fortunes at stake, and we have no intention of ceding them to an unemployed actor and a Waikiki nightclub singer. We already have gambling here. It may be extra-legal but it generates reliable income for certain well-placed individuals. So now you come along with an offer that, frankly speaking, is an insult. Did your employers imagine that we would trade our sovereignty for a measly six figures? Even as an opening gambit, we are insulted. We are somewhat embarrassed for you."

Terry looked at Larry, whose legs were jimmy-jumping. McCabe folded his hands and muttered boyhood prayers. Porky arranged slices of raw fish on a white platter.

"Hundreds of millions of dollars at stake," Spike said. "And you dare to come here with an offer of pocket change."

Spike huffed. "Had I not interceded ..." he cleared his throat and continued. "But I did intercede, and not for sentimental reasons. We want you to take a message back to Nevada. Tell your masters that for a ten million dollar fee, we would be willing to *open*, note that I said *open*, direct negotiations with well-financed mainlanders who were content to be *minority* partners in Waikiki casino properties."

Larry was trying to sip from his beer but his hands were shaky. Terry touched his arm, like to say, Hey, this ain't the time for beer.

"So the key concepts are," Spike said. "Ten million dollars ... only buys a seat at the table ... for *discussions* of a minority partnership. I say again, *minority*. Can you retain those three concepts and transmit them faithfully to your employers?

"I guess so," said Terry. "But they ain't gonna be too appreciative."

Larry shook his head. "They're not going to like it."

"Excuse me," Spike said. "But which of you is the principal here?"

"Me," said Terry. "My brother shuts up."

"Now one last concept," said Spike. "You declined to identify who you meant when you say *we*. But I can tell you who I mean by *we*. There's a Japanese organization, highly esteemed in Osaka, that needs to legitimately invest its huge cash haul outside the reach of Japanese authorities. As part of their worldwide portfolio, they have designated substantial funds for Oahu real estate.

They are very protective of that long-term, completely legal and transparent investment. They are thus wary of any plans to meddle in this island's economic realities."

"Yakuza," said Larry. "I heard of 'em."

"Shut up," said Terry.

"Listen to your brother," Spike told Terry. "He's smarter than you think."

"And the histrionics?" said Porky, looking at them over the dead fish. "They will cease immediately."

"The what?" asked Terry.

"Terrorizing college girls," Porky said, "and all other threats to persons, will no longer be tolerated." He stared at Terry, then Larry. "I take it we agree? Now it's time for kau-kau."

Spike removed his suit jacket and Terry saw, pinned to it, a gold diamond-shaped medal. You didn't see guys with big gold medals pinned to their $2000 suits, usually.

Porky arranged bowls of dipping sauce around the white plate of cut-up blood-raw tuna.

"Attorney Hashimoto," said Spike, "worked summers in the fisheries while in college. He hasn't lost his knife skills."

"Yellow fin sashimi," Porky said. "As fresh as you'll ever eat it. Do we buy ours at the supermarket? We do not. We have a man at the dock in Kona. Just this morning, the predator you're about to consume was a terror of the seas, gobbling every fish in sight. Now he's..."

Using ivory chopsticks, Porky picked up a chunk of raw fish, dipped it in soy and then mustard.

"... he's just a midnight snack." Porky slipped the sashimi into his mouth.

"I never thought of tuna as a bad-ass fish," said Terry.

"Then you don't know your pelagic creatures," said Porky. "Yellow fin! A hundred-eighty pounds of voracious predator. If there weren't sharks in the ocean, tuna would be the apex predator."

Terry gawked at the huge wound in the side of the fish. Its mouth hung open, like it was crying for help.

"You do understand the concept of apex predator?" Porky said. "There can be only one in a food chain." He undermined a sashimi slice with his knife, and held gleaming blade and bloody fish underneath Terry's lips. "Tuna, are they big? Yes. Are they vicious? Absolutely. But their brains are pitifully small. See how easy it was to slice him up?"

Pot of Gold

20

What a beautiful morning it was, with tender light blessing Diamond Head, the sea perfectly calm, the beach free of tourists, and empty blue outrigger canoes at rest on the sloping sands. Doves cooed. Palm fronds rustled in a gentle breeze.

But the beauty was lost on Terry Estonophie, who stood at an iron railing, suitcoat open, waiting for his little brother to quit flirting with the waitress and come to breakfast. Terry chose a table for two, alongside the beach, under flamingo-pink umbrellas. The table was set with white cups and saucers, gleaming glasses, folded napkins, expensive silverware, and a Bird of Paradise flower propped up in a vase.

"How'd you sleep?" asked Larry.

"How'd I sleep?" said Terry. "Since when do you care about my nocturnal emissions?"

"Because I slept like a nightmare," Larry said. Dressed like a beach bum in t-shirt and shorts, he sat in a rattan chair, waved his coffee cup at the waitress. "I'm dry as a desert. I drank like nine beers."

The waitress, in flowered blouse, delivered coffee. Larry said, "Leave the pot, hon."

"You got bagels?" Terry asked her. "I'll have a bagel."

"Cream cheese and lox?" asked the waitress.

"No lox! I'm strictly a land animal. I never eat anything fish-related."

"Nothing for me," said Larry. "My stomach's seasick."

When the waitress walked off, Larry studied her ass and said: "I kept dreaming about that tuna fish. Japanese butchers hacking the poor thing up while it was still alive. That tuna was us, Terry. Raw meat."

"I know, I know, I got the message."

Larry donned dark glasses against the rising sun. "Now what do we do?"

A dove landed near Terry's feet. He kicked at the bird, and it flapped off.

"Now we get tough," Terry said.

"You're losing your mind," Larry said. "This island's lousy with Japanese mobsters. There's probably a hundred guys with their fingertips missing. Face it, brother. Your Vegas buddies threw us naked into the lion's den."

"Indubitably," said Terry.

"You can't go anywhere near Sam now. Sam's one of them, Terry, can't you see? Sam and the fish-eating lawyer and the nasty little fucker Spike. They're all like in a club. It's like the Knights of Columbus, but they got guns."

"I don't give a shit," said Terry.

"Your bagel, sir," said the waitress, and delivered it on a white plate, alongside a pineapple spear and a ramekin of cream cheese.

When the waitress retreated, Terry said: "Back in Philly you get a decent bagel, not here. I can tell just by looking at it. It ain't shiny."

"That's because things are different here, like I was telling you. The bagels, the mobsters, we don't understand island stuff yet."

Terry pointed a gleaming knife at his brother. "And you don't understand the Stairway of Respect. You're at the bottom, looking up."

"And where are you?"

Terry tossed the bagel over the railing and onto the sands of Waikiki.

"Climbing," said Terry. "You want to take the next step up, you don't go crying to the boss that your job is too hard. Respect, Larry. You win respect with guts and honor and loyalty."

"Curiosity killed the cat, but loyalty killed the dog."

"Who you calling a dog?" Terry growled.

"Go back to Vegas, Terry, and get a new plan."

"Leave me to stew on it, little brother."

"I was scared shitless. You weren't scared shitless in there, sitting with a dead fish?"

"I never thought I'd swallow uncooked fish, disgusting." Terry drank coffee, wiped his lips with a pastel napkin. "Not hungry any more," he said.

He left a twenty dollar bill on the table and walked into the hotel's shady lobby. Larry followed him into the luxurious men's room, with its padded walls, tall black empty vases, and flowery smells. Larry stared at himself in the mirror as his brother pissed in the urinal. How would a genuine Yakuza gangster see Larry? As a skinny tourist punk, he admitted, laughable and weak.

Terry stood beside him at the mirror, removed his fawn-colored suit-jacket, to reveal his shoulder rig and gleaming pistol. He hung the jacket on a brass hook and stared into the mirror.

"Failure," he said. "I gotta account for my own failure, brother."

"Just go back to Vegas and explain."

"I'm not bad enough, that's the trouble," Terry said. "I got too much of a sympathetic system. I should be more you know, indimidating. Right in the beginning, I shoulda shoved this gun in McCabe's mouth and demanded: Take me to the candidate Wing."

He pulled the pistol out of his shoulder holster, pointed it at the mirror, and said: "You think Jesse James bowed to the Japanese? You think Al Capone had raw fish shoved down his throat? I should go out in a blaze of glory, avenging Pearl Harbor."

His lips quivered, the pistol in his outstretched hand trembled. "Here, Jap fucks. Eat this!"

The room exploded in a hot white flash. For Larry, it seemed like somebody had punched him in the head. His ears rang, his face stung. He stumbled out of the smoky men's room. The scent of vile chemicals gagged him as he wandered dazed over plush carpets. A fat security guard ran past him. And then somehow he was sitting on the seawall, bleeding a little, from arms and face.

Larry expected to see police cars screeching to a stop in the alleys alongside the big pink hotel. After a few stunned and quiet minutes, with no cops in sight, he recovered himself and wandered Waikiki beach. At Mynah Bird Beach he removed his t-shirt, dunked himself in the ocean, the salt stinging all his little cuts, but washing the blood away. What had happened to Terry? Larry figured in an hour or two, Terry would be calling for bail.

But Terry could rot, because Larry had a date this morning and back at the Tiki Torch he showered and changed into respectable aloha shirt and khaki shorts. The real reason he'd declined to eat at the Royal Hawaiian was that he had a breakfast date with Pua at Eggs and Things, the funky café near the yacht harbor. And the real reason for meeting there was to hide from Pua his embarrassing residence at a cockroach hotel.

After breakfast, Pua drove him in the open-top Thing through ramshackle neighborhoods that gave way to grimy warehouses and rusty junkyards. At the end of the road a sign read:

YOU ARE ENTERING
THE GROUNDS
OF HALAWA PRISON
All Persons and Vehicles Subject to Search

Larry shuddered, even though Halawa Prison looked nothing like Rahway. Rahway State Prison was brick, shaped like a dark star, and surrounded by its trustee farm. Halawa Prison was a long gray slab of concrete, set into a scruffy green hillside. A tower of gray concrete rose from amid the prison yard. Larry knew there were evil guards up there, cradling machine guns, just hoping for the chance to shoot a good guy down.

Rahway had taught him: You thought the inmates were bad, until you met the guards.

A grim, greasy parking lot was jammed with loser autos. At a huge STOP sign, Pua submitted her driver's license to a guard who hid behind the grimy tinted glass of a gate house.

"Kimo Long," she said.

The invisible guard grunted.

"It's so hot," Pua complained, sweat beads on her upper lip. Her words came out strangled, and Larry could almost feel the lump in the girl's throat. Poor Pua. It bummed her to admit her dad wasn't sick, but in prison.

Larry didn't blame Pua for lying about her dad. The truth was like a supermarket, and lies were like the corner convenience store. Sometimes you had to shop at the convenience store, because the supermarket was too far away. Larry had lied to Pua about how he got all these little cuts on his face and arms. Some thoughtless rube, he told her, had locked an innocent puppy in a hot car in Waikiki. What choice did a hero have, but to bust out the windshield and save the dog?

A chick lied to you, you lied to her, that was like, the essence of love.

The invisible guard pushed Pua's license through the window slot and raised the gate.

"I can put you on the list," Pua said as she swung the Thing into a parking spot. "I mean, in case you want to meet Dad someday. It'll take a while to be approved …"

Larry covered her hand with his. He would never be approved because he was on probation. Besides, he still hadn't told Pua his real last name. But here were more examples of how lies beat the truth.

"I'll wait until he gets out to meet him," Larry said. "Prisons spook me."

"Me too," Pua admitted. "But I'm here every visiting day. Dad is so lonely in there."

She draped her black leather purse from her shoulder.

"They only allow twenty minutes," she said. "Except for spouses."

"I'll be fine, sweetie," Larry said.

He held Pua's sweaty hand and walked her to enormous gray steel doors. She wore a bright red flowery dress meant to cheer her dad. It cheered Larry too. She was no willowy Miss America, but she was stunning gorgeous to Larry. It was her eyes. You could fall in and drown they were so deep, a warm ocean of kindness.

How had a Jersey burglar gotten so lucky?

The door slammed after her and Larry retreated across a landscape that had no trees, no awnings, no shade. Larry understood: They had cleared the area to give the guards a better shot at escaping inmates. He slumped in the Thing's passenger seat and sat sweating in the nasty plastic seats. This was nothing, he told himself. Captain Jules Dudoit had battled salty air and tropical sun all his nautical lifetime.

Larry told himself he should buy a hat, though. A Panama hat, like Mick Danger wore in every episode of *Danger, Hawaii.* The Mick was wise to these islands. Kama-aina, that's what they called people who were comfortable with island ways. Pua was teaching him one Hawaiian word every day.

He smoked a Big Tent and remembered Old Lady Tobacco, gardening nude at her estate near the Koshu temple. Every pack of cigarettes Larry bought deposited a dime in her bank account. All around the world, people smoked Big Tents, and the smoke rose into the sky, became a cloud of dimes, then rained money on the old nudist, squatting in her Hawaiian garden.

Where was the justice? Donna Lorris gave the world cancer, and it rained money on her. But doing an entry, and costing an insurance company some of its profits, that could put a guy away for years.

Larry snuffed the cigarette out in the Thing's ashtray. Pua found cigarette butts disgusting but Larry dared not toss this one overboard. He worried that some screw, watching the parking lot for the tiniest violation, would storm out those steel doors and handcuff him.

Although, really, prison wasn't as bad as they said, except for the part about no babes allowed. Once in Rahway, in a fever-sweat, he'd been treated by a nurse. He thought he would die of lovesickness, just from the attention of a homely middle-aged female. After that he went on sick call quite a bit. This was after Karen ran off, and he felt so down and lonely. Surrounded by a thousand loser guys, with Mom dead and Karen screwing a prep cook in Orlando, Larry's last months in Rahway were the most miserable of his life. He'd had the jimmy-jumps real bad.

Larry picked a copy of The Honolulu Record off the Thing's sandy floor, and draped the front section over his head to deflect the sun. Then he opened the back section and read the comics. His favorite was the

Phantom, the Ghost Who Walks, delivering justice in darkest Africa. Comics were read by kids, so the newspapers couldn't admit the truth: The Phantom did entries in his spare time. Larry was sure of it. The Phantom's mask pretty much sold Larry on that idea.

He read down to Ann Landers, where a girl wrote that her father had done creepy things to her. This made Larry red-faced mad. In prison they called molesters *beasts*. As far as Larry cared, beasts could stay locked up until they rotted. And that included Pua's beastly dad.

Horoscopes: The Rooster. Plenty of love and sunshine in your life today, Rooster, so acknowledge your good fortune with a smile. You have been given a tremendous gift, but it will take you a while to realize its value. Direction of your wind: A cooling mauka breeze.

It was almost like that breeze blew open the gray steel doors. Pua walked toward the car, head down, tears sparkling on her cheeks.

"I don't want to talk about it," she said, angry. She started the Thing, jammed it into gear, and peeled out of the parking lot.

"Sometimes I really hate him," she said, and whipped a turn so hard the Thing reared up on two wheels.

"Selfish, selfish man," she said.

"You want to tell me anything?"

"No!" she growled. "All he's ever done is cause trouble in our family."

Larry sighed.

"And now he's just so, so sorry for himself," Pua said. She screeched to a halt at a stop sign, just opposite a warehouse. A crew was using a huge cherry picker to knock it down. Pua stared at the demolition crew. "I should hire them to knock Dad's place to the ground."

"His place?"

"The Ala Wai Rainbow," said Pua, her lips snarled.

"What's the Ala Wai Rainbow?"

"Hang on," Pua said.

And she did mean hang on. The girl drove reckless, weaving on the freeway at 90 mph. The wind, whipping around the windshield, hurt at that speed. The newspaper and its horoscope flew up and out of the Thing like a panicked bird. Larry hunkered in the seat as Pua the lunatic buzzed toward the ocean.

She pulled over at Waikiki's murkiest, dankest blocks. Waikiki was almost an island, one side ocean, and on two sides, a canal. When the canal reached the ocean, it was clear flowing, but back here it was a dirty ditch, clogged with rotting palm fronds, trash and half-sunken coconuts. Larry's view through the windshield was the canal, then the Ala Wai golf course and then the cloud-topped mountains.

"You're looking at it," Pua said.

"I know," Larry said. "You call those mountains the Big Wahine."

"No, silly, the building. You're looking at the building."

Larry looked up at maybe twenty stories of bland concrete. It was an ordinary high-rise except for all the broken windows. Above its lobby doors someone had painted a rainbow, ruined now by some punk's graffiti.

"The Ala Wai Rainbow," Pua said. "The building that ruined my family."

She left the Thing and led Larry across an alley.
Three broad brick steps led to a stone landing and
boarded-up lobby. Pua and Larry put their faces to a
smudged, narrow window beside raw plywood. In the
lobby: flattened beer cans, crushed cigarette butts, ruined
pay phones, a couple of disgusting prophylactics, and
graffiti-covered walls.

"My dad's dream of glory," she sighed.

"Your father built this?"

"Financed it."

She sat on a low stone wall and pulled out of her
purse a scented red kerchief. She wound it around her
hands and worried it.

"My dad was a union officer. There was a pension
fund. Have I said enough?"

"No," said Larry and stepped back to scan all the
way up the twenty floors to blue sky. Why hadn't they
finished this condo? He pictured him and Pua in an
ocean-view apartment on the top floor. Did Waikiki
condos have room service?

"The pension fund was invested," Pua said,
"mostly in real estate, but in this case ..."

"Somebody stole the money," said Larry.

"It kind of leaked away. Some contractors were
never paid. There was a big scandal and ..." She flushed
with anger. "Every few months, they bring it all up again,
in the newspapers."

Larry draped his arm around Pua, but she only
stared at the ground and worried her kerchief. Larry saw a
rainbow developing atop the Big Wahine, then fading, a
tease. A pot of gold lay at rainbow's end, or so Mom had
promised.

Keep digging, Larry, you'll find it.

"I haven't told you the worst part," Pua said. "Land in Waikiki is hardly ever sold. Most of the hotels and condos are built on land leased for 99 years. This land belongs to the Grotton Family Trust. When our condo went bust, Christina's family got dragged into court like they were criminals. I was humiliated."

She let down the straps of her sundress, and Larry thought holy kripes she's going to strip nude. But when she stepped out of her dress she wore a blue bikini underneath. He had never seen her in a bikini before and she was awful cute in it.

"I need a swim," she said. "I'll feel cleaner after a swim."

She led him across the alley to the Thing. "We're walking," she said. "We'll never find parking at the beach."

From underneath a back seat she fetched rolled up beach mats and blue towels and handed them to Larry. For four blocks they walked condo-shaded streets that smelled of rotting fruit, until they reached Pua's favorite spot, where Kuhio Beach met the Zoo.

"Hear that?" Pua said. "Peacocks."

"I shoulda recognized it."

"It's a love call," said Pua. "The roosters make it to attract the pea hens."

"It's the most jungle sound I ever heard," Larry said.

They crossed Kalakaua and traffic stopped to let them pass, another thing about Hawaii that amazed Larry. In Jersey, it was like drivers were actually trying to run pedestrians down.

Pua laid out the towels and mats on the glaring hot Kuhio Beach. Larry removed his sweaty aloha shirt and

held Pua's hand as they waded into pea-green seawater.
The ocean rolled in miniature waves over an ancient dead
reef. You could walk a half mile into the sea and still be
only waist-deep. Pua and Larry sat in the sandy bottom to
let the mini-waves wash them clean.

Larry enjoyed that mauka breeze that had been
promised in today's horoscope. The ocean washed away
every bit of the day's sweat. He worried about Terry for a
moment, and then forgot about him. A night in jail might
cool Terry off.

A couple of goofy tourists tried to surf waves that
could hardly float a popsicle stick. Larry watched the
clouds clinging to the mountains, the daily sun shower
and rainbow forming in Big Wahine Valley.

"This place is magic," Larry said.

"No," Pua said. "It's just Hawaii. It's a hard place
to live sometimes. There's no escaping the island, your
family, or even yourself."

"I want to marry you," said Larry.

Pua gawked at him.

"I been thinking about it since I met you," Larry
confessed.

"Larry …"

"It seems like, you know, predestination." He held
her sea-wet hand in his sea-wet hand.

"Help me," he said. "Help me become a better
man."

Pua closed her eyes and tears leaked from them.
She shook her head. She dropped his hand. She turned
her back on him and waded to a concrete sea wall that
was slimy with seaweed. When Larry approached, she
would not look up at him, it was like she was studying her
nervous hands.

"I can't," she muttered.

"I'll wait until you're ready," he said.

"Larry," she looked up at him. "I'm ruined."

He sat beside her on the seawall, put his arms around her waist and whispered in her ear: "I'm Captain Dudoit, Hawaiian Princess. Marry me, and be ambassadress to France."

"No!"

"Why not?"

"I'm dirty," she said. She scooped sea water up on herself. "I feel so filthy sometimes."

The Sacrificial Jeep

21

"Do I smell?" Terry asked, lifting one arm.

"Like Old Spice," Larry lied.

Dark rings soaked the underarms of Terry's pleated white shirt.

"You know I hate flying over an ocean," Terry said. "So you can imagine. What this trip means to me, I can't even denigrate. You stay here and cover eventualities on this end."

He packed a leather case with crossword books, sharpened pencils, pink erasers, a coffee-stained Webster's dictionary and a gleaming pistol.

"Every three hours you be at the anointed phone," he said. "Around the clock. Three, six, nine and twelve. Get it?"

"Here?"

"Not here, wait at your hotel. They're watching this place. I can feel it like the hairs on the back of my neck."

"What do you expect after you shot up the men's room?"

"What do you mean 'shot up?' It was only one round."

"Good way to bring a whole squad of cops to the lobby."

"They went away, didn't they?"

"Makes you wonder," Larry said. "How smart these cops are."

Terry hefted a suitcase and threw his suit-coat over his arm. "Too hot for the jacket," he said.

"I mean," said Larry, "the guard saw us come out of the men's room, right? You'd think he'd of told the cops who done it."

"Don't think too hard, little brother," Terry said. "It ain't becoming to you." He checked his Rolex. "Ten minutes to noon. Way too early for the plane, but I'm too overactive to stay here. I'm jumpy like you are on a normal day. I'm gonna sit at the airport."

The brothers slipped out of the Kuhio Suite and walked over plush carpet toward the outdoor lobby.

"I'm glad you changed your mind," said Larry. "You're doing the right thing to go back there. I know what's gonna happen. Management pays you off and says thanks for the good job, we're going with Plan C."

"What are you, fucking kidding me?" Terry said. "I'll end up with a bullet in the head. But you were right all along, little brother, I gotta risk it. You don't hear from me in 24 hours, lay low. You're like a ghost on this assignment, officially, you don't exist. Management might suspect I brought you along, but they don't gotta know. Keep a simpleton outlook, I always say. Stay low profile, kid, until I can formulate what you call a scenario of success."

He punched Larry's shoulder, not hard but friendly.

As the brothers entered the jungle of that open-air lobby, a gaggle of lei-draped, sunburned white people staggered off a tour bus.

"You got hours to catch the plane, big brother," said Larry. "Let's get a taxi, take a detour."

Larry walked to a desk that was shaded by a bamboo roof. A skinny dark-haired fellow in purple uniform glared at him. A silver whistle dangled from his neck. His nametag read: MANGO.

"Mango," said Larry. "That's a fruit, right?"

Mango blinked. "Can I be of service, sir?"

Larry palmed him a coin. Mango took it without looking at it. Rube that he was, he probably thought it was a quarter.

"That's a dollar coin," Larry said, "with the Susan B wahine on the front."

"I'll be sure to spend it wisely," said Mango. "How can I help you?"

With an attitude like that, he could work in Jersey.

"A clean cab for my brother," Larry said.

Mango lifted the whistle to his chapped lips and blew it three times, but the first cab in line did not move. A red-and-white car slipped from the back of the line, rolling out of the harsh sunshine into Royal Hawaiian shade.

"Aloha," Larry said to Mango. "I didn't mean no insult about the fruit."

Mango held open the rear door of the cab, then popped Terry's suitcase into the trunk. Terry hugged the leather bag that held his crossword books and squeezed into the back seat. He seemed to know the cabbie.

"What's with you?" Terry said. "You the only cab driver on the islands?"

Larry looked at the woman, a hefty wahine with long dark hair and rough complexion. A license posted on the dashboard read: Prudence Yamanaki.

"I'm first call, Royal Hawaiian," she told Terry.

"First call?" Terry said. "Does that mean you jump the line? What, you pay under the table?"

"Mango's an old friend," claimed Prudence. She pulled out into Waikiki traffic. "He's been here since the days of Arthur Godfrey. In those days, Hawaii Calls was radioed from this hotel all around the world."

"Radio show?" Terry said. "What are you talking, back in the magnanimous days, right?"

"Mr. Godfrey was a very generous tipper. Which airline do you fellows need?"

"Detour," said Larry. "Black Point."

"I need a specific address for my dispatcher," said Prudence.

"I don't know the address," said Larry. "Koshu's temple."

"Good enough," said Prudence, and spoke into her microphone: "Eleven twelve, Grotton estate, Black Point Road."

The radio squawked.

"You're right," she said over her dandruff-flaked shoulder. "It's so private down there, they don't have an address. You boys don't belong to that hippie cult, do you? You don't dress weird."

"Spectacular view," Larry said. "I want to show my brother."

"We don't wish to further converse," said Terry, and poked Larry with his elbow. "Please escort us to our requested destination by the shortest available route."

Prudence drove. Larry fidgeted. Terry looked over a crossword puzzle, but in nervous hands. Larry couldn't stop noticing. His brother, the man with ice nerves, had blood in them veins after all.

When Prudence veered off Kalanianaole Highway, the roads became narrower, then gave way to rutted dirt.

"This is where they live," whispered Larry. "The richest of the rich."

Larry tapped the cigarette pack in Terry's pocket. "The tobacco lady," he said, but to his disappointment, no nude gardener was apparent at the Lorris estate. "Down that road, it's like Hawaii's Hollywood. Bix Sanders and Teddy Hong Kong and maybe even what's his name, Arthur Gottfried."

Prudence pulled up in a cloud of dust at the Koshu beach house, and threw the transmission into park. "Dollar a minute waiting time," she grumbled.

"I should make that kind of money for doing nothing," said Terry.

"We won't be long," said Larry.

He led Terry through a stockade gate.

"What, this is open?" marveled Terry.

"Public access," Larry said. "I found out from the natives. No matter how rich you are, you gotta clear a public path to the beach. Can you imagine? It's like you own a house in Margate, but Philly skids piss on your beach."

The pebbled grounds were shaded by a massive banyan tree. Doves, safe in its branches, cooed love songs.

"This is why I brought you here," Larry said. "So you could see. The pineapple family lived here before it became a shrine. And this was only their beach cottage. Can you believe that?"

He clapped Terry's back. "See, brother, there is a pot at the end of the rainbow, like Mom told us."

"For potheads like you, there's pot at the end of the rainbow."

"No," said Larry. "Hawaiian gold. Look at the way these people live. I seen the light. We don't need Jersey or Nevada either."

"I don't like approximation to the pelagic realm," Terry said.

"The what realm?"

"Pelagic. It means like, pertaining to the sea."

"Live in the mountains, then. Someday you gotta get over that water thing, Terry. According to science, you're 99 percent water yourself."

But Larry understood his brother's watery fears. Once when Terry was babbling drunk, he'd admitted that their old man had tried to drown him. Well, maybe the old man had just thrown Terry into the waves, a lesson in sink or swim. Little Terry had been sucked into a rip tide and saved from drowning only by a stranger. In later years, Terry changed the story to say that it was Dad who plucked him out of the waves.

Larry could easily believe a passing beachcomber showed more love for little Terry than his own father did.

Tiny Estonophie hated his oldest son like poison, but gave Larry an easier ride. The old man delivered beatings to Larry often enough, but no near-death experience.

"Who's this guy?" asked Terry, looking at the statue.

Larry slapped the Koshu statue on its green marble ass. "He's their surfer Jesus." He poked Terry. "Want to see something weird?"

He let Terry into the temple room. There were neither locks nor guards. There was nothing to steal but dinged-up pots and pans, candles, coconuts, a moldy pile of sweet potatoes, and giant sacks of rice.

Sweet-smelling candles burned at the big mural. Terry gawked at the wall painting of Koshu, the man with eyes in his heart.

"Anatomically speaking," said Terry, "that ain't kosher."

"Wait until you see this," said Larry, and led his brother through double doors and into the sunshine. "Lanai," Larry said. "Hawaiian for sun porch. I'm learning the lingo already."

That wide porch overlooked lava rocks and the restless sea. Terry felt seasick, turned his back. He began to suspect maybe Larry had brought him down here as a sneaky way to what you call, demonstrate his pelagic weaknesses.

"The sea ain't gonna come up and grab you," Larry said. But as the words escaped his lips, he remembered: That was exactly what had happened to Saint Koshu. The sea had swept him off and his apostles had stood sobbing on the rocks, helpless, watching him drown.

Larry wasn't going to tell his brother that story. The big guy had enough problems. Larry rested a friendly hand on Terry's solid shoulder. Terry was too tough for high school football, which is why they threw him off the team at Holy Infant. Otherwise, he'd a been a lineman for the Eagles today.

And Larry would be his agent, scamming millions out of the NFL.

Terry led the way inside, into the candle-lit room, away from the dreaded ocean. "What's this?" he asked.

"Shower room," said Larry. "I guess it was already here in the beach house, and the apostles left it. You know who's the Virgin Mary of this religion? Christina Grotton. Grotton! The same Grotton who grows all the pineapples in the world. She's like a good friend of mine now. Can you believe it? Just imagine when we got billionaire friends. They live in a bird sanctuary on top of the Big Wahine. With a hot-tub!"

Terry unbuttoned his shirt. For a crazy moment, Larry thought Terry was going to worship in the nude.

"Why are you stripping?" Larry asked.

"To take a shower, what do you think," Terry said. "Embarrassing to sit next to somebody on the plane, stinking like a longshoreman." He consulted his Rolex. "We got time."

Mister muscles, in his white underwear, stepped into the shower room.

Larry sat on the bench and shook that gold watch. He could swear the second hand had the hiccups. He heard the shower squeak on and the water murmur. He felt himself relax, maybe it was the sound of crashing waves. Or the lit candles below Koshu's heart. Or the beautiful fragrance. Or Koshu's two penetrating eyes above the words: *I see!*

Larry trembled for his brave brother. A man with less honor would have cut and run, maybe for Hong Kong or South America. But he'd never known Terry to run from a fight. It was Terry vs. Dad for house tough guy, and Terry eventually won. The old man, drunk again one night, was whipping Larry with the belt and Terry grabbed Dad by the neck and pushed him out of the house. And that was the last beating Larry ever got.

So in Larry's eyes, Terry was a hero.

And now Terry would fly back to Nevada to face bullies much tougher than Dad. These guys would bury him in the desert without even blinking. Larry didn't know exactly who Management was, which made it more scary. Sometimes Larry hated his brother, often he resented him, but he could not imagine wandering through this dangerous world without a big brother to call for guidance.

Terry stepped out of the shower, swathed in towels, hair dripping.

"I see," Terry said, reading the legend under Koshu's heart.

"His dying words," said Larry.

"Speaking of dying words," said Terry. "Maybe it's the refreshing shower, or maybe it's the perfume in here ..."

"Incense," said Larry. "Good to know for your crosswords."

"But it came to me like a lightning bolt in the shower. Larry, you been playing poker for fifteen minutes, and you don't know who the patsy is ..."

"Then you're the patsy."

"Correct," Terry said. He picked a comb out of his suit-jacket pocket, groomed his wet dark crew-cut. "So in the poker game we are playing, we're a pair of deuces."

He removed one towel and pointed to his chest. A gold cross dangled in his forest of chest hair.

"The lady cab driver is a cop," Terry said. "Or a spy for the Japanese mob, I can't figure. But one way or the other, she ain't wholesome."

He reached into his shirt pocket for cigarettes.

"No smoking in here," Larry warned.

"The voracious clown Mango at the bell desk," Terry said. "He's a spy for the cops. Maybe there's a reason we didn't hear from the cops after what happened in the bathroom."

Terry lit his cigarette. "How was I so slow to see it?" He tapped his head. "Stunod."

He took a long draw on his cigarette, exhaled noxious smoke, flicked ashes on the floor.

"See brother," Terry said, "we're being what you call hung out in the drier. Sneaky cops, spying hotel workers, Japanese mobsters, suspicious cabbies, there's more prevarications to this island than surf boards and sun tans."

"Who's setting us up?" Larry asked.

"Maybe my employer," he said. "The Management. Little brother, they're paying me chump change, compared to the high monetary value of what's at stake. I'm sorry I brought you under my wings, because we're bait fish is what we are. To employ another metaphor, it's like we're the scout jeep, sent in front of a convoy, in case of landmines. What do you call it? The sacrificial jeep."

He tossed the half-smoked cigarette into the shower room, where it hissed. "I'm mixing my metaphors but you get the underhanded message, right?" Terry unjumbled his silky red socks and drew them over his wet feet.

"Larry, they told me don't come back without a deal but they knew their offer was way too low. Now I go back, Management tells me I failed, they owe me ungotz. If I'm lucky they don't shoot me, just pay the veritable expenses. They brush me aside like a mouse with a broom, then make a deal with these tattooed mobsters."

He smelled his t-shirt, wrinkled his nose, tossed it into the shower room. He buttoned his fluffy white shirt over his he-man chest.

"Well, brother, this is it," Terry said. "I might never employ my return ticket. You don't hear from me in 24 hours, get on a plane, go to Alaska or Maine or anywhere, and stay low. Don't go to Florida, it's full of Jersey guys. Forget about me, save your own self. I've known I was doomed ever since I was drafted into the Army, with such a low number. Our old man was right all along. Remember he used to tell me, you'll end up a failure, Terry. You got that stink about you. So yeah, it's my pre-formed destination. All my life I been driving the sacrificial jeep. I'm doomed to hit a landmine sooner or later."

He worked into his trousers and cinched the belt hard. "We'll meet again in Hell, Larry."

"Purgatory at worst," said Larry. "We don't belong with Hitler and Judas."

"They out-clevered me, Larry. All Management wanted to know was, who they gotta deal with in the islands, how strong a hand they're playing, and they found out cheap at my expense. And now they can tell me I failed, they don't even have to pay me."

He picked up the Rolex, his face like a pall bearer at a family funeral. He handed the watch to Larry. "Something happens to me, sell this and get out of town."

He walked into the shower room, and finished dressing in front of the floor-length mirror.

Larry stepped out onto the lanai, stared at the restless ocean, turning that gold Rolex in one hand.

Terry was rattled and he was the brave one, so that spooked Larry even worse. He could see, on the horizon, the shadow clouds above Molokai. Maybe he and Pua could hide out in some Molokai grass shack until this casino deal went down. He tried to assure himself the Nevada bastards would let Terry go, but his gut twisted with the sick, awful feeling he might never see his big brother again.

If Terry was gone, no more family.

"Ready?" Terry said. He looked all dressed up, like an insurance salesman for Mobster Mutual.

"Come on, let's go," Terry said. "Ten million bucks just for a meeting. Can you imagine how this is going to play in Vegas. Like ah, what's my metaphor?"

"Lead balloon," suggested Larry.

"Like the gas-fired Hindenburg," said Terry.

When they pushed out the temple gate, Prudence was standing at the fender of her cab, looking over Terry's crossword book.

"I filled in some answers," Prudence said. "Only one clue left. *Type of stage play*. Ends in Y."

"Comedy," said Terry.

Prudence tapped the pencil on the book.

"One letter short," she said.

"Never mind the verbal challenges," Terry said. "Let's get to the airport."

The taxi doors slammed, and Prudence performed a U-turn in the dusty yard.

"What's your badge number?" Terry demanded.

"It's right there on the license," Prudence said.

"No, I mean your cop badge," Terry said.

"Whatever gave you that crazy idea?" Prudence asked.

"Tell your chief you dropped me at Royal Aloha Airlines, okay Officer Prudence? Then give the suffering taxpayers a break and take a day off. I'm leaving your fair islands, okay?"

Two souls

22

"We have two souls, as we have two eyes," Christina Grotton chanted. "The greedy soul. The wise soul. So Koshu taught us."

She was preaching an outdoor ceremony commemorating Koshu's death. Just a few believers, most in turquoise robes, stood on the lava cliffs, from where the holy surfer had been swept into the sea.

Christina said: "Even the sea has two natures, treacherous and beautiful."

Larry held Pua's hand. She, in a holy mood, wore a turquoise robe. She wiped a tear. Her lips quivered. This Larry understood, because Pua had known Koshu, back before he became a green statue.

Next to Larry stood Donna Lorris, cigarette heiress, in blue jeans and a dirty white shirt. She was coughing, hard, as if she was suffering from the disease her family had given the world. As the ceremony ended, with Chris Grotton dipping a Hawaiian torch into a tide pool, old lady Lorris tapped the pack of Big Tents in Larry's top pocket.

"Get rid of those," she said. "They're poison."

Larry was thrilled, because now he knew two heiresses. Pineapples and cigarettes. If he could meet a rum heiress, he'd cash the trifecta.

"Larry?" said Chris.

She beckoned him toward the pool house.

He tried to lead Pua along by the hand.

"Just you, Larry," said Chris.

Larry let Pua's hand go, but wasn't happy about it. There were too many handsome guys at this temple. California surfer dudes with bleached hair, they were taking off their robes now, showing a lot of muscle. He had the sneaking suspicion that one of these surfers wanted to steal Pua away from him.

In the pool house it was just Larry and Chris, all dark until she lit a fat candle. She sat behind a long desk. Rings of keys were nailed to the wall behind her. A pump was grinding away, making god-awful noise. The room smelled like a factory making dangerous chemicals. There were whole towns in Jersey that smelled just like that.

In the candlelight Chris unhooked the robe and revealed a crisp white shirt and short skirt. Wow, she had nice long legs, and Larry began to puzzle over why she'd never snagged a boyfriend. Maybe it was those bug eyes, and to tell the truth, she came across as a little stern.

She sat behind the desk. "Sit, Larry," she said, like he was a dog.

She pointed to a steel folding chair. It reminded Larry of the chair he had borrowed for Mom's laundry room, the one that said *Property of Holy Infant Parish* on the back.

Christina folded her hands, like she was a teacher about to explain the difference between a "D" and an "F."

"Pua has informed me," she said. "That you've asked for her hand in marriage."

"Yeah," said Larry. "Not just her hand, though, I want the rest of her too."

"Larry, no joking, this will be a very serious conversation."

"Okay, I don't suppose I could…"

"No smoking," she said.

Larry's legs began to jimmy-jump.

"Have you found work yet?" Christina asked.

"I'm working on my resume," said Larry.

Christina cleared her throat, glared at him with those bug eyes. That song played in Larry's head: *She's Got Bette Davis Eyes.*

"I need reassurance that you will be a good provider. Pua desperately wants children, and thanks to modern medicine she may be able to conceive. To be brutally frank, she doesn't need a sperm donor. She needs a husband."

Sperm donor? Something told Larry to shut up.

"What kinds of jobs have you held? Honestly now. Don't try to impress me."

"I worked in a pizzeria for a while," he said. There was no need to mention the fire. That wasn't his fault anyway, he'd been just fooling around with the stove.

"Then I was a room service waiter at the Atlantic Surf Hotel." The circumstances of his dismissal were none of her business, and besides the union had almost taken up his cause.

"And then my brother and I…"

"What does he do for a living?"

"Sells insurance."

Chris nodded.

"But best of all, we had a rent-a-car business."

"You owned the company?"

"No we had like a contract to like, rescue rental cars when they broke down or crashed or were abandoned."

"So you were a tow truck driver."

Larry cleared his throat. "No, we *hired* tow truck drivers.

"And what was the name of your business? I'll have my investigator check."

Investigator?

"T&L Stone Black Horse Auto Rescue," Larry said. "Incorporated. I think. Black Horse is like, the main road to Philly."

"All this is in Atlantic City?"

"Yes."

"You once told me you were from Philadelphia."

"Atlantic City is known as the Lungs of Philadelphia," Larry said. "How come you're asking all this?"

"I'm Pua's financial guardian."

"You mean like she's rich?"

"It's complicated. But the lawyers are going to get most of her dad's money."

"So this is about her dad's condo deal, right?"

"Larry," said Christina, "Pua is a lovely, big-hearted girl. She has been very seriously wounded. The wounds are emotional, not financial. She wants desperately to have a loving husband and eventually children. It's going to take a lot of love and gentle affection to bring her back to us whole. If you're not the man who can love and support her, I won't let you marry."

"Let?"

"She's too fragile right now to decide without advice."

Larry kicked the desk, ouch. He was becoming an Island boy, no shoes anymore, flip flops. And an outrageous tan. When he took a shower these days, and looked in the mirror, his ass glowed like a white neon hill on a dark field. Pua was like turning him into a native and he wasn't going to let this rich blondie step between them.

"Unbutton your shirt, please," she said.

"What's this, a strip show?"

"I'd like to see your tattoo."

"Jesus, lady," Larry said. But he unbuttoned his aloha shirt and exposed the Friendly Devil.

"Where did you get that?"

"On the Boardwalk."

"Not in the Navy as you'd claimed. What's its meaning?"

"I don't know. All the Boardwalk gang was getting tattoos, like to celebrate graduating high school."

"Gang?"

"Yeah you know, from Holy Infant. Not really a gang we just called ourselves a gang."

"And did you graduate?"

"Almost," said Larry. "I had to drop out of summer school to you know, help my mom."

"Were you ever incarcerated?"

He shook his head. "Not me."

Without knowing his true last name, she'd never find the records.

"We'll find out," said Christina. "Have you ever been accused of a sex crime?"

"Hell no. It's embarrassing you gotta ask."

"Would you consider converting to Koshu Kaza? That would be very important to Pua."

"Does she know what we're in here talking about?"

"Larry, I asked you a direct question. Would you convert?"

"What do I gotta do?"

"We send you in with a single candle, you meditate in the nude, for hours, maybe for days, until you experience a vision that purifies your heart."

"Is lunch included?"

"No."

"Meditate for days?"

"If that's what it takes."

"Alone?"

"Profoundly alone. Each of us is terribly alone, as your meditation would make clear to you."

It finally occurred to Larry that the only reason for this interview was that Pua had confided to Christina that she wished to marry him.

"This is what Pua wants, for me to convert?"

Christina nodded. "She is one of us, and she would love to have a husband who belonged. She's had her vision. That's why she gets to wear the seeing heart pendant and the turquoise robe. We'll have one for you too, as soon as you emerge. We live in a world flooded with love, Larry, if only we can learn to open up and accept it."

Larry looked at this bug-eyed rich chick and said to himself: Oh yeah? Well if it's such a world of love, why are you such a hard ass?

"I've got a number of business contacts," she said, "who potentially could provide work for you."

Work?

But Larry shut his mouth and did some figuring. Hey, this was the Pineapple Princess who owned like half the land in Hawaii. Wouldn't it be kind of stupid to piss her off? Let her find him some kind of job, he didn't have to keep it forever. Meditate? Sure, he could sit for an hour in the dark and then claim he'd heard the voice of their surfer god. *Surf's up, Dude!* Could he wear a turquoise robe one hour a week? Maybe for a couple of weeks. Hey, being Catholic was good training for a lot of things. If you could stay sober through a High Mass, you could take any form of torture.

"Fack," he said. "I'll give it a try."

Christina closed her eyes and sighed.

As much as he hated to do it, Larry had to leave the temple and rush back to the Tiki Torch. He didn't want Pua along because, well, it had been 24 hours since Terry had flown off and things might be getting dangerous.

He drove her Thing toward the city. He checked the Rolex that hung loose around his wrist. Damn it, the pineapple girl's interrogation had gone on too long. He was supposed to be in his room at 3, and he would have to speed to make it.

He weaved past tour buses, vans, cars full of surfers, all the while glancing at the rearview. He had to balance the need for speed with avoiding a cop stop. He had good fake ID, but if he got pulled over he'd never make the hotel in time.

He noticed a car behind him, just hanging back there but going as fast as he was. It was a hot rod GTO, dark blue, tinted windshield.

Larry pulled in at a gas station and watched the GTO fly by. He couldn't see the driver for that tinted glass. But his Little Fox told him that was a cop.

A cop who had no choice now, but to report a blown tail.

He nosed into the traffic and raced along, reaching the Tiki Torch at two minutes to three. He was sweating, and not just from the sun. Twenty four hours, Terry said, and if you don't hear from me, run. Well, it was twenty seven hours now.

Larry burst into his dark room. Silence. He cranked open the louvers to let in some light. Down there, dead ducks hung in the windows. He twirled the gold watch around his wrist. His brother trusting him with a Rolex, that was kind of a big deal. It gave Larry a sense of responsibility, like he was kind of a grown up in Terry's opinion now. Okay, five after three, no call, Larry didn't know what to make of things now, maybe run for it.

He climbed down the stairs and behind the front desk stood Carl, the curly headed Hawaiian guy who'd first told him about Captain Jules Dudoit. He was a friendly guy. A *mahu* as they said in the islands. But you know, not all of them were bad, and Carl had never tried any, like, queer stuff with Larry.

"Messages for me?" he asked Carl.

With all the street noise coming off Kalakaua, Carl put his hand to his ear.

"I'm waiting for a call from the Mainland," Larry said.

"I'm not a switchboard operator," said Carl.

He was busy sorting brochures. He ran a little side business from this office, selling time shares, although Larry had never seen him make a sale.

Larry glanced at the clock above the mail slots. Three fifteen.

Hey. He checked his Rolex. Seven after three.

Terry would have called at three exactly, that's the way he was.

This facking watch!

Larry slipped it off his wrist and shook it. Facking Boardwalk Rolex, he shoulda known.

He hustled up to his room, flung the door open in case Terry somehow called late. But he couldn't stay still, he ran back down the stairs, pacing the hot sticky sidewalk in front of the Tiki Torch. It was so bright, he couldn't tell if the torches were lit. It was so hot the welfare loafers had abandoned the steel chairs, even the ones in the shade.

Larry paced nervous outside the big window of the Chinese butcher. He watched a man in bloody apron cut up a cooked duck. Hung all around that butcher were dead ducks and chickens.

The Chinese butcher swinging the cleaver reminded him of the mistake he'd made in his previous life as a sea captain, shortchanging a Chinese cook. He wondered if Jules Dudoit was stabbed, or hacked up with a cleaver? Slam slam slam the butcher cut the duck meat into strips.

If not for Pua, he'd take the next flight for parts unknown.

Come on Terry, call, don't be such a blockhead. Call me. A couple of minutes late, what's the difference? Why you gotta be uptight all the time?

Larry couldn't think any but black thoughts. Terry in deep trouble, and that meant Larry was next.

He wandered to the front desk. Carl was watching a *Danger, Hawaii* rerun on TV, loud with gunshots and squealing tires. Every TV gunshot made Larry flinch. He backed out of the doorway and studied the posters put up by the travel agency next door.

A cardboard cutout showed the jumping kangaroos of Australia. Would Pua live in kangaroo land? They spoke English, right?

He shouted into the office: "Carl!"

Carl was like hypnotized by the TV.

Larry walked in and slapped the counter.

"Carl!"

Carl seemed like he'd just woke up from a dream.

"Do you need a passport to go to Australia?"

"Certainly," Carl said.

"They don't let guys in just to look around?"

"Don't be ridiculous," Carl said.

"And like you get a passport from the federal government, right? Nobody else sells them?"

"You think they sell passports two for a dollar at the K-Mart?"

"Come on, Carl, help me."

"Next door they can take your passport picture."

"But still I got to talk to the government, right?"

"You've got something against the government?"

No. But the government had something against Larry. It had been months since he'd stopped in to see his P.O. Australia, hell. He wasn't supposed to leave Atlantic County without permission.

"Where can I go without a passport?"

"Alaska?" Carl said.

"Too cold," said Larry.

"American Samoa?"

"Huh," said Larry. "I never heard of such a place."

"Or maybe Guam. Don't bring your girl, though. They have way too many Marines on that island. You know what Guam stands for? Give Up And Masturbate."

Larry wasn't taking Pua to no island full of masturbating Marines.

Then he glanced out the window and saw the big address painted on the hotel: 999 Dudoit Lane. Dudoit! That reminded Larry: he was meant to be here. Fate! He was not going to run away.

Koshu Kaza. What did that mean? Welcome fate. Welcome your fate. Something like that. Maybe he was destined to be a chanting, robe wearing Kazan after all.

He took his wallet out of his back pocket and said to Carl: "Let me pay for another week. Can I stay in the same room?"

Carl nodded.

"How do you say in Hawaiian, thanks a lot?" Larry asked.

"Mahalo nui loa," said Carl.

"Same to you," said Larry.

The
Morgue

23

Terry stood on a bridge over the Ala Wai Canal, staring into the water. The dirty water seemed like a thousand little waves, each shining with a threatening point of light. Terry felt like he was back in the Delta.

Mekong River, Ala Wai Canal, same nasty undercutting feeling, like you were nothing, a waterlogged coconut drifting out to sea, a leaf blown into the dirty water by the great winds, twisting blowing, a nothing to be drowned, to be crushed, to be forgotten. Everything he saw seemed to be framed in darkness. Like at a museum, a picture of war, famine, mayhem, surrounded in black, black frame.

Terry was fighting the feeling he was cracking up. He was trying to stare at the water until he calmed himself, the sight of dirty water shouldn't make a tough guy feel so sick. He stood there staring, made himself take it.

It was a personal weakness. You're looking at water flowing out to sea, he told himself, that's all it is.

A flying fish leaped, and then another, slivery splashes. Terry had always figured flying fish were bullshit, creatures of the fairy tale books. Like unicorns. But here they were, in this canal that went right alongside the road, silvery fish leaping, more and more of them as the evening headed toward the interminable sundown.

Couple more drinks, he told himself, and I'll be fine. He walked to the yacht harbor, past a lagoon, and over a sandbar. The Fat Lady, the one Larry called a witch, was blowing the conch just as the sun set. The sun looked like it was dropping into the ocean. You almost expected to hear it hiss. This was what you called an illumination. No, illusion, that was the word.

Terry glanced at the so-called witch, who in pure judgmental terms was just a tired old babe dressed in red. Witch? Larry would buy any kind of fairy tale bullshit. This conch blower had no witchy powers but was just a fat grandma with a two-bit job at a tourism hotel. She hadn't saved enough to retire, that was all.

He entered under the fake-grass-roof of the Mynah Bird. It was just starting to get busy, with the tourists coming off the beach after hosing down their sunburns in the outdoor showers.

This bartender, even tourists knew him, a local legend named One-Lung Pete. He'd played himself on *Danger, Hawaii.*

You'd think he was John Wayne the way people gushed over him. One Lung Pete was just a pale chubby bald guy with a white walrus mustache who wore khaki pants and a paisley aloha shirt. As a bartender, he wasn't exactly of the exemplary nature, being gabby, wheezy and slow on the draw.

Terry sat at the corner of the rectangular bar, whipped out his pack of Big Tents and his First Cav lighter. It was his lucky charm since when he'd been fished out of the Mekong, it was still in his pocket when they got him to the hospital and had worked the first time he flicked it.

"Vodka martini rocks, double olive," he told One Lung Pete.

Drink gin and you stink of it, Terry felt. Vodka, and you could be a sanitized drunk.

He turned his back to the ocean, watching some stunod college basketball game on TV. Who could even watch that embarrassing exposition? If the players didn't fix the game, the referees would do it. It only added to his condemnatory feelings toward colleges. They granted doctor degrees but they couldn't even run an honest playground game? Vegas Management, too, held the game in high contempt, or was that low contempt? All basketball was good for, was fleecing the rube bettors.

His back turned to the ocean and that sick feeling began to slip away. He recovered himself: Terry Estonophie. High school grad, war hero veteran, entrepreneur, negotiator.

Pete pushed an icy drink at him. He tapped the box of cigarettes with a crusty forefinger.

"These are killers," he said. He lifted his head to nod, like he was indicating someone else at the bar. "That bitch cost me a lung. That's all I'm gonna say."

Terry turned shoulder to look. His eye first caught the big handsome Bix Sanders, in aloha shirt, surrounded by four guys. Mainland guys maybe. They were at a table that was messy with drinks, and Bix was sitting back, like a sailor telling sea adventures to a table full of landlubbers. The guys around him were laughing, and then Terry realized one of them wasn't a guy. The only feminine participant at the table had gray locks and was in her 60s, and was dressed like she'd slept in her clothes.

"Donna Lorris," said One Lung Pete. "Tobacco bitch extraordinaire. She's giving money to politicians? She ought to be donating it to hospitals, for all the misery she's caused. I'll say no more."

Pete slipped Terry's pack of Big Tents off the bar and threw it in the trash.

"Do yourself a favor," he said.

Wow, this guy was bitter. Pete was known for this trick. He was like the P. T. Barnabus of showmanship. He'd trash your cigs, but give them back if you insisted. But Terry didn't ask for his cigarettes back. He didn't want to end up huffing like One Lung Pete. Maybe this was the time of life for what you call discretion in the realm of tobacco.

Terry moved to the opposite corner so he could watch the Bix Sanders table. He'd have thought maybe Bix and One Lung Pete would be great friends, having appeared on TV together. Pete's TV role was to feed the detective Waikiki gossip that helped solve crimes. But in real life, Pete seemed red-faced angry at both Bix and the tobacco lady.

Interesting. Terry watched, running the whirling calculator of his cranial mind. Bix had some kind of sneaky doings with Management in Vegas. The Management's whole plan revolved around Bix becoming mayor. So who were all these suits surrounding Bix? And how did the tobacco heiress figure in?

There was so much Terry didn't know. But he couldn't learn too much just by watching the table. He ordered another martini and as darkness rolled over Waikiki, the sounds of Teddy Hong Kong's warmup band leaked over from the Ted Shed.

Teddy Hong Kong was in it too, Terry knew that, but only vaguely. Together, the Management, Bix and Teddy were what you could call the Holy Trinity, the team that would bring in the first casino. They already had a hotel picked out, but which one exactly, that was secretive in nature. Beyond that, Terry could only guesstimate. Watching Bix, Donna Lorris and their ass-kissing minions gave Terry the feeling of being the lowly outsider. Sure he wore nice threads but look at him, within earshot were two guys, Bix and Teddy, who could make millions on this deal and had nobody threatening to put a bullet in their heads. How did you get to that level? Terry couldn't understand it. He had given value for every job, honor and loyalty, and his reward was barely enough cash to buy a Cadillac.

It was like that song in the Army that mocked lifers for re-enlisting.

> Re-up and buy a brand new car
> Re-up, show what a fool you are
> Re-up? I'd rather throw up
> Than be a lifer, a loser, a dud.

Yes, he realized why that song was playing in his proverbial ear. In re-enlisting, the Army lifer throws his life away in return for enough cash to buy a car. Was Terry any different, really?

He drained his martini. As more tourists filtered in, he felt another wave of crazy feeling, but of what you call the opposition nature. He suddenly felt like he was the wise guy insider and these sunburned tourists around him were hopeless rubes, unaware of what game was being played. No different here, it was just like in AC, the whole game was to separate the rubes from their money.

But then Terry began to wonder maybe he was just a better-dressed rube. He was thinking that, take for example Vietnam, everybody knew the name of President LBJ, but it was the unanimous guys who actually fought the war. They came back dead and their name was printed heroic in the hometown paper. After that, forget about them, LBJ kept the war profits going.

So when the casinos came in to Hawaii it would be like LBJ saying, the war is over and we won. And so, victorious, would President LBJ be hanging out with any Vietnam Veterans? No. He would be playing baccarat with Robert Redford and Frank Sinatra in a private room at the Boardwalk Resort, while the wounded veterans were fighting off the nightmares with two Buds for a buck down at the Legion.

"One Lung Pete," Terry said, feeling woozy drunk, "How long you been working here?"

Pete huffed, coughed, wiped sweat off his brow with a red bandana.

"You need another?" said Pete.

Terry pushed his martini glass. "I need a double. The tourists are crowding me."

Pete turned to grab for the vodka and said: "The tourists are just scenery in here. This is a politics bar." He inclined his head toward the Bix table. "I'm waiting for the day Bix and Sam Wing come in for a drink at the same time. It won't be long. Politics in this town is a *shibai.*"

"A what did you say?"

"*Shibai.* I'll say no more."

He paused.

"It's a Japanese word," Pete said. "It's a form of puppet play. What you see on stage is only paint and wood and cloth. All the meaningful action takes place backstage."

Shee-buy. Terry was going to remember that word, and not just in case it came up in a puzzle. Shee-buy. Right! The real movers and shakers watched from the shadows, moving their puppets.

The tourists were beginning to notice Bix, some of them gawking. One drunken fool lurched over begging for an autograph, only to be repelled by men in suits. Terry looked at the barely melted ice in his double martini and realized how fast he was drinking, how drunk he was, and pushed himself away from the bar.

It was true what they said, night was an instant happenstance in the tropical zones. And the breeze was warm, no matter how dark it got. A guy could get to appreciate this little island, he could almost see Larry's point.

Larry, the fuckin coward, wherever he was hiding. Had he been in his room lately? No. Had Carl the Skirt seen him lately? Of course not. The two of them, maybe, hanky panky? Larry was no swish but then again, he'd been in Rahway, where you know, half the men were women, in the so-called balance of nature. And you just never knew, with the little brother.

Terry walked Pirate's Path past all the hucksters selling tourist trinkets, past the great white Ted Shed, and out to the taxi stand at the Ilikai hotel. He made sure before he got into a cab that it was driven by a man.

A bald Chinese type guy. Terry settled into the back seat and said: "You know a driver named Prudence, great big girl?"

"Who?"

"Never mind," said Terry. "I wish to be conveyed to the Honolulu Record building."

He sat back. The driver lurched block by clogged block out of Waikiki past the big shopping center and the dark ocean and the swaying coconut palms.

The driver let him off at the glowing glassy front doors of the Record Building but they were locked tight. Terry walked around the side, down an alley, past a parking lot, where a bunch of guys in ink-stained uniforms were smoking cigarettes around a dark steel stairway. He saluted them. They were his kind of guys. Not pretentious, you could say, just Joe Regularity. He climbed the steel stairs and nobody tried to stop him. To the pressmen, he figured, he probably looked like just another executive suit, but they should think twice, because you don't judge a book by its cover price.

He opened the steel door and entered the first newsroom he'd ever seen. It was not busy and frantic like Hollywood always told. It was quiet and kind of dark. Nobody seemed to notice him. There were a few bored-looking people gathered around a horseshoe-shaped desk. Nobody was shouting out the news, nothing like that. Little computers and clunky typewriters were parked at messy desks, but nobody worked at them. Over in the corner, in a dark tiny office, he glimpsed Lazarus McCabe.

The door to McCabe's office was glass and said MORGUE in golden letters.

That seemed odd since Terry was sure they didn't store mortuized bodies at the newspaper. He pushed into McCabe's office and said: "So, the practical son returns."

The green glow of a computer screen made McCabe's face look sick, like he was a victim in a horror movie. Terry glanced around, what do you know, a lot of big computers, the size of refrigerators, he had seen such things in counting rooms at Vegas.

"So I have come to you…" Terry said and shut the door. … "with the finality of an offer."

He sat across from McCabe, kicked back, put his polished shoes up on McCabe's desk.

"McCabe, you said on previous occasions that you're in charge of the death stories in this great metropolitan newspaper."

McCabe flicked off his computer. Paper coffee cups and crumpled balls of waxy paper littered his desk. No wonder McCabe was jumpy, living vicariously through donuts and coffee.

"Would you have Councilman Samuel Wing's obit handy?" Terry asked.

McCabe looked around like he was hoping somebody would dash in and rescue him. Then he admitted it. "I think we might have it somewhere if I looked real hard."

"Look real hard then," Terry said. "Think of me like a landmine on a two-minute fuse."

McCabe stumbled into a long row of dark green filing cabinets. He picked up two sheets of paper from the top of those cabinets.

"How about that," he said. "Just happen to have it right here."

"Then we publicize it in tomorrow's paper."

"I don't get it."

"It is a maneuver of seldom seen genius," Terry said, and sat back, studying McCabe, enjoying the look of panic on his college-educated face. No amount of book learning can overcome what you call animalistic fear.

"Terry, we can't publish an obit for a man who's alive."

"Would it be precedented in the annuals of newspaper publishing? Maybe it would. However, our purposeful nature will overcompensate for any perceived embarrassment. You could say a mistake was made in all innocent intent. Apologies to the bemused family."

"What would be the purpose, Terry? I don't get it."

"You see, McCabe, it has recently come to my attention that my Management wishes to speak with Mister Wing personally, and without his what you call strategy agents. No lawyers, no cops, no body guards, they want Sam and they want to meet with him end of the week, latest. They want to emphasize that their original offer is not a mere…

He looked toward the door…

"Not a mere lucky spin of the wheel of fortune, but a lifetime of what you call glorious occupation, as an associate attorney for a cash-wealthy corporation, generous in its lifetime benefits. Now how can I get Sam's attention and convey to him the seriousness and edification of our offer? Maybe there's nothing like reading of your own demise in your hometown paper."

"I can't do it."

"Yet you are in charge of obituaries, as you conveyed to me."

"Terry," McCabe whispered, "you have no idea how this would blow up if we ran Sam's obit. The TV stations would go ballistic. The cops would be swarming us."

Terry said: "Put yourself in my place, McCabe. They have cops watching me from the taxi cabs. Can I arrange to meet Sam, either legitimate or accidentally on purpose? No, impossible, since he and his daughter both have private body guards plus the police."

"Terry, Sam's not going to get on a plane and go to Vegas."

"He only needs to go to the Honolulu Zoo. We'll take it from there."

"The Zoo?"

"I have been to Vegas and returned with instructions direct from Management. Honolulu Zoo."

"What about me? If I run his obit, I'll be fired, I'll be arrested, I'll be sued into the poorhouse."

"Innocent mistake. What you call computational error. Oops, you just pushed the wrong button. And when your unemployment check runs out, Waikiki's first original casino would be very sympathetic to your welcome applications for grateful employment."

"You're drunk, Terry."

"So it would appear, however, I urge precautions, because men in a liquidated state can abominate careless acts."

He realized he was slouching, sat up straight in his seat, good posture, as Sister Helen had always complemented.

"You see McCabe I am on the what you call verge of failure poised over the knife edge of success. The Management can crush us both, for them it's like stepping on a cockroach. We're in the same boat, old friends that we are, like back at Holy Infant, when we sneaked into the hedges so's we could smoke between Latin and Algebra class, remember? I bummed a lot of cigarettes in those days, so I probably owe you."

"Speaking of owe, that reminds me of a loan you made me." McCabe used a tiny key to unlock and open his desk drawer. He deposited on his desk the thick wallet Terry had given him, but wrapped in a plastic bag.

"It's all there," he told Terry. "I didn't even count it. Thanks for the loan, but as it turns out, I didn't need it."

So, Terry noted with approval, McCabe was acting more man-like, now that his nurse girlfriend was in hiding. This confirmed that you got results by indimidating women. Meanwhile McCabe rose one step on Terry's Stairway of Respect because of this newfounded courage.

"Cash aside," said Terry. "We got a promissory deal. No broken vowels can come between us."

He reached inside his jacket and drew his Army Buddy from its shoulder holster. He was not the crude type who would point it at McCabe. He simply set it on the desk, not even caring if McCabe made a grab for it.

Although McCabe's office was all dull light, Terry's Army buddy gleamed silver beside the puke-green typewriter on McCabe's desk.

"Can you imagine what is going through my mind, McCabe? I would put this gun to my own head, rather than go back to Vegas yet again a failure. I could blow my brains out right here, and you would be covered in guilty blood and synonymous brain cells. You would have a horrific amount of explaining to do. Plus, the death certificate of a school chum on your conscience."

He drew from his jacket pocket his gold First Cav lighter and flicked it, held it up like a torch.

"Or I could take you with me to the eternal flame, McCabe. It would make no difference to me and spare you from explaining a deceased and highly decorated veteran in your office."

He flicked the lighter shut.

"Could you see us two veterans, side by side among the honored heroes at the Punchbowl? I envision your little nurse, upon your demise, she will be crying the tears of a crocodile, if you get my meaning. Although, when you engage the long term thinking, she's such a cutie she will ensnare some doctor boyfriend soon after your tragedy. They could experience a life of marital bliss together, and on solemn occasions she will remember you with wishful tears. Maybe she would name one of her many children after you. So tell me, McCabe, do you have your own obituary pre-written?"

McCabe's face was quivering. Terry was winning.

"Now what will it be, McCabe? Cooperate with Management? Or eternal death for the both of us?"

McCabe arose from his desk, pulled the shade down over his glassy door, and turned to face Terry.

"I've got a better idea."

"Shoot."

"Sam is a Sheep. Suppose we send him a message in a horoscope. I'll write it up right now."

He strode to his desk, stood over a typewriter that said IBM on its back edge. He spoke as he typed.

"Year of The Sheep. You will be offered a ... business proposition today. A meeting where all the animals of the Zodiac converge. You should accept. Your entire future ... depends on it. A stranger will come into your life, bringing good fortune but beware. It could be a matter ... of life and death. A dangerous wind blows all the way from the Mainland."

He finished typing and glanced nervous at Terry.

"He's going to read this horoscope for certain?" Terry asked.

"Uncle Sam is the one who jawboned our editor into running the Chinese Zodiac. He hectored her for years, at every cocktail party. He's obsessed with these horoscopes, Terry."

Terry slipped his Army Buddy back into its shoulder rig, walked around the desk and slapped McCabe on the back.

"McCabe, you are a verifiable Ernest Hemingway. I have never seen a man of such composing talents since I read about Dick and Jane. So Uncle Sam reads this tomorrow, right?"

"Tomorrow's pages are already printed. We're the B section, Terry. We prepare one day ahead. I mean, Ann Landers and Snoopy aren't breaking news."

"When does it publish then?"

"Day after tomorrow."

"We're grabbing at straws but it's better than ..."

That metaphor sent Terry back into the Mekong, clinging to a soaked straw bale, helicopters flying overhead, two men in a sampan closing in on him, Terry figuring them for VC who would shoot a hole in his drowning head. Instead, they poked his chest with the long pole of salvation.

It was a bitter thought, sometimes, to owe your life to pajama-wearing Commies.

"How about," Terry said, "adding some words. Like: Pay no attention to greedy advisers. Put your own interests first, and as always, keep the family safe."

"Won't fit. It's gotta fit in the little box. Okay, so Sam reads the horoscope, and hopefully …"

"He will be spooked that we have supernatural abilities, and then there is a certain party, very well known in the islands, and trusted, who will go with Sam for a little outing at the Zoo and avail to him all the spectacular awaiting future."

"So you'll call Sam …"

"No no no. The emerging party will call Sam. The what do you call, the celebrity calls."

He saw doubt on McCabe's face.

"It doesn't matter to me McCabe, I died already, and let me tell you it is terrifying, this death event, but then calm at the end. Remember, while you were typing battalion news and sipping from coconuts, I was attempting a heroic swim of the Mekong in order to rescue my men from uncertain death. And this I accomplished, at nearly the cause of my own drowning demise. I have come so close to eternity in the muddy waters of death that I feel I am living on what you call, the extended vacation of life, if you get my meaning."

"I'm running this horoscope in Wednesday's paper, and then you and I are done, Terry."

"You should be delightful, McCabe. We are embarked here on a mission of honor."

"How do you figure honor?"

"You yourself informed me the Island is awash in illegal gambling. All we're doing is introducing legal gambling to your beautiful islands. Above the boards, paying governmental taxes, neon lights winking to everybody, come on in for a friendly game. Legal. Honorable, everybody knows the odds. That's how I figure. Uncle Sam Wing goes to the Zoo, thinking he's meeting a celebrity guy who would offer donator money to boost his mayorhood campaign. He will trust because the celebrity is so well known. Then Sam will experience what you call a twisting variety on the story."

"I think I understand."

Terry gave him a friendly punch on the shoulder. "You're an Army veteran," he said. "All of us, brazen that we are, we should wear medallions of honor."

Captain Apple Seed

24

The rooster scurried out of the jungle and flew at the Thing's fender. Larry swerved. Pua, belted in next to him, shouted: "Slow down!"

Larry braked the Thing in a grassy clearing. The vehicle had raised a red dust cloud, and he began choking on it. Pua held a kerchief to her face. Cautious chickens clucked and peered out of their jungle hideouts.

McCabe sat on the porch, playing chess with an old hippie guy with a gray ponytail. Larry didn't know the old guy, but the Little Fox whispered: pot farmer.

Trust your Little Fox, Mom often said.

He hopped out of the Thing and slammed the door. It made a cheap hollow sound, being about as solid as a soup can.

"Hey, Lazz," Larry said, approaching the porch. "How ya doin?"

McCabe looked panicked. He said something to the old hippie and strode down the rickety porch stairs. They met in the shade of one of those monster trees, banyan, that's what they were called, Larry was learning all about Hawaii now. Or was it re-learning, since he'd lived here in a previous century?

He shook hands with McCabe. It was a sweaty grip on both ends.

Larry lifted a nod toward Pua, who sat pouting in the Thing. "I'm looking for a place to like hang out. With my girl."

"How did you find me here?" said McCabe.

"Oh we knew all along, we followed you twice. Don't worry McCabe, you're like off the hook. You've got to learn to look in the rearview mirror, man. But hey, Terry's back in Vegas, getting it all under control. Relax. It'll all be calm in a couple of days. Look, you could put a guy up for a night or two, right?" He leaned in, confidential, like McCabe was his best friend. "We're getting married. The two of us. ASAP."

He slapped McCabe on the back. "Can you believe it?" He lowered his voice to a whisper. "Keep the money Terry gave you. All is forgiven."

"This isn't my place, you know," McCabe said. "I'm staying here courtesy of a friend."

"Hey, we'll camp in the barn, in a tent," Larry said. "Anything. We won't be any trouble."

McCabe, suspicious bastard, glared.

Larry figured that McCabe, a college graduate, had probably doped out the basics. All Larry could do was put a friendly bullshit twist on the story.

"Our mission is accomplished," Larry said. "Terry he's on the Mainland like cleaning up the details. In the meantime, I met this" … he lowered his voice … "really gorgeous wahine. And guess what? She likes me. Ha ha. Can you believe it? So you know, we're kind of layin' low because her father, he ain't that happy about our sudden romance, and he's looking to kick my ass. So. McCabe. Do a homie a favor, okay?"

"Larry, this…"

"Pua honey," Larry shouted, "come meet my homey."

Pua was dressed modest, in red muumuu. This was one of the things Larry liked about her, she wasn't into showing her T&A to just anyone. Modesty, looks and a high school diploma, this girl, marrying her was like getting dealt an ace and a king at blackjack.

"Honey, this is Lazarus McCabe. Maybe you've seen his name in the newspaper. And this beautiful woman is Pualani Long."

Pua acted shy and then a bad revelation came upon Larry: Ah! McCabe was a reporter. There'd been a big fuss about Pua's dad a few years back, it probably made the evening news. Oh, Jeez, Larry had slipped up. Stunod! Of course, McCabe would know Pua's dad was in prison.

"McCabe," Larry told Pua, "says we're welcome to stay as long as we like. It's such a big house. Looks like there's plenty of room here."

"Well," said McCabe, and shuffled his bare feet in the dust. "I've got to talk to the property owner."

"Why don't you do that?" said Larry.

McCabe mounted the porch and Larry saw, out of the corner of his eye, that the big red rooster was watching them. Jerking his head. Watching. Scratching the ground.

"I don't know who this old guy is," Larry said, "but he's got himself a nice patch of jungle."

"Are you kidding?" Pua whispered. "That old guy is Bobbo Burns."

"Who?"

"Everybody reads his column. I grew up reading *Surrounded By Water*. Seven days a week. I remember he had a slogan back when. Twenty column-inches of the worst gossip in town."

She blushed. "Dad's name was in bold face a lot."

"So this old guy's a famous newspaper columnist?"

"And poet! With a very cranky reputation."

"But he's gotta be growing dope out here."

Pua shrugged. "Probably."

"You ever tried pot?"

"Yes and it made me want to hide under the bed."

He kissed her. "You don't care if I take a hit now and then, do you?"

McCabe beckoned them to the porch.

"Bobbo Burns," McCabe said as they mounted the stairs. "Meet Pualani Long and Larry Estonophie."

"Larry what?" Pua said, her hand flying to her chest.

"It's my former name. Before I shortened it."

Larry leaned in toward Bobbo and offered his hand. "To Stone. I go by Larry Stone now."

Bobbo, cigarette in lips, glared at him. "Businessmen shake hands," Bobbo said. "It's an unsanitary habit, and reeks of insincerity."

"Right," said Larry, and dropped his hand. "I wasn't thinking."

The old guy was ragged. Had he washed his hippie hairdo this week? Maybe. But Larry smelled that perfume, the one that clings to you after a happy smoke.

"I didn't mean to interrupt," said Larry.

He looked down at the picnic table at student papers, like the ones he was supposed to write at Holy Infant. These papers were marked up in angry red, thick writing almost like lipstick. The top one said D-minus. At the bottom of that paper was a gray stain the exact diameter of Bobbo's cocktail glass.

"So you're a professor?" Larry said.

"In a moment of weakness," Bobbo said, "I contracted with a fraudulent institution that claims to be educational in nature."

Larry wasn't quite sure what Bobbo had said, and felt the need to fill in. Fraudulent, he got that part, but... "Yeah, I remember doing them papers back in school. You know like, figure out the meaning of a *Tale of Two Cities*. Did you ever read that book?"

"Dickens was a long-winded son of a bitch. Although his empathetic portrayal of the underclass was progressive, given the reactionary temper of the Victorian Era."

"Right," Larry said. "That's exactly what I wrote in my paper. And like I told Sister Helen back then, why ask me about the meaning? If this Dickens guy meant something, why not just come out and say it? You know. It sucks to be poor, so rich guys should give away turkeys at Christmas."

Bobbo looked at McCabe like they were keeping a secret from Larry.

"There's room upstairs," Bobbo said. "Bring your bags around back. You'll see a separate stairway going up.

There's no air conditioning, I won't have it, air conditioning has destroyed the last shred of honor clinging to this overpopulated rock. There's no television either, for reasons that should be obvious. We don't serve dinner, but you're welcome to assault my refrigerator at all hours. Although I warn you, anything you put in there that contains cholesterol, my daughter will throw out. My chickens lay two dozen eggs a day, but it's been years since I've enjoyed an omelet."

He put his hands in the pockets of his ripped Army trousers like he was feeling for something.

"I've got to finish grading while I'm still drunk," he said. "Never grade sober. Cardinal rule of academia."

By the time Larry and Pua climbed to the hot rooms above the kitchen, they were both covered in sweat. Pua looked especially overheated in her muumuu as she blew stray hairs from her puffy face. Larry opened the windows, and each one took all his strength to move. Pua used her red kerchief to dust a Formica-topped table that was pretty much like the one in Mom's kitchen long ago, only a lot dirtier.

Pua ran water in the stained porcelain sink, it came out rusty. For appliances, all the room had was an old chrome toaster. No fridge, but Larry figured he could put beer on ice.

"How long do we have to stay here?" asked Pua.

"Oh honey," he said, and put his arm around her. "Just until the wedding."

She shrugged his arm off. "I'm hot."

She wandered into the dark hallway and opened the door to the bedroom.

"I have to sleep on that?" she said.

Larry looked over her shoulder. A mattress lay on the floor, no sheets or anything, along with two nasty looking striped feather pillows.

"I'll get sheets. I'll go to town and buy us new ones."

"Larry, a mattress on the floor?"

Oh he forgot. She was royalty, back in 1800-something, so what could you expect?

"Try it for one night," he said. "If you don't like it..."

She pushed open the bathroom door and said: "Yuk."

"Princess," Larry said. "I'll get down on my knees and scrub the toilet, if that's what you need."

"Why do we have to hide in the jungle, Larry? I don't understand."

"It's just temporary," said Larry. "Trust me. It's best not to be seen around town until we're married. You know. Superstition."

"I never heard that."

"It's a Jersey thing," Larry said. "Lay low while you're living in sin."

She huffed. "Sin? There are no sinners and no saints, you'd learn that if you meditated on Koshu."

She shut herself pouting in the bathroom and Larry wandered to the kitchen. He had to admit, even the Tiki Torch Hotel might be better than this dump. But he couldn't risk being seen around Honolulu and he couldn't stop worrying about what the hell had happened to Terry. A postcard had arrived at the Tiki Torch this morning, postmarked Las Vegas.

It said in Terry's scrawl: *Lay low, another postcard in three days.*

He'd been hoping it would say: Mom Sends Her Love. That was the code he and Terry had arranged. Mom's Love would mean that everything was all right.

Larry couldn't help but worry. The Rolex around his wrist was a constant reminder. What was Terry up to? Desperation, that he knew, but what exactly? It must be real dangerous if he wanted to go it alone, like the war hero he was.

Larry wandered to the window and looked out at the jungle.

This Bobbo dude was Johnny Appleseeding that jungle, Larry knew it. Just a plant here and there, nothing the Feds could swoop down on, no big field of green to show up in their binoculars or scopes or whatever they used to spot marijuana.

Larry was hoping for a hit of good dope that would relieve this feeling of worrisome doom. His gut felt like he'd swallowed a cactus plant and it was working its way through him. He made the Sign of the Cross over himself and prayed for his brother. Ten Hail Marys and a Glory Be. He prayed to two saints he was sure had gone to Heaven: Mom and Sister Helen.

He looked up at the kitchen wall just above the window and there was this tiny green dragon clinging to the wall. Good Christ! That's all he needed, Pua to come out of the bathroom and see dragons on the wall. He removed one flip flop and moved the kitchen chair across the floor so he could swat this slimy disgusting green creature.

He had just, wobbly, mounted the chair and was raising his killer flip-flop when Pua appeared in the doorway.

"What are doing?"

"I'm killing this lizard for you."

"Are you *pupule*? That's a gecko. It's good luck to have a gecko in the house. They eat bugs. It's a year of bad luck if you kill a gecko."

Larry stepped off the chair. He felt a little embarrassed. There were so many things about Hawaii he didn't remember from his previous life.

"*Pupule*," Larry said. "I've heard that word somewhere."

"It means crazy."

A yellow Volkswagen Beetle rolled to a stop in the yard and Pua stared out the window at it. Two local gals got out of it. One was dressed in overalls and another wore blue-jeans with a nurse's green scrub top.

"I know that nurse," Pua said. "Reiko. I've seen her at the temple. Larry, I'm going down there, you don't mind, do you, if I make girl talk with them for a while?"

Hell no, he didn't mind, but he was determined to stay out of sight. That nurse would recognize him right off, a horrible danger.

"Go," Larry said. "But our romance, you know, the wedding plans, all gotta be held secret, right?"

Pua blew a kiss at him on her way down the rickety stairs. He watched the three women talking in the yard. The strong-looking babe in the overalls led them to the wide open doors of the barn, and into the darkness.

He glanced up at the gecko, who now was clinging to the ceiling. Hanging upside down was a pretty good circus trick, Larry figured, and maybe he could get used to disgusting lizards in the house someday. Although it might be hard to sleep at night, knowing lizards were out there in the dark, tongues flickering.

Larry wanted to give that lizard a Jersey Swat. But you're not in Jersey anymore, he reminded himself. He chirped at the gecko and said: "Eat a lot of bugs, you lucky bastard."

With a glance over his shoulder at where the ladies had disappeared, Larry rounded the corner of the house. Where the hell McCabe went he couldn't figure. But the old hippie Bobbo was packing a leather briefcase with term papers. As Larry climbed the porch steps, Bobbo poured rum and Grotton Pineapple Juice into a coffee cup.

"Make your own," Bobbo said. "If you add orange juice, it's a Captain's Paradise."

"What's a Captain's Paradise?"

"The drink," said Bobbo. "Drink all you want, but replace the bottle if you finish it and wash your own glasses."

"Thank you," said Larry and began mixing a drink. "This is like the most courteous thing that happened all day."

He raised a glass of Captain's Paradise to Bobbo and said, "But you know I'm not really an alcohol man."

"No?"

Larry mimed, thumb and forefinger, putting a joint to his lips.

"Just where are you from?"

"Miami," said Larry. "Florida. You know, near the Gulf."

Bobbo looked like he didn't believe him.

Sometimes, when you talked, you couldn't hide your Jerseyness. "But before that," he said, "I lived in

Jersey, the nice part, like Cape May, down with all the classy people."

"Is that so? Navy man myself. San Diego, Subic Bay, Yokohama, Norfolk. The only parts of the world worth living in are those blessed with salt water." He drank the dregs of his cocktail. "Too many so-called Christians in Norfolk, though."

Larry sipped easy at his Captain's Paradise. Pua was already annoyed with him, no need to get drunk and make it worse.

He asked Bobbo: "You know where a guy could buy a little good weed?"

"How little?"

"Like a gram? Just for now?"

"I might know someone who has a little more than he can use."

"If I were you and I had this nice property..."

Bobbo jerked his drink.

"I'm not looking to rip you off or anything," Larry said. "That's not me. Ask McCabe about me, he'll tell you." He held his hand up like a boy scout. "I'm just jonesing for a little hit, that's all I've been like ..."

"I'm off for the University," Bobbo said, and grabbed his briefcase. "If Journalism students had any sense, they'd take one look at me and switch majors." He tossed down the last of his drink. "Come to think of it, perhaps that's my purpose in life. Someone's got to disillusion young journalists, and send them off in a useful direction."

He stared at Larry.

"That's assuming life has any purpose at all."

"Purpose?" said Larry. "You mean why are we here on this planet, you know, running scams on each other?"

"Precisely," said Bobbo.

"I been wanting to ask a professor," said Larry. "But I never met one before."

"Ask what?"

"Do you believe in reincarnation?"

The old guy didn't answer. He just gave Larry the Evil Eye and mounted a rusty old motorcycle. It spewed blue smoke as he rode it down the jungle driveway.

Larry looked around in fear of meeting that nurse, and decided it would be a good time to wander in Bobbo's jungle. He trotted off the porch and eased into the shadows. The only moving things he saw were the chickens. Back in among the trees was this dark little cabin where McCabe and his nurse were staying. He sneaked past it and into the bush.

A well-worn path has gotta lead somewhere, Larry figured. He walked, sun, shade, dusty heat, buzzing flies, blazing blue sky, some kind of big rat scurried along the path and then, up against a bunch of trees, he spotted it.

Might be booby trapped, so he walked careful, sweaty. He reached out, pulled a branch to his nose, yes. Pinched a leaf and smelled his fingers, stepped back and looked it over. This plant was as healthy as he was, and taller. Larry didn't know a thing about marijuana cultivation but he knew a small fortune when he saw one. Imagine that. You throw a couple of seeds over your shoulder, and a few months later, you come back, and Mother Nature has ten thousand bucks waiting for you.

A tiny seed grew up to be $10,000!

So there was a God, like Sister Helen always said.

Six, eight, ten plants, a guy wouldn't need a job. Larry began to rethink his priorities and also wish he had worn a hat. He gazed up at the sun, great for marijuana plants, but it could, like, melt a human being. He stepped back, found some bushy shade.

He couldn't help but wonder about Pua's freak-out. Okay, he'd asked her to stay in these lousy, dusty rooms, but it was only for a couple of days. He began to figure that having a princess for a wife might not be so easy. He might have to get serious about pulling in some coin.

A marijuana patch was the obvious answer. A guy could get a little plot of land. Gentleman farmer. Hadn't Captain Jules Dudoit run a sheep ranch? Well, times had changed. The second coming, Captain Larry, would run a pot ranch. Handful of seeds, couple of pit bulls, shotgun, that's all you'd need.

Hands in the pockets of his shorts, in deep thought, Larry ambled back toward the houses. He stayed in the jungle and peered through the heavy bush so he could hopefully avoid seeing the nurse. The thing to do was get the nurse alone and convince her not to say anything to Pua.

But the nurse's yellow Beetle was roaring away.

McCabe ran down from the lanai of his cabin and Larry stepped out of the bushes.

"Pua," McCabe huffed. "They're driving her to the emergency room."

"What?"

"She'll be okay," McCabe said. "The rooster got her."

"What do you mean *got* her?"

"Slashed her on the foot. With his spur."

"So that means emergency room?"

"Reiko talked her into it. Puncture wound. Could get infected."

"Where's that fucking rooster?" said Larry.

"Never mind that," said McCabe. "I'll get you out to Castle Hospital. But you've got to drive."

Larry ran up the back stairs of the main house to look for the keys to the Thing. He couldn't find them, maybe Pua had them in her purse. He scampered down to the barn, where, it was some kind of shop in there, welding stuff, somebody had twisted metal into dolphin shapes or maybe those were sharks. And there he found the only tool he needed.

He ran out to the Thing, jammed the slot-head screwdriver into the hub of the steering wheel, pop. Twist them two red wires together and touch the black one.

"McCabe," he called over his shoulder. "You coming?"

25

Top of the I

Now that the horoscope trick had worked, Terry was feeling very clever. He felt even more clever after the third martini. He was atop the Ilikai Hotel, thirty stories above Waikiki, at a swank restaurant called the Top of the I. He sat at the bar, facing the mountains. Even from way up here, he never liked looking at the ocean, especially at night. How black it was! Just a couple of cargo ships winking out there, waiting for daylight so they could enter the harbor.

The ocean gave him the creeps.

So he concentrated on the Honolulu Record, open on the bar, booze-wet on the edges. He tried to imagine the meeting at the Zoo. Sam waiting at the flamingo pond. Being watched careful by Teddy Hong Kong's paid

informers. Then the meeting. It was not ideal, no. Plan A
was that Sam would sign on with Management before it
was revelatory about Teddy's involvement. But now, no
matter, because the plan had worked. Terry wished he
could have been at the Zoo, to watch his handiworks
unfold.

Sipping his martini, he worked the crossword
puzzle just below the horoscopes. In his profession, with
the time you spent alone, waiting, the crossword puzzle
was a life saver. Unfortunate. Six letters starting with D
and ending with D.

Damned?

He penciled it in lightly, not so sure. Didn't check
out, crossways. Crossword puzzles were half, you could
call it intellectual brainwork, but the rest was superstition
or that other word, inner tuition, is what it was.

"Someone's sitting there," he said to a babe in a
glittery cocktail dress. She certainly didn't look like a
Hawaii tourist in that dress, silver with skinny straps.
More like a Vegas call girl. She put her hand on the back
of the empty chair, glared at him and backed away. Was
she a call girl? Who knew, but she looked too classy to be
alone by herself.

He refocused on his puzzle and started to get that
dark feeling again, you could call it eminent failure. Like
when the little ball rolled into the red and you had bet
everything on the black.

It was just about closing time, the barmen stacking
glasses, the bus boys collecting ash trays. Wouldn't they
be jaw-dropped when two of Hawaii's most famous men
arrived via the glass elevator exactly at 2 a.m. Terry
himself was what you called irascible that he was about to

enter the ranks of Management. He wondered what his old man would think of him now.

Terry, with that punk attitude, you'll amount to nothing.

Too bad the old man died before Terry could climb his Stairway of Respect. And in what you called the prospective of adulthood, who was the old man, anyway? A waddling-fat shopkeeper of a Mediterranean Avenue surplus store. Half his customers were welfare queens, pulling up in their Government-issued Cadillacs. You'd think the old man owned a hotel on the Boardwalk, the way he lorded it over Terry.

He lectured his old man now, even though he was long in the grave. *Take the cigar out of your mouth when you talk, old man, and have a little class.*

Now, with the Zoo deal safely locked down, he allowed himself to think the true name of the Management. Arthur "Big Art" Cruz. A name he had kept even from Larry. Would Cruz be at this meeting, which ... he glanced at his wrist, but no Rolex, he couldn't get used to that. Two a.m. this meeting and it was almost that now, because the barman asked him to drink up so's he could swipe the glass.

It happened in Terry's mental vision before it happened in what you call reality time. He pre-pictured this yacht harbor meeting, the look on Sam Wing's stunod face when he realized he was up against the full rostrum of Management: Teddy, Bix and Big Art Cruz. A combination of formidable existence!

This was planned to take place aboard Bix's yacht, *The Danger*. Sam's sweaty hand would clasp with the hands of Management, and then they would all share Havana cigars and a $2000 bottle of brandy. Big shots only would be allowed on the party deck, alongside

maybe a few babes, decoration purposes only. Cruz
would clap Terry on the back, and say congratulations,
Director of Security for the Desert Skies, see you back in
Nevada.

Disgraced? He counted squares using his pencil tip.
No, too many letters.

He looked up. Where was the call girl in the glitzy
dress, the bartender, the bus boys? Distracted. Begins
with a D and ends with a D.

Was Sam already on board *The Danger?* This was
not Terry's problem. Terry's job was done. Sam was the
Sheep, and Terry the Shepherd, who, what was that,
shorn right, when you fleeced a sheep?

Doomed fit. And as Terry penciled that in, he began
to have the lousy muddy Mekong feeling. So he roused
the troops of his mental Army against the very notion of
doom, and began to erase that word.

But there was no erasing the fear gnawing
underneath him like a hungry rat. The fear that he had
now become the Missing Link. All because he had
thought, in all due charity, to bring Larry on this job,
teach the kid some class, and Larry's bumbling had
caused them to mess up. Requiring intervention of the
executive nature.

No, this job had not gone as smooth as they had
hoped. The whole purpose on this job had been to keep
Management – Cruz, Teddy and Bix – in the realm of
clean hands. And that had not exactly been accomplished,
although the main thing, the money thing, that could be
all right.

What if Cruz now thought of Terry as the Missing
Link, the same way Terry had once seen McCabe?
Because when you pondered the Management business

model, Terry could cost Cruz a $1 bullet in the head, or a small fortune as director of security, and a risk always to run his mouth.

Terry began to wonder maybe he had served his purpose, providing a cheap way for Cruz to find out who his opposition would be in the Islands. It turned out to be tattooed mobsters, a lawyer who ate raw fish, and a nasty little real estate guy. And it was that real estate guy Spike who put on a *shibai,* great word, a *shibai* behind which lurked a gang of tattooed mobsters.

You and our famous friends will meet with Sam aboard a fancy yacht, Cruz had instructed him.

What do they need me for?

Because.

So I am the muscle, Terry concluded. Okay.

But the yacht, even floating at the harbor, would be rocking and that alone could make Terry sick with Mekong fever.

Just as he was breaking out in fear sweat, the elevator door opened.

He should have known: It was neither Teddy nor Bix but two guys he had never seen. They would never pal around in the bright lights, Cruz and Teddy and Bix. Their only meeting would be in privatized darkness, a yacht moored in a harbor.

One of these gentlemen was short with very dark skin and a nasty case of acne. The other was tall and could be Russian maybe, pale with the blond hair and blue eyes and hollow cheeks. Both were dressed in the appropriate splendor of full business suit and tie.

They nodded at him.

Down the glass elevator they descended, the three of them, thirty stories to the green glowing courtyard, empty now except for cleaning crew, all the deck chairs upended at the spot-lit shimmering pool, a stunod in hotel uniform hosing down the big deck.

Across the courtyard they walked, thick man in front, thin man behind, and down the hotel's back stairs into the darkness. Here cars were parked along the silent yacht harbor road. The full moon made everything look a dark shade of blue. The lights of the hotels showed the crescent of Waikiki Beach. Like the lights of Vegas, the lights of Waikiki never went out. And Diamond Head rose in its world-famous shape against the moonlit sky. Cinder cone, that's what McCabe had called Diamond Head, a good word to have in your armory in case of volcanic clues.

And so the three of them walked solemn-like, over the wooden boardwalk that led to the yacht. Was this Bix's famous yacht *The Danger?* Terry could not see the name, because they were approaching from the front, where it was roped to the pier.

The smell of dirty water hit Terry's nostrils, encroaching.

Of course he'd have the easy part, sit silent while the others did the talking. Would Big Art Cruz actually have made the journey from Vegas, or would this just be Teddy, Bix and Sam?

Terry would be honored, to be in the same room with the big man. Cruz had sealed the deal with Sam, cut out the Japanese mobsters, that's what Terry could sensibly figure. So Cruz would be happy, in the ultimate sense.

Once again Terry was driving the Army scout jeep. The convoy rode safely behind him and all of a sudden, filthy brown Mekong rising to his belt, his gut, his chest, his neck, his lips. He reached for his Army Buddy, empty holster. He tried to scream but gagged on water.

Once again he tried to steer that jeep for dry land. How many times in his nightmares had he tried to steer across the Mekong for the dry shores of salvation?

Stunod!

Down down down he couldn't see light no more, this river sucking him down, endless depth of eternal water, just like he'd always feared.

North Shore

26

David Shimada drove. The chrome Hurst shifter between him and McCabe shuddered with the power of his hot-rod engine. The police radio sat awkward, silent. A blue police flasher on a giant suction cup lay between McCabe's sandaled feet. Shimada and McCabe occupied the front leather bucket seats. Reiko sat in the rear bench seat, keeping one hand on the precarious, shifting luggage.

Shimada sped along Kamehameha Highway. A twisting, narrow, dangerous two-laner, it was the only road to the North Shore. When they passed the sprawling Turtle Bay Resort, David said: "You remember, McCabe?"

"What do I remember?"

"You remember, don't you, Rei?" Shimada called back. "The Kuilima? Del Webb? The political fireworks?"

"I'm afraid I don't follow ..." Rei said. "I'm afraid I don't follow politics."

"Years ago," Shimada said. "Nevada developer Del Webb built this resort and called it the Kuilima, remember? People said, you're crazy building a big tourist complex way out here. Then the other shoe dropped. Webb and his buddies got a bill into the legislature: casino gambling at the Kuilima. Gambling would be exclusive to the Kuilima, and would do no harm to tourism, since it was a ninety-minute drive from Waikiki. You don't remember?"

"I'd forgotten," said McCabe. "Democracy worked. The bill went down."

"Big margin," said Shimada.

"I forgot how beautiful the North Shore is," said Rei. "So quiet out here."

They passed between scrub hills and Turtle Bay Resort's sun-blasted, seaside golf course. Built for haole gamblers, it was now clogged with Japanese tourists. The highway cut just inland of the golf course, then between a volcanic hills and stunted bushes. The plants at this edge of the island had scant chance against the salty air. The winds blew unhindered from the Bering Strait, in winter pushing monster waves ahead of them.

A mile or so down the road, a sparkling blue bay appeared alongside the highway. Modest homes worth a fortune lay behind lava rock walls. Shimada slowed The Goat as they neared a parking lot and strip mall. Outside a ramshackle café, people, half of them in bathing suits, ate lunch at umbrella tables.

Just opposite Sunset Beach, Shimada turned The Goat up a narrow one-lane road into the hills. Near the crest of a hill he turned and now the homes were grander, set back against a lava-rock hillside that had grown lush.

"I didn't even know this was up here," said Rei.

The road ended in a lollipop circle and at the last house, Shimada nosed The Goat up a short concrete driveway to a locked solid steel gate that jutted out of a high stone wall.

By mysterious means, the gate slid open to reveal a house engulfed in tropical plants, the deep greens splashed with red, white and purple flowers. The front of the house was a long deck, set with tables and loungers and three green beach umbrellas. Parked in shade under a carport were a neglected maroon Mercedes Benz, with a sheen of salty dust, and a shiny cheap black Ford, an obvious unmarked police car.

Detective Prudence Yamanaki awaited them on the shady deck. She wasn't quite the size of a sumo wrestler, but she had worked up the same fierce countenance. She was dressed in a red blouse and blue corduroy trousers and wore a white cowboy hat. She watched with a scowl of contempt as David and McCabe struggled up the staircase with suitcases.

David, sweating, stopped at the deck to take in the view of Sunset Beach.

Prudence glared at them as she worked wooden chopsticks over the remains of a bento-box lunch. On the table beside here sat a picnic cooler and a hand-held walkie-talkie.

McCabe and Rei, burdened with luggage, stepped into a home of simple elegance. The house seemed to be half windows, and at the biggest one, a telescope on a tripod was pointed toward the sea. When McCabe and Rei claimed a breezy cool bedroom, they were just steps away from the backyard, where a sunken tub lay in the shade of palm trees.

"McCabe," said Rei, "what do the owners do that brings in this kind of money?"

"I don't know, Rei. Some dirty business."

She slid open the French door and stepped out onto the redwood deck.

"Someday, McCabe, someday…"

"We'll be rich?"

Her eyes filled with tears, but she shed not a drop. She sat on a bench between two potted trees. "We're here, aren't we? If you're alive, you're rich for the moment, aren't you?"

"McCabe," Shimada called from the living room.

McCabe walked into a dark living room where three lazy overhead fans turned silent and relentless. An S-shaped path of bleached, crushed white stone ran like a river through the elegant polished floorboards.

"Who's yin, who's yang?" David asked.

Only then did McCabe realize that river of stone divided the room, lighter, near the windows, darker near the backyard.

"Who built this place?"

"Royce Hashimoto. Senior."

"So this is Porky's…"

"Retreat," said David.

"A magnificent house like this, and he doesn't even bother to live here?"

"Long way from town, blala." David shrugged. "But if you want to impress a client, where better? Come over to the light, McCabe."

The two Army buddies stood looking out the windows. The shore they were looking at was the Banzai

Pipeline. Had it been January, thirty-foot waves might have been pounding that beach but now, the Pipeline was as calm as a duck pond.

"World's most isolated land mass," David said. "Nothing out there for thousands of miles. Doesn't it ever get to you, McCabe? Island fever?"

McCabe sighed. "Perfect place for a man like me, with no particular ambitions. I like the idea of having nowhere to go. It's relaxing."

"That's the last word I would choose to describe life on this island. Perpetual scramble, that's what I would say."

"What do you think, David? Okay, I know I'll never own a home this luxurious, but what are the chances Rei and I could end up with a modest cottage on the Windward Side?"

Shimada gave him the Evil Eye.

"Yeah," McCabe admitted. "Pretty much zero. I've got a townhouse future at best."

"Depressing," Shimada said. "I get that trapped feeling worse when I think about my daughter. I'm determined. Rachel is not going to end up a Waikiki waitress. She will get off this island, at least to taste life on the mainland. The sense of limits here, it gets to you. Around and around every day, same old thing, tourists, druggies, surfers, scuba divers, trinket sellers, t-shirt shops... The whole place is just one big roadside attraction. For her 8th grade graduation, I'm taking Rachel for a tour of the mainland. Hopefully it will open her eyes."

He looked McCabe up and down like he was measuring him for a punch.

"You've been all around the world," David said.

"Eh," said McCabe, "Air Force bases. They're pretty much the same, wherever you go."

"My wife, soon to be ex, cleans teeth eight hours a day. Except that I got lucky, I'd be thumper patrol, Waikiki, trying to keep the sailors and Samoans from killing each other. The one thing that made a difference, I woke up. Life is a war. You take sides if you want to survive."

He gave McCabe a friendly slap on the back.

"Finally after all these years," David said. "You're with us, McCabe. You've picked a side in this war."

McCabe, in baggy shorts and t-shirt, sat at the shady edge of the hot tub, his legs dangling in burbling water. Part of him was hoping the danger would last at least the weekend. A whole lifetime of donkey work awaited him once this affair was over, and he was in no hurry to get there. Life in this safe house amounted to a paid vacation, with catered meals, in an exclusive home with a magnificent view no tourist would ever see. Estonophies on the loose? He was confident that the brothers would never get to him and Rei here.

What did this mean, the police using Porky's north shore retreat as a safe house? It meant the police chief had taken sides, and saw the Sam-Spike-Porky-Yakuza contingent as the lesser evil, compared to Nevada mobsters. It meant *us* was the local crooks and their Japanese allies, and *them* was the haole gamblers.

From a cabana surrounded by upright surfboards and boogie boards, Rei emerged in a modest pale flowery bathing suit. McCabe had been in love with her since he first met her, when she was tending her bonsai on the back lanai. She'd been humming to herself that morning, unaware he was watching her from the next lanai.

Coffee? He'd offered.

She'd poked her beautiful face around the wooden divider.

Oh yeah, McCabe had said to himself, I've found her.

Now Rei wielded a straw broom and began sweeping the hot tub deck.

"You don't have to do that," McCabe said. "I'm pretty sure they have a maid here."

"I've got to have some use," she said. "Work is how we justify our existence."

"Existence is how we justify our existence." McCabe slipped into the hot tub. "I could get used to this."

Rei set the broom against the cabana wall and joined him in the hot tub.

"You're amazing McCabe. I wouldn't call you … I wouldn't call you lazy, but you can just sit."

"All things come to those who wait."

"Hmmph," said Rei. "I don't buy it."

"What does your hero Koshu say? We have two souls, the greedy soul and the wise soul, right? Maybe he's wrong. I don't think you're the least bit greedy, Rei. What are you greedy for?"

"Don't you want to be useful McCabe?"

"Not particularly."

"What do you want?"

"I want to take it easy."

"Even if it means … aren't the owners of this house criminals?"

"I wouldn't put it that way."

"Well, who are the owners and what do they do?"

"Big picture? They're lawyers, players in the real estate game."

"Selling houses?"

"Oh no." He spun her around in the water, put his arms around her waist, and whispered: "Whole islands."

Shimada appeared on the deck, and McCabe climbed out of the tub for a huddle near the cabana.

"I'm headed back to Waimanalo," David said. "To see your friend Bobbo. Sergeant Yamanaki, she'll take good care of you."

"To see Bobbo Burns? He'll sic his rooster on you."

"No more," said Shimada.

"Speak plain, David."

"Secret handshake meeting between Chief Abreu and Bobbo Burns, later this afternoon."

"The Chief and Bobbo?"

"Bobbo insisted, face to face. After the meeting, Bobbo will file for mayor."

"The Chief wants him to run?"

"In return, the Chief gives his word of honor, no cops with machetes hacking down Bobbo's plant life."

"What's the point of that deal? Bobbo takes votes from who?"

"Bix. Bobbo and Bix split the haole vote, better chance for Sam, and Sam promises no interference at HPD."

"So the Chief has taken sides too."

"Selfish, I told you. It's like gravity."

After Shimada roared off in his GTO, McCabe and Rei changed to dry clothes in the cabana and wandered into the kitchen, looking for lunch.

Sergeant Prudence Yamanaki was leaning on the kitchen island, watching a small TV. A reporter McCabe hated was doing a stand-up from the Ala Wai Yacht Harbor. He could not forget how she'd mocked him on air for falling asleep at the governor's press conference. Now she stood for a close-up in front of a row of yachts. She said into her microphone:

A Canadian tourist couple has told Honolulu police they saw the body in this very spot, just hours ago. But so far, the search for a victim of drowning, or perhaps foul play, has come up empty.

Aloha

27

Christina Grotton called for Larry at noon. He peeked out the Tiki Torch's louvered windows and saw her down there, pacing, tapping a ring of keys against her trousers. She wore sunglasses that hid her bug eyes. Khaki trousers shielded her long pale legs against the broiling sun. The Pineapple Princess, Larry said to himself, and stepped over to the cracked, clouded mirror. He'd been coached on the proper attire for a Hawaiian wedding: pure white trousers and tasteful aloha shirt. He'd chosen a blue shirt with a nautical theme, schooners, in honor of Captain Dudoit. Although the captain's boat was a brig, not a schooner. Was there a difference? Amazing how much knowledge was lost during a reincarnation.

"Oh don't you look handsome," Carl gushed when Larry arrived at the foot of the stairs. Carl wore a red lava-lava, white shirt and fragrant purple lei. Christina's mouth set hard, like she was a pissed-off nun back at Holy Infant.

"Acceptable," she said, and brushed something off Larry's shoulder. What exactly she brushed, Larry couldn't see. "Okay, go upstairs and change back."

When he passed the butcher's display of dead ducks and mounted the stairs, Larry remembered a dream from, was it last night? Captain Dudoit, with his flame-red hair and his pirate's eye patch, appeared to Larry in this dream. The Captain was holding a dead duck by the neck. *I never learned,* said the Captain, *to treat people right.* And he didn't talk like a Frenchie at all, but more like a Jersey accent.

Christina had followed him up the stairs, and waited just outside his open door while he, in the bathroom, changed back into blue-jean cutoffs and a workman's blue t-shirt. He hung his just-pressed wedding clothes from the shower curtain rod.

"You're not going to see her until you meet on the beach," Christina called in. "It's a superstition, but I see no harm in honoring it."

Larry searched under his rumpled bed for flip-flops.

"I killed a scorpion in here this morning," he said. "I know it's bad luck to kill a gecko, but scorpions sting, so they gotta die, right?"

He wished he could see Christina's eyes, because the rest of her face did not look happy.

"Okay, we're off," she said.

Larry was astonished, how modest they lived, these pineapple moguls. Christina drove him in a little white Honda, its only luxury an air conditioner. The car stammered through Waikiki traffic, Christina's hands tight on the steering wheel.

"You said you had a brother," she said.

"Unfortunately, he was called away to a business meeting."

"What is his business? Towing?"

"Protection," Larry said. "He's in the security business now."

"My security team couldn't find either of you. Lawrence and Terrance Stone of Atlantic City?" Her lips puckered. "Nope."

Larry whipped out his Jersey driver's license.

"Documents are easy to forge," Christina said. "Birth records, not so much."

"Maybe there was something mom didn't tell us," Larry said. "Maybe we're adopted."

"Larry ..." Christina started, but if she was going to give him a lecture, she bit it off. After a deep breath she said: "Open your heart to love Larry, and you'll find it's all around you. Put yourself in Pua's place, instead of thinking selfishly. She's been terribly wounded by those she's trusted. To make it all worse, she's been embarrassed in public by her father's financial misdeeds. It's going to take a while for her to heal. You'll have to be special man, Larry Stone. Can you step up and be a special man?"

Larry recalled Mom saying many a time: *You're my special man, Larry.* Of course, Mom was lying, because she said that to Terry too.

Or were they both special?

"I can promise you one thing," Christina said. "If you hurt Pua in any way, I'll have you banished from these islands. Believe me, Grotton Pineapple's security team can do that."

"I believe you," said Larry. "But I swear to God, I really love that girl."

"You've known her less than two weeks."

"In this lifetime," Larry said.

"What are you talking about?"

"Kaza," Larry said. "I've wised up and, like, welcomed my fate, you know, like your surfer Jesus advised. I was destined from birth to live in these islands with a beautiful Hawaiian woman."

"Part-Hawaiian woman," Christina corrected him. "Who's Hawaiian, who's merely an islander, it's a sensitive issue. If you're going to live here, you should know the difference."

She pulled up at Ala Wai Rainbow, the tall junker condo that failed and put Pua's father in prison. Christina's window looked out on the condo building while on Larry's side was the Zoo's jungle.

They stepped out of the car and Larry could hear the zoo peacocks call. He followed Christina around to the shady side of the condo.

"You do know what a time-share is?" Christina said.

"Yup, Carl explained them to me. He said they're hard to sell."

"But you," Christina said, and thumped his chest with a thin forefinger. "You have the salesman's personality."

"I do?"

"Don't be coy."

"Coy what's coy?" Larry said. He snapped his
fingers. "Oh them big gold fish. Don't be all wet, like a
fish, is that what you're telling me?"

"Coy is pretending you don't realize something
when you do realize it. And you must realize you are a
natural born salesman. You sold Pua, and no other man
has broken through her defenses in all the years I've
known her."

Larry scuffed his flip flops on the concrete. Hey,
he was good for something, he could melt a girl's heart. A
good girl, too! Pua wasn't one of those, you know,
Boardwalk floozies.

In a planter filled with barely-alive bushes, some
rude tourists had deposited empty beer cans and cigarette
butts. Christina shook her head, as if the trash disgusted
her, and walked into the deep shade of the lobby
overhang.

"Ultimately, this land will revert to the Grotton
Trust, but we're stuck with this condo for 94 more years.
In the meantime, it's got to earn its keep, just like you do.
We're a utilitarian family. If we Grottons know anything,
we know to how to use. When the lawyers finish settling
bankruptcy claims, this condo will be turned into a time-
share. Eventually, we'll set you up here, in this lobby, with
a sales office. You will be trained, especially in the
legalities of the time-share business. It's a morally dubious
business, but you, in your employment by a Grotton
subsidiary, will maintain scrupulous ethics. Until we get
you underway, you will work with your best man Carl, for
a few hours every day, getting practice in time-share sales.
Understood?"

"Sure," said Larry. But he already was thinking of his under-plan, of someday buying land out Windward way, and establishing a weedy enterprise, like that columnist-professor guy.

"Pua's in therapy, as you know," Christina said, "and hopes someday to return to gainful employment. Until then, you will be the sole breadwinner. That means no tall tales, no excuses, no flaky behavior. Ultimately, we will expect hard, steady work, five days a week. Understood?"

"I'm working class all the way," said Larry.

"Good," said Christina. "We'll hold you to it."

Larry was tempted, that afternoon, to get drunk as a sailor, you know, like they did back in the days of Captain Dudoit. It was tempting to get stinko, because he really had nothing to do for hours, except worry about Terry. The postcard ending with *Mom Sends Her Love* made him feel better, but only for a while. He wished he would get a phone call from Nevada. Terry didn't like the island life, maybe he'd never be back here, but Larry felt in kind of a low funk knowing that his brother would miss the wedding.

Although, if a guy was superstitious, he might think, hey, Terry's been my best man three times and all those marriages blew up. So...

He went for a long walk along the Ala Wai Canal. Joggers detoured around him, women pushing strollers cut in front of him, homeless men sat on sun-splashed benches drinking cheap wine. Everybody complained about this canal but it looked pretty clean by Jersey standards. Floating coconuts and palm leaves, was that so bad? And it all went out to sea anyway. Larry followed the canal towpath to the edge of the yacht harbor, where flying fish leaped, where dirty canal water gradually became pure ocean blue.

He turned around and took a gander at the Big Wahine. The yacht harbor poked out into the ocean, so this view must have been pretty much what Captain Dudoit saw when sailed up in The Clementine. It was easy for Larry to imagine the mountainside without all the houses. Yep, a whole mountainside full of marijuana. Did they have marijuana back then?

Captain Dudoit, in his excitement, must have looked at the Big Wahine and furled his sails, or whatever sailors did instead of saying fack it. The Captain must have told himself: Wow, only an idiot would sail back to France.

Larry, sweating in the blazing sun, strolled the edges of Mynah Bird beach, wading in warm, clean ocean water. The gentle waves washed up over his ankles, tourists splashed in the ocean around him. He felt like an insider now. A kama-aina! The dumb tourists would go home in a few days but he would be a kama-aina for a lifetime, planting good weed, snuggling with Pua, and making happy babies. He told himself nope, not even one drink, because that would lead to him showing up drunk to his own wedding. That had happened the first three times, but he would be clear-eyed sober for this ceremony.

He didn't want to bring any curses on himself now, not with dream captains holding dead ducks and a real Witch performing his wedding.

Of Larry's four weddings, this was the simplest, sandiest, windiest, and least Catholic. He stood feeling handsome as the sun sank toward the ocean, and the Trade Winds whipped sand into his eyes. Beside him stood Carl, wearing trousers and an aloha shirt that matched Larry's exactly. Carl held a little box with Pua's wedding ring, and an armful of leis. On the other side of Carl stood Kapuna the Witch, dressed in flowing red muumuu, looking like a queen with her long gray hair and weathered skin.

From out of the coconut grove limped Pua, in white muumuu patterned with tropical flowers. She wore sandals but her left foot, still enflamed from the rooster wound, was wrapped in a soft sock. She was both wincing in pain and bursting with happiness.

Larry made her happy, how about that?

Alongside her strode Christina Grotton, staring off like she was marching to her own execution. She stopped Pua to adjust a garland of red flowers that lay like a crown on her princess head. Tears flowed down Pua's beautiful face.

Larry, barefoot, kicked at the sand. He had the feeling Christina was giving Pua one last chance to change her mind.

"Pua lani," whispered Carl. "Heavenly flower."

Carl handed leis to Larry, and he draped yellow plumeria, red carnations, and white orchids, over the future mother of his keikis. He kissed her on both cheeks. When Larry draped Christina with a beautiful orchid lei, she allowed herself a flicker of a smile.

"Auntie," Pua said to the priestess-witch, "will you give us your wisdom?"

"You'll be happy for a while," Kapuna said. "And that's all we can ask."

Kapuna started muttering in Hawaiian. The sun began to disappear, like it was dropping into the ocean. Half-naked men in lava-lavas ran up the beach lighting tiki torches. Kapuna, with powers vested by the City and County of Honolulu, broke into English to pronounce Lawrence and Pualani husband and wife.

Larry kissed Pua full on her delicious lips. Man, this chick was a thrill. He couldn't explain it. Stunod! A man doesn't cry at his own wedding.

Just as the sun disappeared, Kapuna stepped back and sounded her conch, the sweetest note Larry had ever heard, or at least the sweetest to come out of a seashell. Then like magic came the green tropical flash and the almost instant night. He and Pua hand in hand walked the surf line of Mynah Bird beach, Pua careful to keep her wounded foot out of the water.

Tourists on the beach applauded. For this one magic sunset moment, Pua and Larry were stars.

They entered the Mynah Bird and left their tiny wedding party behind. Almost smothered in leis, the newlyweds ordered, light beer for Larry, ginger ale for Pua. One-Lung Pete asked if either of them smoked. Larry lied and said no. Non-smoking newlyweds? Pete approved, and insisted on buying the first drink of their marriage. Drunken tourists toasted the newlyweds and offered to buy more drinks.

From somewhere appeared a noisy helicopter, with a searchlight piercing the darkness, and its red navigation light winking. It prowled the Ala Wai Canal, then did a turn over Mynah Bird Beach.

An escaped criminal? Larry suggested.

"In Waikiki?" said One-Lung Pete. "I'll tell you who's a goddamn criminal, that tobacco bitch Donna Lorris. If you don't smoke, don't start."

He coughed.

"Police chopper," said Pete, and shrugged. "Noisy son of a bitch. All that noise, and it'll turn out to be just another drowned tourist."

Outside in the alley between the low-slung Mynah Bird and the tall Ilikai Hotel, a limousine idled, and Larry was surprised when Pua led them to it.

"Christina ordered it," Pua said. She sighed. "She's my hoaloha."

"That sounds sexy."

"It only means good friend."

Up the Big Wahine the limo traveled. Showing on its little TV was the episode of *Danger, Hawaii* where The Mick was searching the yacht harbor for bales of smuggled drugs. Strange, but when Larry looked out the limo windows, the police helicopter, only a point of light now, was still down there at the yacht harbor, circling. It was like TV and real life were almost the same.

Must have been a real bad guy slipped out of Halawa, Larry figured. Maybe, he wondered for a stunod minute, it was Pua's dad broke out of prison, trying to make the wedding.

Nah. He sat back and held Pua's hand and took her in, appreciative. It was like his mom's ghost spoke to him. *We can't all be alive at once, Larry. Appreciate your life and thank the dead. They have died so you can live.*

The limo pulled into the bird sanctuary, then up on the gravel road in front of the Grotton guest cottage.

"Beautiful keikis," Larry said, holding Pua's hand across the big seat. "That's what you want, right? A house full of kekis?"

Her eyes glistened, her lips twitched, she glowed with pleasure. "Yes, but…"

"There's a but?"

"Larry, I was thinking, you know." She raised her rooster-wounded foot. "About Reiko Nakamoto. The nurse."

Larry was ripped by a bolt of fear. Had Rei spilled her guts? Larry would have a truckload of explaining to do.

"You know, she's from such a poor family," Pua said. "Her father worked in the cane fields. And she doesn't say it, but I get the feeling her dad was really mean. But Rei raised herself up to become a professional. She's so … she has such character. She's so quiet, but she understands so much about human nature. When she drove me to the ER, I told her I wanted to be treated under another name. You know, because of my family shame. And she didn't judge me. She said lies were okay sometimes, lies were like bandages, they cover up our wounds. Larry, she inspired me."

"To be a nurse?"

"No, to you know, to be somebody. Somebody who counts. Not just somebody's daughter."

"You still want to have keikis, right?"

"Silly, why do you even ask?"

He drank the entire bottle of champagne, since Pua would only let the bubbly touch her lips. You can't drink alcohol with my medications, she'd explained to him. All that bubbly had put him to sleep, and his thoughts drifting off were: Man, who'd have believed I wouldn't get laid on my wedding night, but I'd still be a happy groom.

Pua was balled up under the sheet. Night birds were calling spooky in the Grotton family jungle. Owls, did they have wise owls in Hawaii? Larry, naked, dark tan except for the pale outlines made by his bathing suit, stepped out onto the guest house deck. Way down there in Waikiki that helicopter had come back on patrol. What they heck were they looking for with that searchlight?

He slipped into the steamy hot tub. He had been so uptight all day and now so relaxed, with the champagne in his blood and his wife inside sleeping all peaceful and such, and now the hot water massaged him. Cool trade winds of the Big Wahine blew through his wet hair. The stars above just, hard to explain, but they looked friendly.

Yep, Kapuna the Witch was right. He'd just arrived in Hawaii when she told him this was his lucky year, the Year of the Rooster. Maybe next year it would be Terry's turn. Larry wished his brother would ease up, and take Mom's advice and just be happy to be alive. He should find a girl, he was of that age now, over thirty. Terry could settle down, once this casino deal came true, go back and find a Jersey girl to marry. Because the truth was, Larry was a roamer and Terry was a homer. Terry would end his days in Jersey, Larry was pretty sure.

When he was all air dried, Larry walked into the bedroom and crawled naked under the sheets with Pua. Warm and sweet, with the luxurious long hair, she still smelled of the flowers she'd been draped in. Heavenly flower. He fell asleep happy, his arm around her waist.

It was who knows what time in the deep night when he awoke. Maybe it was the hooting owls that woke him. Or maybe he'd heard a sound in the room, someone walking across the floorboards, someone heavy. The Phantom, the Ghost Who Walks?

Or maybe Captain Jules Dudoit, come back from the dead to congratulate Larry?

It sure wasn't Pua walking. He had his arm around Pua.

Creak creak. Was that the wind? No. For a stunod moment, he thought: Maybe Terry has figured out where we are. Then another thought gave him sweaty palms. A maniac has broken in, the Honeymoon Killer. And Larry without even a shiv to defend them.

No.

Silence now.

Sweet wind whistling through the louvers.

Another ghostly creak. Larry sat straight up and could see in reflected moonlight, nobody, nobody else in the bedroom.

But something was giving him goose-bumps.

"Mom?" he whispered into the darkness. "Mom is that you?"

www.ingramcontent.com/pod-product-compliance
Lightning Source LLC
Chambersburg PA
CBHW030016180626
46810CB00001B/59